SCÆDREIN INFILTRATION

BOOK I: SCÆDERIN SERIES

PUPPET

iUNIVERSE, INC.
NEW YORK   BLOOMINGTON

Scaedrein Infiltration
Book I: Scaederin Series

iUniverse books may be ordered through booksellers or by contacting:

iUniverse
1663 Liberty Drive
Bloomington, IN 47403
www.iuniverse.com
1-800-Authors (1-800-288-4677)

ISBN: 978-1-4502-3896-0 (sc)
ISBN: 978-1-4502-3897-7 (ebk)

Printed in the United States of America

iUniverse rev. date: 6/8/2010

F⊕RWARD

The earliest civilizations like the *Kyban* from the *Klovia* system on the planet *Kyban*; the noble citizens of *Jilix*-two; the *D'neirie* and *Dwaelioc* helped establish universal order on a cooperative level the galactic market and stable trade routes. There was still one dilemma the ability to travel great distances in space in less time, this feat wasn't meagerly accomplished until sometime after first contact. The D'neirie and Dwaelioc reside from the same system and traveled on parallel paths light-years apart all ready knowing of each others existence before the cooperative space exploration mission. The D'neirie and Dwaelioc first encountered citizens of Jilix-two; the Kyban didn't come into the picture until one year later.

The four expedition teams worked together and developed a faster method of space travel establishing artificial wormholes that would open up the earliest trade routes, and more direct routes to their home worlds so many light years away. The four teams worked vigorously to expand their reach and discover several more systems with sentient life, and all close by, the artificial worm holes only bridged very small gaps at least by the standard measurements of space.

DDS (Dynamic Drive system), or DMS but that applies before it's actually installed into a ship, doesn't come along until the Myie enter the picture a few years later carrying the earliest versions of a DDS.

The Myie spent a long time in space looking for a new planet to call home after being forced off their planet when the larger of two moons exploded. The Myie traveled in space for an undisclosed amount of time before entering the outskirts of the growing galactic industrial empire of the Kybans. The Myie used a makeshift DMS that was hooked to the old drive system, DDS was a bit more tricky but in the making. The Myie were integrated into the working galaxy and given the opportunity to terra-form a planet and begin establishing a population.

The Myie were one of the few races of humanoid liked by a majority of the known systems, and DMS (Dynamic Molecular Sequencer) wasn't the main reason. A couple years later DDS technology is made available for the first time and takes its place as the top product in every known system. The Myie are making loads of much needed money, as with the other systems that picked up a contract to mass produce the DDS (most of them did.). Several years went by before the Myie lost all the respect they gained from the known systems, why and when is what some of this story covers.

A race of insectoids called Scaedreins begins assaulting the galaxy. Assaults turn into a wide scale conquering of over eighty-percent of the known galaxy. The Myie are wiped out first and sadly most would say the Myie had it coming to them, and the Scaedreins didn't stop until every Myie was killed. The Scaedreins knew only the Myie would be able to stop them, as soon as the Myie were out of the picture the rest of the galaxy surrendered to over 999 billion Scaedreins. Not possible, but when you see three systems filled with nothing but Scaedrein ships so many you can't count them it's safe to say there are A LOT of Scaedreins. The sentient insectoids take control of the smaller systems leaving the larger systems alone.

Despite the economical girth of the larger systems they couldn't match the Scaedreins even with the rest of the known systems backing them. They let the Scaedreins have their way with those who couldn't seal their borders and hold off an attack at such a large scale. The smaller known systems are beneath the oppressive hand of the Scaedrein Empire with no choice but to obey their leaders.

There are some who have hidden themselves from the Scaedreins massive empire, which is possible but very difficult. Most who tried to hide have been caught and killed, only a few have succeeded. However, success can be doctored to look like failure.

Eighteen years later...

The skin splotched with marks of disapproval showing as scars beneath fresh wounds, a lifetime of captivity. The last of his kind born a slave to an alien species, he's ugly in appearance to his oppressors for he is a humanoid. An embellishment to his people his family labeled a pariah before the destruction of their race, with no links to his past he has nothing to live for and does not foresee escape. His spirit broken pride no longer has any meaning he will not live long in these conditions after age settles in, being young around 18 human years. His captors are relentless and vindictive; they killed his parents after he was born. How he knows this, they told him.

His strange-blue hair kept short his captors like too pull and yank him around, the hair was the easiest route, now it's not as easy too grab being only a couple inches. His captors have somewhat stubby fingers and small hands for their, size. He really dislikes being grabbed by the hair and has reacted harshly once or twice, depending on the situation, plus their grubby little fingers makes his hair greasy. "Dirty ass alien take your stinking hands off me." Steel he thought he never had, he often wonders where that came from? He had no intentions of hitting the alien yet, he didn't fear the punishment like he usually does. That was the last incident it happened about a year ago and all that started from the constant yanking and pulling at his hair over the years. He'd cut it, it would grow back the pulling would commence but not any more! An act of defiance, his shaved head, against his owners a subconscious desire for something he didn't know existed for his kind, freewill; but why? He would never entertain such notions because the only way to free himself of his captors would be to destroy them because running from the Scaedreins is near impossible their reach spans the known galaxy, hell they run it, and him being the only one of his kind hiding would be nearly impossible. He currently has no qualms about his predicament a caged rat happy with his surroundings making the best of his situation.

The captain of the ultra-medium frigate with a once filled manifest she is the only one left. The others died when the rear cargo hold door blew up, unable to engage the force field in time all were lost. The bandit that surprised them almost finished the job. She was quick enough too save herself and not the crew. What kind of captain is she, apparently not a good one? Two entire crews in one year is not a good record for any captain to have, usually its additions or single replacements not an entire manifest. It might be harder too pick up another group of able bodies unless of course there are individuals who ultimately plan to mutiny when the time is right, which is what was going on before the cargo door incident. Three quarters of her crew decided to do so. The smaller portion was her first officer, and lieutenant. The other four were new additions about six months back, working in conjunction with the bandit planning the scenario weeks before the incident. Needless too say her past situation has put her in this present predicament neck deep in crew negotiations by a commission from the United Networks of Interplanetary offices for Outfitting Networks, or UNION.

"Your crew manifest will not be filled with any of our people," the old fossil of a bureaucrat glaring with suspicion. The others appear to feel the same way; they know the reputation of this particular captain.

She feels the chair holders are overly paranoid, so much so they can't see,

"Your people were responsible and accountable; furthermore, I am eligible by your contract to receive compensation for such occurrences."

"Young lady you will not address this commission in that manner again. The decision has been made you can accept or appeal but I seriously doubt you'll win."

Not taking to the condescending tone he delivered she gave them the finger and left.

Lousy bearcats always making it harder than it all ready is, if she had some sway with the local district judge she might have won. With no crew she could make more money it's just a bit more dangerous traveling alone in space dealing with the shadier types for high-risk jobs, which is what she likes to do but without a crew it's out of the question; unless it's.

Amongst the crowd of passers-by, a familiar face. Someone with diverse networks and extensive resources a *Dwaelioc* with his own angle on the universe and how he could manipulate it; not very honest but when you're desperate...

Can't remember his name, she's experiencing mental block, the words hanging off the tongue.

She approached him thru the pack drawing attention to her self. The *Dwaelioc* recognizing her turned in the opposite direction. In an act of evasion he goes deeper into the crowd. He is swallowed up by the masses into the belly of the beast, only to be caught before he could leave. He was at the top of his ships cockpit ramp when stopped by the captain; smiling at her persistence he turns to face her.

Perhaps he was seeing how desperate she was? Or maybe he knows about the loss of her crew? He could have very well been responsible for the mishap he's capable and has the reach to do it, and if he needed her bad enough he would concoct such a scenario. His devious reputation is no rumor and is not exaggerated merely being in his presence is dangerous, which is why working for him can be a lucrative venture and he doesn't kill to avoid paying anyone.

She still couldn't recall his name. 'Colde,' that's what it is!

"Why did you try and avoid me."

'Colde' shrugged his shoulders not saying a word.

"I would like to offer my services if you have anything for me."

"Where is your crew?"

"It's just me for now."

"I have nothing that small lined up and I don't like port loaders." 'Colde' set in his ways.

"Well. I guess I'll look elsewhere." She turned around beginning to walk away.

"Now that I think about it I may have something you can do for me."

She grinned before turning back to face 'Colde.' They entered his vessel to discuss the job and terms, little does the captain know she is about to experience one of the most significant and dangerous parts of her life.

The reference to port loader is a person or persons who work outside normal, but not necessarily illegal, channels. It's not illegal to port load.

'Scaedrein' space. A closed section of the known galaxy where visitors aren't welcome unless of course you have a death wish and crazy to boot or you have something of value, but, then you'll be deceived stole from and finally killed. Nothing like being reduced too nothing, literally, by a high powered sub-atomic blaster. How about the Multi-Phasic-Frequency-Scrambler-The MPFS is a weapon that de-polarizes living beings molecular frequency ultimately canceling one out, evaporated at a molecular level. The sub-atomic weaponry is usually attached to larger 'Governor-class' vessels, which occupy the boundaries of 'Scaedrein' space at all times. No window of opportunity no point of entry, this is the popular belief. The horrific thing is Governor-class vessels aren't half as big as the *Tarsuon*-class. There are ways in and only a few outsiders possess this information and only one would actually apply it.

"You expect someone to take this, job..." She smiled believing 'Colde' made a joke. Wrong...

"I need money but not that bad." Pushing away the data file 'Colde' has in his hand, shooing away an asteroid of trouble.

"If anyone can do this it's you."

'Colde' out of character from his known reputation; what are his motives behind the flattery? Besides he doesn't know her well enough to make such assumptions about her.

"What are your reasons behind this *Scaedrein Infiltration*?"

"Let's just say idle curiosity."

"Better be a little more than that if all you want is one humanoid slave."

"You don't understand my dear he is the last of his kind."

"Why does that concern you?"

"If I told you I had reason to believe this one slave and his people were once "the" mortal enemies of the Scaedrein race."

"Everyone hates the-" She suddenly stops realizing the emphasis on 'the'.

"Yes captain I have strong instincts that this slave is a Myie."

Seeing Colde, the devious eyes, the mystery of his intentions becoming clear what he so boldly assumes. The *Myie* destroyed by the Scaedrein's some years back, it's quite possible that one still lives on. The *Myie* another up and coming super power what some would call genetically superior. An extremely aware society of beings that resided from a planet called *Mieveodrin* translated as: Mighty eve of our greatness. More like eve of extinction. She will not believe or assume until she has some type of visual proof, surely the Scaedrein's wouldn't be stupid or arrogant enough to keep one alive.

"I know what you're thinking because I had the same thoughts. Its true DNA doesn't lie I had the sample verified by a geneticist in the *Naeasus* system."

"I still don't see your reasoning and refuse to take part in such a conversation."

She cuts 'Colde' off.

"I can guarantee your safety-"

"You obviously think I'm stupid too."

"I don't think you're stupid," raising his voice some.

"If I thought that I wouldn't have presented the option. You are known for your radical and fiery spirit...Are these things I hear wrong."

"Well everything I've heard about you has been contradicted. The last time I worked for you, you killed your book keeper for being one cent off-"

"Let's just say there is more to this Myie slave than what is seen, just like the book keeper incident."

She can see that 'Colde' is holding something back but knows she will not get this information out of him.

Perhaps 'Colde' was having trouble silencing his conscience? Whatever his reasons may be, obviously it affected him personally. Against her better judgment she decides to work with the *Dwaelioc*.

When he had the time to sufficiently cover his tracks he spent time in his secret hideout. Drawing tight fashioned knots for a fishing net something he just sorta started doing a few years ago, strange thing is he never learned it from anyone just picked it up one day. Paranoid, looking around, he knows there is very little chance of his oppressors finding this place. More like a habit taught by fear but why would he have such a place? A question he often ponders while there.

He put his hands lightly over the water that encompassed his secret hiding place, a small cave near a waterfall. A metallic type glint within the slow moving water heightened his paranoia thinking his oppressors discovered him, and the glint is the point man's MPFS.

There is so much fear cowering in that corner it would be better from now on to never come back forget this place ever existed. Will he fail to realize that what has kept him alive is the effort into making this his real home, a basis for freedom?

Realizing the allure of danger is false he re-directed his attention on the reflection. Unable to locate at first he soon rediscovers the mysterious little glint; a piece of metal resting at the bottom of shin deep water near the mouth of the entrance to the cave, about ten-foot from his original position. The wind blowing through some of the foliage covering the entrance allowing a ray of the mid day sun thru the tiny openings and in intervals, causes the sun to reflect off the metal. Strange though it's covered in rust how come it gave off such a revealing glare, like it wanted to be found and was calling to him?

The metal shard about three inches square held its own significant value, more than he could imagine. The surface rust came off quickly.

On the metal is a picture of some sort, a number of small stars with a blue backdrop surrounded by words written in another language. He can only read 'Scaedrein' and barely any of that. Below the stars are stripes of red and white. What manner of imagery is this, some sorta flag?

He gazed off while studying the estranged piece of metal. What or who did this represent? How did it get here and why did he find it now? Did he somehow need this scrap of metal? Perhaps it's a scrap of knowledge a one-page book with thousands of different views all with one common meaning?

This moment of pondering finishes the time slot covered for his stay at home meaning he was late and his oppressors would ask him why. What would he say, how would he react? If he's smart he'll just shut up and take the punishment. Then again, being humanoid you just can't tell most of the time. He could just flip his lid and start shooting as he quickly pulled the gun from the Scaedrein's holster. What's he doing; waving the MPFS about the area pointing with intent to kill. A fire in his eye's blazing a rising inferno every time he triggered the weapon. Dumb fuckin' Scaedrein's burn-burn.

He shook his head looking around; what just happened? Standing outside the entrance of the cave, an epiphany? Is it delusions from a mad mind? The sun setting he was really late, he must be stupid and crazy.

Running as fast as his adrenaline, idealism reborn, as he supplies his oppressors with misinformation describing the details of his lengthy disappearance...

He was collecting Rhazbid when he noticed a *'Veareein.'* Veareein's are large aggressive and bird like with six-foot talons capable of picking up a Scaedrein.

A full grown Scaedrein will range from seven too nine feet tall and weigh between two, and five hundred pounds. Infancy for Scaedrein's is like instantaneous evolution. After a year, which is two of ours, they are young adult males or females. Some are even bi-sex and can procreate without a mate. Most Scaedrein's procreate at random times of their later years. (The bi-sex are about one in six hundred billion out of a total of 2 zillion 459 billion 309 million 106 thousand and 6.Give or take a few million.). Not seeing a Scaedrein is like not seeing the sun from the planet you inhabit. In literally every corner of the known galaxy lives a community of Scaedrein's; so why is he conspiring to lie having visions of revolt? Besides, *Veareein's* don't usually mess with humans because they're too small there are bigger things that aren't as much trouble as humanoids. Scaedrein's are so tall these Veareein's usually end up ripping their heads off before swooping them up and enjoying a freshly killed Scaedrein, a way he would like all Scaedrein's to go.

However, their isn't a main kill switch and would be virtually impossible to wipe the race off the face of the galaxy, running and hiding is definitely out of the question.

Avoiding the bird he fell and knocked himself out. Showing no visible damage they took the story. What, they slipping or something? He didn't even get any lashings or the slightest accusatory look. In fact his open wounds were actually closing things must be going his way this won't last, because it has never happened before.

He should have brought the chard of metal with the funny looking drawing on it; he'll just go back and get it.

The embers of freedom burn igniting a dried out log producing a crackling hot fire. The source of this burn is the image with five pointed shapes in a blue square above red and white stripes. Not knowing what this image represents will he soon learn? He all ready feels the answer, the heat from the fire in his mind, a hammer driven nail of determination straight into the heart awakening a sleeping beast within the spirit. One that says: "Punish me if you will but if you ever let up I will show you a new definition of punishment." A driven yet focused spirit can achieve a universal change. A kinetic wave of one single thought so true and so persistent can and will have a tidal wave effect. Others will hear and react, join they will, become new leaders of a new era.

'Colde' shuttered upon the thoughts. Where the hell did that come from? He wasn't planning a revolution all he wants is the one single human so he can extract all the information this slave knows about the Scaedrein's and if necessary, kill him. Besides it would be next to impossible to hide this human slave who didn't even have a name. A nameless one with the most intimate knowledge of the most feared race in the galaxy.

"Are you gonnah' answer my question?" Knowing 'Colde' wasn't listening to her; men.

"I have a lot on my mind and don't have time to discuss things I all ready know, that you don't need too know."

"Since I'm flying this ship it would be useful if I had some idea of the direction." She disengaged the Dominant Drive Systems (DDS).

The technical name is Dynamic Molecular Sequencer (DMS). This system is capable of opening up lanes like connecting space, augmenting all ready present sub-atomic particles to create a more controlled and direct route. Not to mention 1,000 times more stable than worm-hole technology, sewing a path in the fabric of space. But does it create instability within normal space? The theory is of course, yes. What has been discovered in this fictional galaxy is these particles are in constant flux anyhow and are replaced by other particles, which by nature help produce the particles that were compromised by the ripping effect. If an accident should occur some of the bigger ships can collapse the lane with an engineer capable of performing such a task. The procedure isn't safe and only few know how to do it, and even a lesser amount of those who possess this knowledge would actually go through with such a dangerous option.

They just stared at each other seeing if the other would compromise, neither would have it.

"This is ridiculous. We've all ready had this conversation. "Colde' trying to use reason more than he ever had in his whole life with this female captain.

"We never technically finished it." She cuts 'Colde' off.

"I know the way and it's not necessary or safe for you to know it." 'Colde' cut back in.

"I'm not go-"

"Can't you see that I have been up front with you on everything else, and have agreed to pay you more than enough-."

"Even enough too hide from the Scaedrein's. Yeah you've told me that..."

'Colde' actually waited for her to finish.

"But what I need to see is a tactical layout to be more prepared and organized."

"Remember I am a Dwaelioc. I am very capable of getting us in and out others aren't as crazy." Colde' momentarily interrupting the female captain.

"You've made this personal. Why?"

'Colde' said nothing...

Against her better judgment she re-engaged the DDS (or DMS) and continued. The pre-set coordinates encrypted into the hardwired navi-computer's core processor virtually impossible to decrypt, this is the most popular opinion.

This mission could very well prove that *Dwaeliocs* are indeed the most kick ass beings in the galaxy at this moment in time. *Scaedrein's* have two-zillion citizens their rule is self explanatory. She only hopes it doesn't kill her. Not that she's brooding but let's face fact, for once it's a dangerous step. But all things face the inevitable either by their own hand; from arrogance; a more powerful adversary or by those who have had enough. Has 'Colde' finally said; "enough." Is she saying this herself by going along with 'Colde.'? Battling with her conscience, a moral dilemma, why now of all times and is 'Colde' in the same ship but for different reasons?

How come she agreed to be part of this 'mission,' oh yeah the money? Colde has somehow made her forget that with all his annoying little annoyances that are concocted and perpetrated to annoy her beyond annoying so much so she blows herself out of an airlock to get away from his putrid presence. If you haven't noticed she doesn't hold a high opinion of him or his ideas.

The medical personnel droid (MPD) pricked the subject with one of its many needle like appendages connected to its right arm. The twitching subject has no effect on the droid's reflexes, meaning the MPD doesn't compensate for the twitch, thus driving the needle just a bit deeper into the arm. Why, this droid doesn't like humans and this particular subject personally offends the robot. A guinea pig, but what do his creators want with this humanoid. It isn't its place to question but the droid is capable of curiosity, whether or not it destroys the MPD is another question.

What's going on here? Lying there strapped to the table unable to move, at all. Why are they suddenly so concerned with his health? Why is the droid tending to his less serious wounds as if cleaning them and why hasn't he received any new marks of disapproval? Have his oppressors been over taken by some mind control device, who or what happened to them? First he gets no lashings for being late and now this. Feeling more nervous than ever he can't help but wonder what the Scaedrein's intentions are it can't be as good as it looks.

Hard to figure out these Scaedreins this is why they currently control three-quarters of the known galaxy. Their actions seem random but are actually focused, like how they were able to gain control of so many systems in such a short period of time.

The rooms in the medical wing, dreary, t'would drive a mad man insane. Why he has never seen this before is beyond him and why he cares now eludes him even more. Last time here he was so afraid they were cloning him or giving him horrible afflictions, now he's seeing stagnancy and monotony. What is fueling this dreary mad man? Running in and out a shuffling trail corresponding with the hate controlling his retribution at war with his fear turned to cowardice the yellow streak down his mousy-back, squeak-squeak. So angry at himself humiliated, a tear fell from his eye. They couldn't kill him even if they cancelled him out at a molecular level. Is he beginning to realize what it is he really wants? Is he finally saying he's had enough, and why now of all times? A second tear fell from the other eye so many of these inner questions he can't answer, the tyrannies of oppression you don 't know yourself; you don't like yourself; you are ashamed and afraid..

His body tight as if experiencing pain at a physical level, yet, there is no devices inflicting this pain. What, if anything, have the Scaedrein's done to him now. Gave him a new strain of *Beigelipis?* Or maybe he is telling himself something, but what could that be...

On the outskirt of The Scaedrein's home world, two systems from *Scaedrei*, lies the mid way point this is the last time they can change their minds and turn back. 'Colde' didn't have any problems with not turning back but she on the other hand has been wrestling with the thought since day one.

Her only obvious benefit for going is of course money but it's no good if she's dead. However, 'Colde' is right about one thing it's a lot of money and it would move her up the financial wrung. She could start her own transport or distributing company? With this money she could have more options than she does now maybe the question to ask is: Are the intentions of this Dwaelioc worthy enough to risk her life? Because she can tell that 'Colde' is being driven by something more than profit margin, and expenditures.

So much wear on the Dynamic Drive System (DDS.) is not an economical thing to be doing. At the present time most would not use there's more than twice a day. The current price of fuel is and has been .25 for 2.5. She has an account set aside but not near enough for so many convergence points in such short days, and not to mention fuel used while traveling in normal space.

The average commercial ship spends 2-5 hours in normal space before acquiring 'convergence' on most of their longer routes. For bigger companies it's around four too six hours moving in normal space. This is a combined total between changes in course and heading.

There is a rumor that 'Colde' has a considerable amount of money and owns a number of companies in multiple systems seem quite a bit for one person, who has that kind of freedom and time.

This age of un-discovery dictated by Scaedrein law and restricted sectors have gobbled up most of the known galaxy. There are established routes that ships have to take.

The silence of the cockpit still uncomfortable even after days in space, though not intimidated, she has no qualms about asking uncomfortable questions.

"Are we stopping to refuel before we're inside the inner-perimeter?"

"We don't have to my fuel tanks are accessible from within the cargo hold." 'Colde' implying that he has fuel on board and a way to pump it.

"You've got every thing covered don't ya?" Applying sarcasm has needed. She did not like the idea of an excessive amount of fuel on smaller ships.

Even the one's that could afford larger ships couldn't buy one or have one made it's illegal for anyone who possesses a space born vessel more than fifty meters long and most of that is engines and internal functions of the ship. Other options like defensive packages and DTR's (Dynamic Temporal Re-sequencers) are options you must pay extra to get. DDS (or DMS) is a standard Convergence Package with limited capabilities and designed for only short trips into Convergent space.

'Colde' remaining quiet leaves the cockpit, gazing off out of it, as if he never heard what she said.

Wow not even a come back as she watches the door slide shut behind him. What is up with 'Colde'? Not that she cares but they hadn't argued in a few minutes she was getting bored.

That 'Colde' is full of surprises next thing you know he'll be back in the cockpit preparing for 'convergence.'

Colde stepping back thru as the door slides open.

"Prepare the ship for convergence."

She smiles as the door closes shut leaving her alone in the cockpit.

Several minutes later 'Colde' is back in the cockpit.

"This is our last jump for the day," Colde' sitting down in the co-pilots seat.

The coordinates coming straight from the navi-computer prevents her from attaining the knowledge. She doesn't want the knowledge anyhow. Most of the routes taken she has never seen but still lacks any curiosity about the exact coordinates. Heavily restricted sectors have certain penalties for any outsiders who attain such knowledge; you are killed by the *Scaedreins*. By now she is an "accomplice" an equally detrimental penalty; still it would be nice to know where she is going...

Scaedrein-seven, a once uninhabited planet, terra-formed several centuries ago has three distant moons. On one of these moons rests a hidden garrison beneath the surface, a hidden secret for over fifty-years. Scaedrein-seven is one of the most strategically placed planets in the system, another reason why the Scaedreins were able to take control of the galaxy. It is located on the opposite side of the galaxy but it was perfect for the circumstance. A network that has become so vast that one sector doesn't know what the other knows and even if they do they won't even tell each other. It is all for the Scaedrein race and no one else. They are committed and dedicated to the cause of conquering and expanding, two-zillion is not nearly enough.

The command post located on this moon has a high success rate when it comes to their job. Patrolling, Scouting, and investigating anything that appears on the high-resolution sensors.

'Colde' the possessor of such secrets, avoiding the system completely, was the reasoning behind the multiple trips into converged space. (Or 'convergent space.'). The intentions of Colde going over the head of the captain, she has no idea about the moon base.

Her name still unknown by most she is plainly referred to as 'Captain.' She's no ego maniac it's one of her emotional defenses one that keeps her from getting close to anybody even her first crew and they were on board for almost three years. At times she can be as cold if not colder than Colde one of the reasons why he chose her for this top secret mission. She has no reasons for deception he never burned that bridge he has never given reason to provoke such an action out of her. Colde met and worked with the captain a couple years ago, she knocked out a *Threpp* a very large intimidating biped with course skin and natural body armor that covers the Threpp and breaks at the joints to allow free unencumbered movement, with the exception of their natural armor that isn't very heavy, despite the agility of this Threpp and the size it dropped like a rock. To this day he still doesn't know how she did it, and he isn't going to ask because she probably wouldn't tell him anyway.

"What do you expect to gain from this?" The Captain briefly glancing at 'Colde' as if trying to casually easy the information out of him, sneaky, but it doesn't work.

He simply replies, "An edge."

Half the answer is better than no answer; the captain not wanting to talk anymore leaves it at that.

The rooms more like a prison the walls closing in on him, a sudden attack of claustrophobia wrapping its fingers around his neck. Why and where are these feelings coming from? It has only been a day since his stay at his hideout and all ready he's feeling a need to go back usually a lengthy stay, which is never as long as yesterday's, satisfies him. Why didn't he bring that piece of metal with him? He could have all ready cleaned it up, clearly seeing the picture beneath the rust. Maybe he can find a way out, an excuse or way of doing it without them knowing. An answer to his anxiousness is marked by an opening of the door.

A fellow slave enters the room holding shackles; behind him two Scaedrein guards stand in front of the doorway. This particular slave became a traitor to his own people the second he started working for the Scaedreins. One who traded the will of millions for his own well being becoming a pariah to his people, by his choice.

The shackles now resting heavily against the flesh of the humanoid he is a pariah not by choice-by bloodline. His descendants were all outcasts captured by the Scaedreins during the extermination of their kind. His descendants were the last of his people to be killed, the planet's population fell several months before that. Of course this is his view of the events that unfolded all learned thru rumor and what little information he could acquire himself. Questions he often asks himself are: "Why am I the last of my people?" Surely I am a poor representation of my race." How can I ensure my survival much less our blood-line?" At this point in time every question has an impossible answer. Is he capable of seeing thru this realm of impossibility-a darkness that consumes hope with fear and despair a deep and sorrow depression caging the ambition of the soul a forgotten way driven out by self-doubt insecurity and fear, too afraid to be who he really is. Yet, he doesn't know himself. So who can, or what is he supposed to be?

A slave, that is all he'll ever be but he knows this all ready. Has this part of his life come to a full-circle is he facing the issue again no longer accepting the answer. He's been restless to sleep and groggy upon waking perhaps this is the reason why, and he is just now realizing it. Perhaps this is the day of his birth or death of his mother who ever she was. He's never seen her, just as he would never see the sun setting on another planet other than this one. The sun isn't so bright underneath the hand of 'Scaedrein' oppression even more so for one of their slaves.

The entire galaxy isn't enslaved but believe me it's probably part of what the Scaedrein's have in there plans, control of the entire galaxy major powers and all. A move of such proportions is going to cost a lot of lives and natural resources.

There is a rumor involving confirmation of an entire system of asteroids? This could be the source of the Scaedrein's reasoning behind this suspected wide scale campaign of domination and why it has the Scaedrein's looking and waiting for confirmation of this system of asteroids.

Questions are how and why the Scaedrein's have not discovered such a system? The Scaedrein's could have artificially made it and they are reacting as if they never knew it was there. That is a likely scenario when it comes to dealing with them, unscrupulous and conniving. If it wasn't for the few remaining galactic powers the Scaedreins would have stomped all over the galaxy by now. Of course with the rumors of this system of asteroids the Kybans are the second to react; makes one wonder if the two are working together, not likely but you never know. The other galactic powers are at a level beneath the Kybans, and Scaedrein's, but still in no immediate danger. A majority of the known galaxy is lower middle to poverty. Most planets that had magnificent cities are now depleted, dilapidated, or no longer functioning. This so-called system of asteroids could change all of that for everyone, if the Scaedrein's were no longer able to control that resource.

Colde avoided the real danger, so he thought, being humbled by surprise as a patrol of scout ships entered the system. Ships that represent the Scaedrein army and not directly from Scaedrei so at least they weren't actual Scaedrein's, as if that matters.

"Have they picked us up on their sensors?" Colde quickly initiated the tactical array.

"I can't tell. Either they're jamming us or their AJS has deliberately done it for them."

AJS being the Auto Jamming System that is always active in scout ships in the event they cannot see an intruder, like now.

"If we can get behind that asteroid they will never see us," Colde studying the read-outs from the sensor array.

The captain performs her job admirably as she corkscrews thru two asteroids fixing to collide with one another. The impact of the two asteroids is enough of a distraction to the pilots and their ship sensors.

The sensors garbled by high concentrations of metallic fragments within the colliding asteroids. The scout pilots avoided the distant shock wave but enjoyed the spectacle from afar.

"What's the matter 'Colde' you look a little tense." She smiled coming out of the corkscrew maneuver just outside the shockwave of the colliding asteroids and its debris.

"You did that on purpose," Colde looking at the captain angered and startled; perhaps feeling vulnerable.

"Now why would I have any reason to do that," applying once again her sarcasm for the general distastefulness she found in Colde's methods.

"I could drop you off at the next port and have you deal with the Scaedrein's on your feet, and without a ship."

'Colde' meaning exactly what he said and she knows this.

"Why don't you lighten up a little," the captain once again showing distaste for Colde's methodology.

'Colde' remaining silent, again. She is beginning to wonder if the criminal tycoon has gone soft mushy like lablur, or as you earthlings call them bananas.

Colde leaving the cockpit again his type don't like to be alone for too long the screaming of the conscience is heard during these moments of dead-silence. Colde having heard his conscience is now dealing with it in an attempt to regain what little rationality he needs to keep him psychologically balanced? Is the burning-cold ice within his being now melting away?

One thing she knows for certain Colde is going through some changes she is not sure what will emerge from this change; he could turn out worse? Maybe it is his attempt at keeping her off-balance so when he kills her she won't suspect it. Of course that won't ever happen she won't let her guard down for that long. There is another rumor amongst the galactic criminal worlds: Supposable Colde killed his parents when he was six or seven the reason has never been revealed some would say its because he's Colde, but as with any rumor the facts are more than likely buried in exaggeration and lost in multiple translations passing from being to being; ear too ear; mind to minds all with their own opinion and way of seeing it. Makes one wonder how and why people even start or listen to rumors?

The whole galaxy is pretty much enslaved one way or the other. The only difference between being a slave, prisoner (or both.), or citizen is the fact that citizens don't have the bars in front of them. However as oppression goes it's bad for both sides. You see what happened is this: The Scaedreins hostile takeover was challenged by a couple of the other galactic super powers. Certain rights are in place for the so-called free citizens thanks to the treaty negotiations conducted by these two merciful galactic powers. The first united voice came from the *D'neirie* in the *D'neirie* system accompanied by the *Dwaelioc* who all so reside from that system, and though not revealed just how much ass this race can kick, the D'neirie are a close second. Not to mention neither are considered galactic super powers because their economies, even combined, don't amount to one-quarter of what the other's yield. However, and this is a big however. They both have the strongest armies in the known galaxy. Not by numbers but by sheer determination. They have better training, are more equipped and are known for the durability of their war machines.

The D'neirie, Dwaelioc, and the other true galactic powers combined would probably be less than half of what the Scaedrein's army is equaled to. Remember there are 2 zillion 459 billion 309 million 106 thousand and 6 Scaedrein's in the known galaxy. Most would say that isn't possible but some how they have achieved it. Of course *Scaedrei* makes our earth look like a meteor, a very small meteor. You could call Scaedrei God's basketball still they did not want to be on the field of battle with all of the galactic powers at once, especially the Dwaelioc.

The Dwaelioc have the most conventional tactics throughout the known galaxy but their machines of war are not as durable as the D'neirie. The Dwaelioc are masters of strategy, now that the Myie are no more.

The D'neirie are the master of metal. D'neirie steel is one of the highest priced metals in the known galaxy. The Kybans have been known to endorse and use D'neirie steel and the Kybans are masters of industry period.

The Scaedreins are master terra-formers.

The Kybans actually helped out a little during the negotiations for the surrender of virtually the entire galaxy. The other super powers didn't or don't care as long as they know there in no danger from the Scaedreins it's okay to sit back and watch the rest of the galaxy fall under tyrannical rule, nice.

Years have passed since the treaty was signed, and with each passing year the treaty is forgotten bit by bit. The collective parties of the treaty have taken notice and are awaiting an opportunity. This opportunity may never present itself, but how long can so many ignore before they 'all' finally say: "I've had enough." A day will come when Scaedrein rule is a thing of the past a bad memory for all to learn from and remember. Remember that control at such a level is indecent and against the rights of every being in the known galaxy.

People have to do what they must to survive. People make bad choices, sometimes. Lifestyles such as this will gain a lot of enemies known, and unknown. You're always looking back startled by the sound of sirens, paranoid upon the sighting of law officers, which is exactly what she'll be doing if this mission fails and she does somehow manage to get away.

How long would she run before being caught? Where would she go, live in space for a few years or in some mining colony? (The mobile ones.). What the hell is she doing here? Just get up and walk away simple as that if she really wants to why isn't she acting on it. The ship still maintains it's heading, Scaedrei. If she chooses to believe that, which she really doesn't, bringing her back around to why or what is pushing her onward? She smacks herself literally. The ship on autopilot she is doing absolutely nothing. Everything that is needed done is done now she is looking for something to do, she's thinking too much. Colde's spell of morality is beginning to affect her. Her conscience is not only screaming its babbling and wimbling. Fickle; indecision, fuckin' moral dilemma, why NOW of all times? She personally believes Colde is making up the story about this slave being a *Myie*.

"What have you gotten yourself into?" She speaks under her breath before leaning back in the seat propping her legs up on the edge of the main drive console. She will take this time alone to think about her own intentions.

She doesn't know what they are, at the moment.

The Scaedrein dragging the body of the unconscious humanoid slave, by one leg, just passing the fixed ventilation shaft positioned at the bottom of the wall.

The slave opened his eyes at that very second; catching in his barely aware mind, the realm of possibility revealing its light within the darkest levels of his hopelessness.

Grabbing a hold of his consciousness, now aware, he is violently thrown into a small room landing by a bench built into the back wall. This bench is what the Scaedrein's call a bed.

In a daze, again, pulling himself up as he hears the door locking from the outside. Why have they re-located him? Has it been that long, sure doesn't seem like it?

The room barren and dark it doesn't seem any different than his previous location. If he hadn't woken up he probably would have never noticed the change, at least until the next day.

After a day and they still have not moved! What is going on and why has Colde decided to park his ship within the crater of this small moon? Has this "fail safe" plan of his fallen apart. She hasn't seen him much within the last day, is he hiding this failure. Whatever is going on his intentions are conveniently obscure. The sensor probe he had her launch yesterday was the first obvious clue why didn't the light bulb appear over her head then instead of now. This whole mission has been one massive ball of confusion. Why didn't she hear the warning bells in her head before she even agreed to help one of the most ruthless, conniving, vindictive, and devious people in the galaxy?

She's hearing the warning bells now except it's not in her head it's coming from the sensor array. The sensor buoy (probe is the common term.) is actually a product of stealth technology, not phasic technology. It is possible to see but it is black with no visible lights and is invisible to even the most sensitive sensor technology.

She quickly activated the 'smart chair' that works off cerebral scanners and anti-grav mounts (when activated.), an easy access foot switch or a personal activation system (PAS) thru the seat cushion. The PAS is only optional if you have a neural link adaptable to the chair.

The video uplink image of the sensor report showing the scout ships they encountered before, now circling an area of ninety thousand kilometers. Of course the path of their sensor sweep would happen to be directly above them, I mean directly.

"Colde you better get up here."

"What do you want I'm busy?"

"We've got company," her tone now a bit more urgent quickly taking notice to the scout ships hovering around the crater.

The scout ships trying to triangulate location or do a focused sensor sweep of one particular area.

Question: Are they focusing on the crater or in space away from the planet? Perhaps they have discovered the buoy or in the process of?

Problem: Sensor buoys can be dead give a ways. Opposing ships can trace the data stream (or signal) directly to the receiver, it takes some time but it can be done.

"What is it-" Colde quickly noticing the events unfolding above stops the question.

"Is the buoy still active?"

"Yeah, I was about to trigger the self destruct. Do-" "It's hot," Colde answering the question before she can finish.

Her eyes grow amazingly wide as this look of "are you insane" pummels the face of obviousness, which in turn pummels the strings of levity within Colde's warped sense of humor.

Laughing while responding to her next un-asked obvious question he is slowly growing, hysterical. Merely pissed off, she suddenly grows irrational and violent as he falls to one knee because of his fit of hysteria.

"Am I amusing you?" Her voice unheard over his unusually loud annoying and stupid sounding laugh, sounded like a *Dumra*. An equivalent to what you earthlings call a jackass.

Colde still laughing and trying to talk she is unable to catch a word of it.

"If the laughter doesn't stop immediately I am going to take off." She directs the chair back in front of the main drive console. How stupid is he setting a hot- buoy so close to his own ship.

"Sure take off but it's a far walk," Colde still laughs. "Oxygen is an expensive commodity while in space," Colde's laughter growing even louder.

"DDS on line in ten-seconds-better buckle up," ignoring the overbearing and annoying pompous *umra*. (Ass.).

Colde begins to stifle the laughter taking her seriously because she will, and is starting the lift-off sequence.

"Okay captain. Just lighten up I have everything under control," Colde suddenly becoming serious and focused.

"It's hot but we're out of range from these buoys particular effects," Colde pushing the self-destruct button.

The view screen suddenly flashes but comes back into focus as a blue shock wave slowly dissipates.

Her eye's blinked in amazement. That is sub-sonic technology. Where does he get all these high-tech gadgets?

"I have one more that is all," Colde releasing a heavy breath.

She can tell now, that one hurt Colde's pocket book.

"We better get a move on. You can bet that attracted attention," Colde getting back up to leave.

"Where you going?"

"To my quarters."

"Where are we going?"

"It's all in the navi-computer," Colde's voice fading out as he exits the cockpit leaving the door open.

What the hell is his problem?

Suddenly remembering the question she was going to ask, again, because Colde never answered her the first time. It was in reference to why the ship sensors couldn't accurately scan the surface of the moon they're lifting off of.

During the landing she was uneasy about doing so without some kind of visual aid.

In normal space once again she is much happier now watching the moon slowly disappear from the retractable view screen hanging down where the cockpit window meets the ceiling, if she never sees that moon again she will be happy.

She sat there pondering the name of the system and the other systems they had previously entered, the same thing she's been doing since they entered the restricted zones.

In a place he has never been before surrounded by a numerous amount of Scaedrein guards is where he wakes up every time. A reoccurring dream ever since the age of fifteen, nightmare is more like it. In this sub-conscious imagery are feelings of terror the ultimate decision. This place is a large room with indented archways in intervals of eight. A long balcony going around the second and third level of the entire room, a gaggle of guards looking down from both balconies with weapons drawn; the target, him and two other people he has neither seen in the dream or in person. He feels their presence and interprets their emotional state while in the dream, fuzzy blobs mostly. He knows one is a man and the other is a woman. There isn't much to tell because the dream is always the same he wakes from the dream tense groggy and un-rested, irritable to say the least. He never feels irrational, why does he now?

The sliding of the door wipes away the groggy but tightens his all ready taut body.

"Nyeek anui tu," the Scaedrein's voice deep with a static like effect behind it, like mucus bubbling in the throat.

He knows what the guard is implying but doesn't understand all he is saying. Not feeling as fearful and compelled to obey these orders, he will not get up just yet. Where is this antagonism coming from? He should know by now that any of the guards are allowed to disintegrate him if he becomes a problem. He has no concern or care for his own life but being evaporated by a MPFS is a whole other concept. The rumor says it's very painful for being only one second.

The guard stepping into the room grabs a hold of the prisoner throws him out of the door. A few feet thru the air is followed by a heavy thud as he hits the floor, outside the room.

The pain does not sway his intolerance; in fact, it fuels a fire now burning in his eyes. This kissing the floor is getting tiresome. Subduing this fire for now he reluctantly adheres to the commands of the Scaedrein.

Escorted in the opposite direction of the ventilation shaft not a clue of where he's being taken, having never seen this particular building, not sure if it's within the compound.

A military outpost somewhere outside the nearest city: The outpost is about six-grids (miles) long with several large buildings, and heavily congested areas.

A push from the guard sends him on the floor again taunting his tolerance. He gets back on his feet and is now staring at the guard as if taunting the Scaedrein.

The Scaedrein not taking too kindly to the behavior slams the slave down onto the floor.

The fire growing in his eyes he spits blood as he gets up.

The guard laughing at the sight of this pathetic excuse for a life-form, pushes the slave back down demanding he kiss the floor.

The Scaedrein pressing the slaves face to the floor in an attempt at dwindling whatever amount of dignity and pride this one has acquired.

The laughter growing louder and louder as he lays there underneath the heel of humiliation; the fear no longer turning to cowardice has manifested into a new form. A ringing in his ears the sound of his pounding heart being pushed by adrenaline drowning out the laughter, the snapping of tolerance and consciousness as the mind and body act on its own instinct.

The guard is distributing his weight forward every time he pushes down. This means there is less weight on his back legs during the peak of the push.

He can see out the corner of his eye the realm of possibility, a target on the area of possibility. When the momentum is just beginning to teeter back; now! The Scaedrein is suddenly trapped within the phases of momentum falling to the ground straight on his back.

In an out rage the guard reacts quickly trying to pull himself up.

The slave standing above the Scaedrein delivers a punt style right kick directly into the path of this Scaedrein's forward motion. The Scaedrein goes out like a busted light. There are no other guards around, in fact the whole corridor is barren; what shall he do.

He procured the guards MPFS and fragmentation devices not to mention a couple of other things he found but don't know what they do. He knows exactly where to go, back up the corridor.

Standing before the open ventilator shaft; is this escape or is this death; only one way to find out he can't stand around for too long.

The cover to the ventilator shaft is put back into place before he starts moving through the elaborate maze like network. A system probably so expansive that he might end up getting lost for days or even worse dying. He feels different but he can't rely on how he feels in this particular moment his euphoria and paranoia are conflicting something awful and he may be suffering from fits of false hope, delusional by the prospect of escape. What ever it is he can't stop now he has taken the step now he must follow through even if it hurts or, in this case kills him.

No slave or prisoner has ever escaped the Scaedreins. In fact I don't think any have ever gotten as far as lifting off the surface of the planet they were prisoners on; if this is so then he will be dead in no time. Won't be so bad at least he will never have to look at another slime-sucking filthy ugly Scaedrein, anything is better than that in his book.

A junction in the network so soon three different directions two rights one left and the shafts are smaller than what he's crawling in now. Curious?

"Its not that complicated, pick one," the captain irritable at his lengthy decision-making process.

Colde remaining silent still continues to ignore her, completely.

"Are you still pissed at me; you are angry for what I said." She now fully realizes that for once in his life Colde is telling the truth.

"I never said that I believed the rumor. I just implied that your reputation is what started the rumor."

"It's not important-" Colde cutting the captain off only to be cut off by her.

"It is important. No one could have known your parents were explorers and they were killed during the *'Black days'* of space exploration," the captain showing perhaps for the first time remorse toward Colde.

"I need no pity or sympathy from you," Colde now irritated leaving the cockpit.

Taken just how she thought he would take it, oh well, can't say she didn't try. If this mission doesn't play out in favor of Colde he will try and kill her, she knows this. And she knows that Colde knows that she knows this. Question is: What is his next move?

The corridor has been sectioned off and is now under investigation. One single Scaedrein leads a group through the scene of the crime using a bio-signature scanner. The lead investigator quickly takes notice of the route used by the escapee. With little time to work the team of investigators have their case cut out for them, find this one slave before he realizes where he is. Why this building was chosen for detaining this slave is still not quite clear someone gave the order but no one knows who. This building has a hanger and ships, not to mention weapons. Why this slave was put here in the first place when it isn't even equipped with a holding-cell, is absurd.

There is one thing he doesn't understand the department heads are making a big deal out of this fleeing bird as if this slave is *Myie* or something, at one time they were the most dangerous enemy to the Scaedrein race.

The lead Scaedrein stops his team in front of the vent and rips it off the wall. The next thing down the shaft is a mobile remote video scanner equipped with repulsors and an anti-grav nodule this small device hovers and moves at a substantial rate it will track this one lone slave in no time this case will be wrapped up by the end of the day.

Downloading a schematic for the entire building the investigators now have a map and know what escape routes to cover, a sector wide alert will ensure the re-capture of this human as well.

Taking mere seconds to communicate ideas the group breaks up in smaller teams of two, in unison calling for additional support to surround the building. He couldn't have got out of the building by now it is of fair size at least by human standards it will take time to move down five levels especially using the enviro-system shafts, at least as far as the lead Scaedrein can tell.

What a confusing system to follow if this schematic is correct the only way out of the building is literally thru the front, door. The only way out of the vent system is through one in the ceiling on the second level. The rest of the vent work is too small for a human to fit. Emergency exits and two elevators are the only things leading to the bottom level.

The lead Scaedrein speaking into his personal communication system relaying info, positions, locations, and orders to the field units as they move thru the building at intercept speed. A drive that takes them down stairs as fast as an elevator; a determination that keeps them moving even when tired their graceful yet massive bodies moving swiftly down each set of stairs.

Now on the second level the two teams separate; one continues down the stairs; the other stays on the second level and covers the vent and the exit. Typical Scaedrein tactics which are good but don't always work. What if the prisoner went with something less conventional like for example entering the vents on the fifth level and exiting them on the fourth then climbing down the building from the backside, the side partially covered by a near-by maintenance hanger.

Of course he didn't abandon the vent idea on purpose he just sorta got lost and came out on the fourth level upon which he noticed the open window and scalable wall. Down he goes without hesitation jumping to the roof of the maintenance hanger, not one minute later teams of Scaedrein guards surround the building he just jumped from.

Ahead of the search party he has very little time before they send in the air units for a more thorough sensor sweep. He needs to find a way down that doesn't involve him being discovered and molecularly evaporated, and before the air units show up, because soon enough the guards will realize the prisoner is no longer in the building.

Across the backside of the roof he goes where there is a lot more vegetation, but he is all so racing against two guards moving between the buildings directly below him. Their hearing is impeccable so he is moving very quietly and he is good at such things. He has been known to sneak up on Scaedreins and they do not like being startled in the least bit. He got severely beat one time for supposedly sneaking up on a group of them but he was merely walking and not even attempting such a task.

Across the roof undetected by those below he quickly jumps from the roof to a treetop below. Thru the air he goes landing on the tree he grasps for his meaningful task something he is clinging to more than even his own life, his balls. Ouch, unable to vocalize the pain because you need air to talk and he doesn't have any at the moment. He sits atop a tree down wind from a group of three who are rounding the corner from the front of the building, his gonads sandwiched between himself and the tree.

The realization of capture subdues the pain long enough for him to lift his hanging legs above the leaves of the *Klarjm* tree. Heavy thick leaves with a faint fragrant odor, comfy to.

The guards directly below the Klarjm tree look up see nothing, smell nothing, or hear nothing.

Through a tiny crack in the leaves and branches he spies the three looking up the tree realizing they can't see him.

He releases a tense breath as the three Scaedreins leave luckily he dumped the MPFS if he hadn't he would have never been able to conceal himself amongst the leaves and branches. He still has the small gadgets recovered from the guard he knocked out all he has to do now is figure them out, no time now.

The area as clear as it will ever be he is now climbing down the tree a set of bushes near by will be his next stop.

It's a long way to go from here but even a thousand mile journey begins with the first step.

Out of sight behind the bushes just avoiding the next wave of patrols, circling both buildings, he knows what they are going to do next.

The next available concealment a sewer more than likely there isn't enough vegetation around to sufficiently conceal him. The closest thing is a building just beyond the other half of the clearing he currently occupies, he must go now.

The first ship arrives giving him the motivation to move faster and faster across the clearing; will he make it? No idea where he's at or going, the rest of the six grid (mile) military post is a mystery he has been to certain sections but it usually involves him not seeing where he is going. No sense of direction he has only instinct to lead him.

In the shadows of uncertainty he swiftly moves against the odds the clearing is coming to an end but not soon enough. Two Scaedrein guards apparently still unaware of his escape are walking down a paved road beside the plot of open land. Maybe if he keeps running they will think he is on an errand or something, probably not.

The two taking notice to the running slave raise their weapons.

He suddenly stops. Why? He knows the weapons are short to medium range and he is just outside of that spectrum. However, he is still in plain view. The somewhat distant patrols behind him are spreading their search and getting closer, let's not forget the air units. At a dead stop in the great wide open during the middle of the day is not a good thing and what is he doing, fondlin' a box. One of the gadgets he got off the guard. What it is or what it does he isn't sure but he's out of options one of these has got to work.

Maybe this will do something, holding up a hinged gadget pointing it at the two advancing. The box type gadget erupts with a couple electrical beeps, and whistles. In a frenzy he continues to dig in this large pouch, he made on the move.

The next gadget looks rectangular with grooves for grip. He points it toward the guards and pushes the button. A small laser shaped blade pops out of the top, well that's not going to help. He is almost in MPFS range.

His tolerance now filling with terror he is frantic fumbling through the make shift pouch, by accident he triggers a device while it's still in the bag.

A short electrical whine is followed by a couple beeps then complete silence, this is just friggin' great, in a panic he pulls out the now active device pointing it at the two guards.

Wait. What's going on? The two are no longer advancing and are looking everywhere except where he is as if he is no longer there, can they not see him.

Now the two are doing something with their head gear, what ever it happens to be it's making him very nervous.

One of the guards is kind of close the other is circling around he does not know why they can't see him but he knows they can't, he must act now.

The distant guard must have honed in on his position using one of their gadgets. Firing the weapon did nothing but evaporate his fellow comrade as the slave dove out of the way. Furious, the Scaedrein fires his weapon again just missing the slave by mere inches.

The shot going above his head as he gets up off the ground, quickly notices the grubby scumbag calling for back up.

Momentarily stopping to call for back up has given the upper hand to the under-dog.

An opportunity that grabs his grit and fear focusing the duo into one trajectory point, while instinct determines accuracy and distance. Lead by his heart he throws the small laser shaped blade.

The guard looking through special sensors in his head assembly sees the throwing motion and feels nothing as he drops to the ground dead with the hilt of the weapon sticking out of his head.

The haze now clear he stands there in disbelief, did he just do that?

No time to think about such things-gotta' go.

Swarming around a hostile who is currently undetectable by conventional sensors they know something is there. They're real Scaedrein scout ships. Upon entering the system their initial sensor sweep detected nothing but a focused sensor sweep revealed the anomaly they currently surround, although getting a fixed location is another story. Whatever it is, it seems to be moving.

"I told you we should have kept going," the captain sitting at the controls just waiting to be discovered and destroyed.

"You told me nothing. One chance in a million is what the odds say." Colde practically befuddled by this situational circumstance happening all over. Except this time it isn't the buoy the scouts are surrounding.

"Is that one chance in a million that we encounter Scaedrein scouts in 'their' space or is this on account of you being wrong," She's looking directly into the eyes of Colde.

The four scout ships tightening their circle focusing in on the source of this suspected hostile. Perhaps it is a sensor glitch despite the self-diagnostic system. (SDS).

"Something isn't right, they shouldn't be able to detect us at all," Colde checking the ships systems.

That's odd when did that happen, must be ship fatigue from excessive trips into convergent space.

"The ships leaking," He plainly replies, "and we can't possibly out run them now." Colde pointing at the sensor read outs making clear the tactical advantage of the four scout ships.

"We can't just sit here boxed in."

"They can't see us. Nor can they determine who or even what we are, we can take advantage of this situation."

"I hope you have an idea I've been lost since we started." The captain making it clear that it might not have been such a good idea to keep her in the dark about the entire mission.

"Out of your league," Colde sort of grins.

Is he making a joke or being an asshole, she can't tell.

"I have an idea. If I can send them a message in Scaedrein saying that we are conducting experiments with phasic shield technology, and we can't phase-in without compromising the validity of our experiment we might get away with it."

"So why aren't you doing it."

"Well there is one problem."

She knows what it is.

VST, Voice Scanning Technology. They can scan the voice pattern of the transmission, and determine whether or not the source is authentic or synthetic.

The four scout ships come to a halt in a cube around what they know now to be a ship.

"We have one other option that I can think of."

Hearing the deep reluctance in his tone she is assuming the worst.

"Engage the DTR drives-" "Motionless with four other ships around us," she cut him off with a bit of logic. Hell phasing in and fighting is a better option than that. "You're completely insane aren't you."

Colde smiles easily replying, "hopelessly is more like it."

"What are you doing? Your not-"

A bright white flash and explosion is the last thing seen or heard in that small section of space.

He has been subjected to some volatile smelling shit but these sewers are the worst. It's better than being locked in a room, now sitting down and holding the device that saved his life earlier; the one that made him invisible to the eyes of the Scaedreins. What is this thing; how does it make one invisible? Guess he won't know that because its now broken must have happened after he ducked the second shot maybe it can be fixed, regardless he is going to keep it.

Setting it to the side he has found a new interest the one thing he couldn't use during earlier events because of the noise factor, fragmentation devices. He smiles hoping to use at least one having seen the damage they can inflict scary and probably painful, he may just find out the painful part before this incident is over.

This is a strange device, thin rectangular and shaped so that it may fit around an arm or leg, by a strap. The face opens with the push of a small green button located on what would be the bottom side when strapped on. A red button is positioned on the top side. Beneath the now open face are two bigger yellow and blue buttons. However none of the buttons seem to be doing anything, is the device busted. A faint odor draws his attention.

It's not the sludge, mildew, or rats. He's having trouble distinguishing between shit and Scaedrein there are similarities but Scaedrein is worse by a small margin and the smell is doing exactly that getting worse, must be heading in his direction.

On the move again he has but one objective, get as far as he can before dying. Not sure if he is going to make it for the path is long with many different routes and endings.

Not to mention that everything looks the same down here in the sewers. The only thing really different is the degree of stench seems to vary down every corridor sometimes not so bad and sometimes worse, like this small intersection with a set of steps leading to a ladder. To the right is an archway somewhat bigger than the other two tunnels. The steps are to the left, and straight ahead are two separate tunnels.

Ladder, no. The two tunnels is two too many routes. The right seems to be the most plausible option he knows the Scaedreins all to rationality? Is that what Colde wants? This could be the very thing that knocks her off balance. Is Colde intentionally pushing her buttons?

Weaving its velvet fabric a quilt of darkness sewn by the laws of time from star to star, or so it seems from his perspective. Never once has he noticed how vast the sky is. A pattern that appears totally random from a 3-D perspective yet we have discovered patterns amongst this spontaneity; constellations. From a fourth dimension perspective would we see the lining up of stars and planets on a much wider scale? A thicket of trees looks very different from a distance. Yet from above the same thicket of trees you see a clearly defined pattern. In fourth dimension physics could we see planets and stars with such clarity actual shapes and patterns with some idea of depth? The abstract image of space from a third dimension perspective could be a reflection of the fourth dimension. We see it as space but on another dimensional cosmic frequency it could be something totally different, who's to say. The opinion is as vast as the scope of individuality.

He's out of the sewers, momentarily, taking a peek above ground. Where exactly is he heading in relation to the compound? What will be his best escape route?

At the moment he seems to be in some residential area because there is no activity, whatsoever. They are similar to the ones back at his section of the compound, the one he never left. He has never been in one but he knows they are homes for Scaedrein families. A fragmentation device would do well here and he could do it but such a small and remedial move is not a productive step in an escape scenario.

If he keeps moving in his current direction he will exit the south side of the compound in less than an hour, however he does not know the south side. He knows a small section of the north side and that is closer to his secret cave by the waterfall they would not find him there but that's clear across the compound back the way he came. The Scaedreins may never suspect it, could give him the edge he needs to get out alive. Is it worth trekking back through the sewers or should he take his chances on what he doesn't know, been doing that since he started the escape and it's working out just fine.

He figures his best route is the sewer but he can't go back to the tunnels he just left because it's a dead-end where he came up from, must find another entrance into the sewer system that continues south.

Ever so cautiously he steps out the alley and begins moving down the front of the building, the alley behind him blocked by a high wall is the reason for his up front approach. Another sewer entrance should be within the next couple blocks. Question is how long can he stay out in the open before being discovered?

Now at the corner of the building he quickly notices there isn't an alley or sewer grate in this small area, only a quarter of the way thru he has to keep going.

This residential section is a lot bigger than the one on the north side, higher as well. He can't even see the roof or even the eaves. One single Scaedrein guard comes out of nowhere; he can see this because the guard walked into the light at the corner of the second adjoining building a block and a half away. His entire body going stiff he is afraid to breathe, not one sound.

What's he doing just standing there, move. Why isn't he moving? It looks as though the Scaedrein is looking right at him. The chaos of adrenaline pumping thru the veins straight to his heart, so much that it makes his chest hurt. Up against the wall cringing in fear; the pounding of his heart growing louder and louder with the passing of every single second, intensifying every bit of reality into this one seemingly indecisive guard.

A moment of non-action before any life-altering situation can be as fast as light or stretched beyond the boundaries of time, as the sheer truth of that circumstance reveals itself.

The truth is he will not go back alive it's either live, or die trying. The pounding once so loud has now grown faint and the fear is now focused initiative.

The guard suddenly on the move again, leaves the area.

An astounding amount of tension lifts off his chest and is released through his breath so much that he is light headed, and still wired from adrenaline—or as he calls it, "adrenalive." Because for the first time in his life he felt very alive and in fear for his life before it didn't matter, now everything matters. Is this his first meaning for life or is it the fact that he not only wants to escape but he wants to devote his life to

"And what if it is," Colde becoming somewhat defensive.

"I'm not saying anything," she's suddenly serious. Maybe Colde is changing as a person.

There it goes again. Why is she looking at him like that it's as if she cares?

"I don't know why I'm going to say this," she paused checking for some kind of reaction from Colde. Here it goes.

"If you need-"

"Say no more." Colde seeing how difficult of a time she has being nice to him, who could blame her.

"I appreciate your concern."

"Think nothing of it," trying as hard as she can to avoid an awkward moment.

"No," Colde taking a hold of her hand before she can start walking. "It's a gesture I have never honestly heard from anyone your sincerity is taken well and for that I have to thank you."

"Can we discuss this another time? We have to get this Myie off the planet"

Colde very glad she has decided to participate in the mission.

Still, she can't help but feel Colde is deceiving her. Is it her nature to be untrusting or is it Colde's untrusting nature? She has a certain amount of trust for a couple people in this vast galaxy, does Colde as well. Is he merely playing on her sympathies? With Colde it's hard to tell either way.

They disappear into a dense section of woods at the north end of the embankment heading toward the six-grid post hoping to find the escaped Myie slave before the Scaedrein's do, if in fact he has escaped..

Broadening their search has yielded no results yet they remain alert and determined they will find this lone slave and when they do they will rip him in two and feed him to the *Veareeins*, as bait, then capture and eat the large bird. Veareein wings are rather tasty and filling, after all, they have nineteen-foot wingspans. The talons are great for making foundations for small yet elaborate tables despite the savagery of the Scaedrein's they seem to have an eye for decoration, go figure.

The search progresses thru the night into early dawn with no sign of this slave. Where the hell could he be hiding? The entire sector is mapped and known by every Scaedrein on the post the events have really upset the lead Scaedrein heading the investigation, this stupid human is making him look even more stupid. The *jid* commander is watching and isn't very happy with the results thus far.

Not wanting excuses the lead Scaedrein is dismissed with a warning; find this slave or die.

He couldn't have gotten out that far all ready the lead Scaedrein over looking the search and projected results from a three dimensional map projected from what is called a strategy-center. Each of the teams is marked as moving real time images with shape and solidity linked to the units in the field. Each and every Scaedrein has one of these and all are implanted with a tracking device. Come to think of it, the guard that was knocked out during the escape reported that his was missing. Strapped around his arm is where it should be. If the human took it then it's probably still on he isn't smart enough to work the Wide Band Relay (WBR), it's not like he's *Myie.*

Myie were very adaptive and had what is called an accelerated learning ability. The Scaedrein's seen the Myie as a threat which is one reason why they were wiped out before they declared their control over the galaxy. If the Myie would have been around during that time the take over would have never happened.

Inputting the transponder signal of the missing WBR into the strategy center directed the lead Scaedrein to nothing, a big fat miserable zero. Who is this human? He must find out some background information to better understand who he is dealing with, pulling up the archive records he will learn what he needs to know; hopefully.

Saeius (Say-us) city is where he was born from a slave woman who died six years after his birth. Up till twelve he moved around until finally he was placed at the post he escaped from a day and a half ago.

Question is why he was moved after his mother died, he would have been fine exactly where he was a city prison is a much better detainment facility. Is there something special about this slave that he isn't aware of maybe the captain's first officer should be leading this investigation after all that crew is one of a few remaining survivors left after the battle of *Cly'ruk,* the only major battle before the Myie came to an abrupt end.

The search perimeter reaching beyond the post about seven miles requires reinforcements to cover the additional ground. Soon after a number of security command posts will be established in the field housing these additional units as well as the units who started the search. They will remain in the field until the slave is captured or killed. These command posts will fortify their forward position and keep strong their newly established boundaries.

As of the moment the main focus is around the central post where the investigation is being directed from, the lead Scaedrein standing before a mobile strategy center within a temporary structure delegating authority from the wide band relay. The still of night is bringing with it an allure of doubt in the lead Scaedrein's methods but not from the others, from himself. If he has not captured this 'one' slave by day break he will more than likely be relieved of duty then severely punished by demotion or death. His fate will be in the hands of those who wish to see him gone, he must find this slave!

He can see the outskirts of the perimeter, all thanks to this gadget which allows him to see far distances at night. He doesn't know what this device is called only that it takes a mere push of one button to work it. There is all so a knob but he has not found any use for that yet. There are at least three separate patrols at any given time and remote sensor probes are all over the place he isn't going to get through that very easily, who said anything was ever easy. In his case it may be easier than being a slave yet there is a small amount of apprehension just touching the surface of his reluctance. This could be the last moments of his life perhaps it is time he used the fragmentation devices? Only thing is it would be nice to have the devices go off at a particular moment a series of distractions set to go off as he makes his way toward the opposite direction of the explosions. Of course he has no clue of how to set the traps to effectively work and he still has not yet reached the perimeter. It doesn't seem that far when looking through this gadget but it's pretty far and the terrain is kind of open. One thing is for certain he is becoming more and more convinced that he will and must survive.

Meanwhile the front side of the perimeter is under observation as well, except these observers are much closer to the numerous patrols walking their routes.

"Get down," Colde pulling her back behind the rocks as three guards walk by.

She looks at Colde knowing he just saved her life.

"How did you know those guards were coming you weren't even looking hell I don't think you were even paying attention."

Colde smiles, "Call it astute instincts."

"Do those astute instincts know what we're going to do next," she smiles in return as if saying thank you for saving my life.

There is something else in that smile, coy attraction.

A strange look in Colde's eyes is followed by one single word. "Yes," answering not one but two questions. A silent confirmation delivered through his eye's yes he can see how she is looking at him, and he knows what she is really asking.

Staring into each others eyes both unknowingly draw closer together.

Their hands touching, ever so briefly, an assurance of mutuality, she can't believe she is doing this; why him of all people? Trembling, fearing vulnerability she attempts to push him away.

Taking a hold of her hand he places it on his face. "Do not be afraid."

His skin feels warm. She feels warm and is no longer trembling, as if she is in...

"No I can't do this," turning away from him.

Colde not sure how to react just leaves it alone, for now.

What just happened is far from over whether either of them like it or not a connection has been established.

Abandoning the idea involving the fragmentation devices deciding to maintain zero presence he is now within the perimeter standing by the side of a temporary building in what he knows is the main command post. If he wants to damage his enemies strategic advantage he must attack the heart if it comes down to that, hopefully it won't.

The snapping of a twig from behind him severely changes his state of mind. He doesn't need to look to know what it is, he can smell'em.

"Nyeek tu alou," the Scaedrein standing behind the slave about midway down the side of the temporary command center.

Slow-ly raising his hands in an act of surrendering he is being directed to move into the open.

The MPFS to his back he begins to take his first step. Before he can even plant his foot he hears a thud which turns him around. What the hell-

"Do not be alarmed," Colde puts away his weapon.

"Du ogu," Colde trying a bit of the Scaedrein language on the suspected Myie slave.

"Do you think he understands you," the captain slowly revealing her presence.

Abruptly the slave begins to point at her and then Colde.

What the hell is going on here?

He knows who they are, the two from his dream.

They seem to be saying something but he can't understand what it is they want. Abruptly the two begin to motion the way he just came from, shaking his head in disagreement.

"Mu deenak," Colde knows a very small amount of the Scaedrein language.

The captain looking at Colde, "you never fail to surprise me be it bad or good."

The slave studied Colde for a second then replied with the same words, which means don't worry.

"Shal va luoh mu deenak," a Scaedrein steps from around the front of the temporary structure.

That's just friggin' great all three now holding up their hands.

"Don't panic," Colde whispering, "we can still get out of this."

"You have something to say Dwaelioc?" The Scaedrein throwing the slave out of the way is an inch from Colde's face.

Scaedreins don't like the Dwaelioc because of their reputation given to them by the other galactic races, all Scaedrein's entertain the notion of proving the galaxy wrong one Dwaelioc at a time.

"You actually speak a civilized language you must not be as stupid as the other bug heads," Colde staring back at the Scaedrein.

The Scaedrein showing his teeth jagged white fangs retracting from the upper and lower jaw followed by a disgustingly large amount of bile like saliva not dripping but hanging off piercing nightmares. The Scaedrein roughly pushes the Dwaelioc into the side of the building holding him against it.

"Don't even think about it," the Scaedrein using his other free hand to point the MPFS at the woman thwarting her attempts at blind siding him.

"She has not dealt with Scaedreins but I can tell you have," staring into Colde's unwavering eyes.

Abruptly another Scaedrein's voice enters verbal melee breaking the moment. Colde can tell that the Scaedrein roughing him up is surprised as well. The guard standing at the front corner of the building is wondering what the hell is going on.

"This is not over yet," the Scaedrein turns around grabs the slave and drags him while holding the other two at gun point.

Dwaeliocs don't like Scaedreins either and they too entertain the notion of proving the universe wrong one Scaedrein at a time. Colde wants to confront that Scaedrein and cram those teeth right down that fat ugly throat.

Out in the open the three are surrounded by Scaedreins. Where is that bag of goodies the humanoid slave procured from the Scaedrein guard?

The captain and Colde are beside one another in perhaps the last moment of their lives and all they can do is argue.

"What took you so long we could have escaped," Colde referring to the moment at the side of the building.

"Don't worry; our new friend is bearing gifts," the captain quietly revealing a sonic pulse grenade. The escaped slave gave them to her when the Scaedrein was focused on Colde.

"It'd be great if we had two."

"Actually there are three on me as we speak," the captain kind of grinning glancing ever so quickly at a giddy Colde.

"Now that's a gift a Dwaelioc can really appreciate," Colde replying with a smile.

Oh-oh the lead Scaedrein is coming, the other Scaedreins parting behind the circle of guards.

He steps between the two pointing at his eyes and then to the forest. He then looks at both of them and walks off shaking his head those two just can't get enough of each other.

Both look at one another shrugging somewhat defensive and in unison replying; "What?" An intense second later both are still wondering why they haven't moved, before practically running to catch up with their new friend.

Thanks to the guide, they are now standing on the other side of the thicket looking at the lit up command post on the edge of the same exact field he used to escape, almost two days ago. It took him a full day of mostly waiting to get clear of the base now they're going back to it, oh-oh, suddenly stopping in mid-thought. What's going on with them two, they're approaching him.

The man seems to be trying to communicate with him. He is flapping his arms as if he were a bird. Birds fly, flight! Suddenly realizing what is being asked of him he begins to slightly lunge forward motioning them to follow him.

"Do you think he fully understands?" A questionable look upon her face, "I don't want to be staring up at some bird nest because you're flapping your arms like an idiot talking to someone who could be an idiot himself."

"You know you have this way about you," Colde cracking a grin hardly seen thru the darkness and his beard saying nothing else continuing forward.

Not sure of how to take that she remains silent and continues walking.

Swiftly making their way across the field they have very little time to get off the planet if they want to do it before day break, the main command post isn't far now. If all goes half well then they should be off the planet in the next two hours, at the most. Maintaining their steady pace they are across the field in about five minutes and are now standing at the side of a building on the south side of the somewhat small military base.

Only knowing the path he used during his escape he is reluctant in wanting to take the same route it's a good way to get your self caught, now he has two others and the Scaedreins know this. Security in the base on full alert it will not be easy to get through and if this crazy one, who wishes to infiltrate the Scaedrein home world, is asking him about their flying metal crafts that is another obstacle.

Thirty-minutes! That's all it took Colde in disbelief something isn't right looking around standing in an alley on the north side of the base, the only alley they've seen. One thing they have seen is patrols everywhere, yet, it seems as though none are paying attention. They should be? An attack has been made on their soil there should be activity everywhere and not just units on conveyer belts so to speak, which is what the guards look like. Still looking about and contemplating Scaedrein strategy the other two are held up behind him and I say held up because.

"What the hell?" Colde suddenly turns around noticing a darkened form at the rear of the alley from where they entered.

He quickly pushes both out of the way and proceeds to draw his weapon, only to stop mid-way. The form is there and it's facing the alley, why has it not moved? He can see the beady little eyes not to mention the outline of its head, as he moves closer to this motionless Scaedrein.

"What are you doing?" The captain anxious to move forward and not back is perplexed by Colde's behavior.

On point she is unable to distinguish anything at the rear of the alley.

He can see what the crazy one is doing, at the moment he's just too scared to breath.

Ignoring her Colde is now crouched, advancing.

Not more than five feet from the Scaedrein and the bug head just disappears. No walking any movement what so ever just vanished right into thin-no wait, he's back again. However this time his back is toward Colde.

Suddenly relaxing he feels a certain amount of relief, boy that was close. Wait, why is the guard only a hologram, are the others as well?

Feels like forever. What is he doing, just standing there is what it looks like. The slave looks genuinely confused yet terrified all at once. What has he seen that she hasn't? I mean he has reason to be terrified but he just looks as if he's been re-terrified by something new. A tap on his shoulder and a point in Colde's direction should be enough for the slave to understand. Wait, maybe it won't be necessary. Here comes Colde now but why is he running?

"There is no time," Colde pretty much forcing them to run with him.

"What about the guards?" She kind of slows down and watches Colde run into the open.

"It's a trap."

The captain taking a hold of the distraught escapee, hesitant at first, but he trusts the woman more than he does the man.

Colde noticing the hanger right off just knows the Scaedreins didn't leave a ship because this base has been evacuated and is about to be ripped apart by a very large and violent explosion it might be better if they get as far away from this base as possible but he just knows that it's too late for that, five minutes at the most before boom!

What is he doing he just passed the hanger.

"Colde, what the hell is going on?" She suddenly stops.

Colde stopping as well, sigh. He runs toward her and grabs her arm, adamantly staring into her eyes.

"Will you keep running there is no time to explain," Colde practically pushing her. "Come on if you desire your freedom," Colde extending his hand to the slave.

All three running once again Colde is now fully focused on the task at hand; find a ship of some sort to get them out of here.

What happened to all the patrolling Scaedreins they seen before coming out of the alley it's as though they are all gone; have they left and if so, why? Unless they're closing it down or. Oh no, suddenly she can understand where Colde is coming from, there may not be a ship here.

There's no sign of a ship anywhere they're beginning to lose hope, there isn't much of anything left lying around.

"Separate," Colde motioning that she take the slave.

"What," too busy looking around to hear Colde.

"Take him and go look for something to get us out of here. I'll go this way." Colde being as level headed as anyone could in such circumstances.

The seconds ticking into wasted minutes as neither can find any means of transportation the whole place is shelled, nothing remains. The three realizing exactly why the search party was so big it wasn't to keep them in but to keep them out a distraction big enough to disguise an evacuation. Question is why are the Scaedreins destroying this post? There's new construction and it looks as though a lot of work has gone into maintaining and updating the command base, it seems a bit irrational to blow the entire base up for three people. Utterly hopeless the three are just staring at each other.

In one moment of silence one person thinks even more when they aren't talking. This splurge creates a build up of metaphysical energy if induced by tense situations these thoughts can often project intent which can be felt by another close by, or even far away. In his case he's close by and the two want to get far away but the Scaedreins are gone; why are they so worried? Here comes the crazy one he's holding something-it's one of the exploding devices. He's pointing at it now and emphasizing with a wave of his arm, the entire base. One of those things couldn't destroy the entire base; wait now he's pointing to the sky.

"Boom," Colde simply replies waving his arm once again.

Suddenly realizing the girth of the situation, eyes as wide and big as the planet he is beginning to panic, the next instinct to run is put to a halt by the crazy one.

"Eenue do'shoo," Colde placing a hand on the shoulder of their panic stricken friend in an attempt to calm him down.

Take it easy; this one is definitely crazy. There has to be another way to get out of the impact zone in time, which brings about his next epiphany. I say epiphany because it's a vision of his free will a place the Scaedreins don't know about, the cave.

The captain observing the interaction quite impressed with Colde's communication abilities, but.

"What is he doing?" The escapee walking up to Colde.

"He wants us to follow him," Colde momentarily looking back at the captain.

"It's a noble attempt but he must know we will never make it that far out of the impact zone," directing his statement at her then breaking it down to their eager friend.

Dawn laying a blanket of sunshine on the charred smoking remnants of aftermath, not nuclear but sub-sonic bombs designed to do more damage beyond impact point. The cave and water fall a pile of rubble and most of what's beyond that is gone. The seventeen mile rock shelf is now about fifteen miles and there is a steady drop in elevation starting from the remains of the command post leading to the north east coast line, now even more jagged than before. There is no way any one could have survived that.

Scaedrein drop-ships entered from the south and east dispatching three squads of six to investigate the impact zone. One of these Scaedreins, a rare breed, is a specialist in high order high impact ordinance. He is to gather sample evidence and compare with test readings to better quantify simulation results, a better understanding of bombs and how they work. Most Scaedreins aren't concerned with how things work, only that the thing works when using it.

That bomb really did some damage, looking about the area, why did high command destroy the post in such a violent manner on their home soil. He must not concern him self high command knows what they are doing.

The ground still feels warm as he takes a sample and places it in a Limited Field Scanner (LCS.) to get readings on composition and a rate of molecular deterioration in organic compounds at a sub-atomic level. This research gives basic figures to build on and helps when defining high and low order explosives, a minimum and maximum of each degree of bomb.

His hand is on a tree before quickly pulling away, still too hot to touch. He's getting better at his job the warrior class impressed showing their appreciation with a pat on the back, nodding in reply he continues with his assigned duties.

Watching his step, having learned from the tree incident, he seems brisk and cocky walking toward the outer boundaries of the explosion toward the north east knowing of the treacherous jagged coast line, anxious to see how it looks he has preoccupied himself with estimated images.

The waterfall gone and rock everywhere all kinds of h-oles, his foot now lodged between two rocks before giving way and swallowing his whole leg. Great, only a moron would let this happen. The Scaedrein attempting to pull his leg out-abrupt vibration-oh shit, Ahhh!

He didn't fall very far but far enough to be trapped, the surrounding patrols out of visual range he will have to use his com-link.

No luck there must have been damaged in the fall, removing it from his arm, no sense in further damaging something that is not beyond repair. Seeing the size of the hole he decides to try and verbally scream for help.

No response from above. He activates a small tunnel light built into an armored helmet looking around to sum up options. The rock wet and the smell of mold and stale air indicating this tunnels presence before the bombing took place, like way before. This tunnel could lead to the coast or go further inland attempting to use his geographical mapper-oh no it can't be should have guessed that one, entirely too predictable, it's broken to.

A dead end about ten-feet to his right the left is definitely accessible but does it open at the end, and more importantly is the route safe. He will stay right here they will realize he's missing and come look for him, Scaedreins don't leave anyone behind unless it's completely unavoidable. There is one place he is considered important, as with every Scaedrein, MPC. (Mass population Count.). "There can never be enough" is his assurance they will find him, besides he's part of the reason they are here. His other teams of researchers are on the south-east side taking samples from the remnants of the base.

He gave them the real reason why they are here. The slaves were left behind and used as live test subjects to see if trace evidence was left behind, probably not even a tooth. Perhaps this is the reason why they ordered the destruction of the base in the first place. If so why didn't they offer up more subjects? Would have made this job easier but that is not what it's about it's about obstacle, and challenge. The validity of the situation doesn't matter as long as it's for a good cause. "Naik Teil ly'dien."

Still standing after an hour not losing hope he refuses to sit down, as if sitting down means giving in, instead he's trying to find a way to use the larger rocks to hike him up closer to the hole. He piles the rocks one on top of the other ultimately crumbling under the weight of his first step, so much for that, remaining patient he will wait-they'll come.

Strange that none of the patrols have headed up this way, they should have by now checking his-That's broke to! This day is turning into his worst day.

There is one thing that is a constant in life and that is death either it be early or later in life we all face that great unknown the 'X' factor of mortality. In this case it's the 'H' factor as in how are they still alive? One minute the three are about to be crushed and ripped apart the next minute the cave floor buckles and they fall helplessly into the darkness then comes the water, an underground reservoir within a deeper hidden tunnel about thirty feet beneath the cave they once occupied. In complete disarray for an hour the three are just now getting a grip on the situation initially having to deal with the gap in communication between the two and their freaked out friend, in complete darkness. All is clear now and they are currently working on a means of light combining pieces from both their broken flash lights trying to get one, working. Question is did the water cause the damage or was it the fall?

"Don't move so much it won't stay in. Bad enough I'm doing this in the dark," Colde feeling his way through the small wiring connected to the circuit board in what is called a clip-light.

"The reminder isn't necessary any idiot can see that it's dark, even you."

"Woman," Colde not taking light of her almost condescending tone.

"It's not me you keep pushing," the captain sounding somewhat tickled.

"What do you find so amusing?" Colde looking up only seeing her silhouette.

"I'm sitting watching you work in complete darkness on a clip-light and I ask will this man ever cease to amaze me. One way or the other I hate ya; in another way," she hesitates, "I wonder why I feel the urge to kiss you right now?"

Colde abruptly stopped; what did she just say, and why now of all times? He's heard those words before but why does he feel different when she says it?

His heart pounding through his chest a moment of overwhelming emotional currents crashing against the shores of his glaciered conscience now beginning to melt away and expose the hardened ground beneath, soon to be softened by the wet and warm waters of mutuality a tidal wave of emotion as there lips meet.

Beautiful while it lasted the two now feel more awkward and violated and stupid for dropping the flash light in that moment of vulnerability gladly using it as an excuse to put an end to the perhaps mistaken kiss. Besides they got things to do other than each other. If the kiss was a mistake something good did come out of that moment the flashlight is now working, the two avoiding eye contact start looking for possible exits.

Abruptly Colde remembers that Myie were excellent cavers by instinct what a way to test their friend.

Of course with no prompting from Colde this former slave is all ready partaking in the search for a way out. That's a good sign if Colde has ever seen one. If Colde's source is correct then they will be on their way in no time.

As predicted he passes the test and discovers a small crawl space at floor level directly center of the wall to the left of the reservoir, which may seem kind of strange to an untrained eye seeing how there are two larger tunnels winding in virtually the same direction as the crawl space.

The captain somewhat familiar with spelunking can see this is a rational choice but could never have found it on her own; could Colde?

The crawl space small and coarse with very little room to move may more than likely poke and slightly rip skin while maneuvering thru the small opening about six-foot long. This is going to hurt but if it's the only way it'll work.

Colde shining the light down to the end sees the edge of the crawl space but nothing much beyond that.

More and more impatient as the time passes beginning to question the validity of his importance, or the jealousy of his associates. Paranoia isn't healthy for any being it disrupts reasoning and makes one act irrational and eventually drives one crazy. He isn't going to let that

the inside displaying an image of the terrain, it's like having one eye working as two. (D.Lo: Digital Layout.).

Magnify image. A mere thought is all it takes after HQ has established a link, which isn't really good because if any one is listening they can use the signals to triangulate both of their locations.

"I'll be damned." Taking notice to a patrol of Scaedrein's moving in his direction about a grid (mile.) behind him. Why are they going out so far could they be looking for him or are they aware of the southwest tunnel?

"I've got six Scaedreins moving toward my position."

"We just picked them up," a reply from HQ is abruptly silenced.

"You there," the uniformed humanoid beginning to feel his instincts push on his chest as if telling him to get moving.

Static is all he hears and the Optical Terrain Scanner is no longer linked with HQ. Quick on his feet he switches to the camera attached to the MPFS. This doesn't work as well as the direct link but it'll have to do.

A quick scan of the area before he's en-route to the south west tunnel, he will have to get there before the Scaedreins reach the clearing he currently occupies to sufficiently cover his tracks. He has what the Miscreant call a 'pace-lead' that means every time he moves thirty or so yards he stops to look around and check his back, make sure he isn't being snuck up on or moving when an enemy walks up from in front of him. The 'pace-lead' is used when the threat level for enemy presence is minimal. No sign of the Scaedrein patrol he is still feeling pressure on his chest, unable to determine the center of this anxiety his attention is drawn to his itching hand-Oh no what is this, he's been cut, dried blood on the back side of his hand. Damn *Strail* bushes and there tiny thorns, thought he was out of harms way, now the patrols may be able to compromise his zero presence-via bio scanners that pick up traces of blood. All Scaedrein patrols are equipped with such devices along with several other handy little gadgets; sub sonic grenades; WBR (Wide Band Relay.); bio-phasic shielding device (How Scaedreins seemingly vanish before their enemies eye's.); nucleic compounds with HGD's (Hot Graphite Detonators). In the event they need to blow something up and do a lot of damage, as if the sub-sonic grenades wouldn't be enough. If he could take out all six Scaedrein's he could procure some badly needed supplies that will later help the war effort, seems unlikely though. Killing one isn't so detrimental to the project killing six is a whole other story; where's a *Veareein* when you need one?

"You there," he speaks into a mini com-link attached to the collar of his uniform.

The sounds of static and a low whistle could be an indication of AJS technology at work; the source this Scaedrein patrol (Auto Jamming System.). The only loop hole is the Scaedrein's haven't yet realized the AJS is active because there are no indicators to tell them unless they take the effort to look, most don't because it tunnels there attention away from everything else around them. There have been many Scaedreins that lost there lives because the old AJS used to make a beeping sound; if anyone other than an ally was close enough to hear it they would be aware of their presence and/or location.

The entrance to the south west tunnel located within the back wall of a small cave on the bottom of a low rock out cropping is hidden using the same technology based on his holo-suit, except it looks like rock and is hooked to a bio scanner using remote sensors so any unauthorized personnel would just walk into as if it were rock. The area seems to be void of Scaedreins if they had found any blood there would all ready be drop ships and troops all over the terrain, from the blood they could discover his true heritage. Checking behind him he knows the Scaedreins are close, communications still jammed. The area well covered with trees he should be able to up his pace and be there in half the time, unless the Scaedreins key in on his position. 6 to 1 on any terrain isn't good unless you have an edge, his edge is the outcropping; can he get there in time?

He only moved a mere ten feet before the com-link opened back up but it was still fuzzy.

"What's that, I can barely hear you?"

"I said the Scaedrein patrol is falling behind they have altered their course. We had to shut down they were attempting to trace the signal we had to re-initialize so we could re-direct the signal to a Knock Box located to the west of your position."

"That still leaves them kind of close," he replied.

"It was necessary to do so because any other direction would appear too random from their initial readings."

"Understood," he finished.

"One more thing; the cargo is getting closer to the exit." Kelmu referring to the three moving through the tunnel that leads to the cave in that rock extension.

Without another word he begins a steady run toward that cave at the bottom of the outcropping, he isn't worried he'll be there before the cargo can reach the exit.

It didn't take long at all now standing at the entrance to the tunnel checking his back from inside the cave; those Scaedrein's can be pretty sneaky sometimes.

Area secure. No time to waste he points his MPFS at the back wall using infrared to check for heat signatures behind the false wall. No sign of anyone he cautiously walks thru the holo-wall by passing the force field that is deactivated when bio-scanners have confirmed matching DNA profiles, like it has always been since the system was installed some fifteen years ago.

Maintaining infrared status he cautiously takes his first few steps into the winding tunnel, staying against the left wall. He can't just run up on them might cause a small fire fight in the process and in the tunnels that is prohibited, besides he doesn't know how the other two are going to react.

A loud whine and crackling static draws him to a wincing halt as he places his hand over his ear startled and annoyed, he hated those earpieces for that one reason. Question is why all the interference?

"What?" Only needing to whisper into the transmitter located on his collar. The line goes dead.

He knows what is going on; they're being jammed and maybe on purpose this time. The whole network may be in danger of visual verification from the Scaedreins. That patrol must have changed directions from west to south; inevitably he will have to face the six but maybe not by himself.

The tunnel on a steady incline all three half expecting to see a light at the end of this jagged nightmare and on softer ground, suddenly the suspected Myie stops.

"What's the matter, why's he stopping?"

Colde shinning the light further up noticing that the corridor has come to an end and no light is near; however, the trusty guide seems to be focused on something else. Please be an exit because Colde has no idea where to go from here.

She hates to wait for an answer and Colde is always good for doing that, making her wait. He could at least say hold on or assessing the situation or something, just acknowledge that he's listening.

"We have come to a wall," Colde looking back feels the captain's frustration.

Not again. Question is why's the former slave so concerned he seems to be focused on something else maybe it's an exit, hopefully it isn't one of those jagged crawl spaces.

"Don't move," a human looking form emerges from an unseen nook in the corridor near the tunnels dead-end.

All three jump with a startling fear that stifles and stiffens the nerves.

"Just take it easy. I'm not here to hurt you. He's all I want," pointing to the slave.

Colde shaking off the shock of surprise, "you're humanoid how'd you get here?"

"I ask the questions for now my presence is of no concern to you," raising the MPFS and pointing it at Colde. "I haven't got much time and neither do you."

"And why is that," the captain inquires standing beside Colde.

"Keep that light down," the humanoid assailant emphasizing his demand with the barrel of his MPFS.

Colde failing in his attempt to blind the humanoid with the flashlight, having noticed the assailant adorning a night vision receptacle.

"Why you here Dwaelioc?"

"I'm an archaeologist," Colde being a smart ass trying to make this aggressive man angry.

"You obviously want to be evaporated don't ya," taking his attention off the three momentarily upon receiving a slap from his instincts. The Scaedrein patrol must be getting closer to the cave.

Colde noticing this split second motion is all so seeing the same reaction from the former slave, both seemed to be pre-occupied with

It would seem obvious if the others were thinking that but only she had such thoughts on her mind, she's quickly realizing this could be the beginning of something great. The Scaedreins number is coming up and that number is going to soon be zero, as in zero Scaedreins left. It was rumored that the Myie knew something about the Scaedreins no one else did and that was another reason why they were annihilated, she isn't sure exactly what the Myie knew or if the rumor was even true but it could possibly be a weakness.

Abruptly she glances at Colde then to the former slave, Colde is shining the light in the Myie's face.

"Ank u."

Both surprised and overcome by this great amount of gratification and effort put forth by this Myie who couldn't speak any language other than a minimal amount of Scaedrein, as they realize what he is saying. "Thank you."

"Your welcome," Colde speaking slowly so the Myie better understands how the words flow phonically.

"Y-our wel-come," He looks as if curious about the meaning.

Colde going through the steps shows this Myie the meaning of returned gratification.

"He is slowly realizing who he is," Colde looking back at the Captain with a large smile, knowing that very soon Scaedrein rule will end.

There was a brief moment of silence between the three as confirmation settled into acceptance of what will be and how it will come about, this lone Myie clan all that is left of a once great culture will show the galaxy that you cannot silence true grit and determination. That very soon these oppressors of free will, these Scaedreins, will be driven into the ground like a spike driven by a massive hammer- A hammer of good will and of justice.

Colde and the Captain get this chill up their spine at the same time and acceptance builds up determination, persistence and drive-There isn't anything that can stop what is unfolding and the Scaedreins will experience this from the sharp jagged side of the stick.

That moment over all three are escorted into the underground network for questioning. Colde feels it more of an interrogation from a Myie on the senior staff, and rudely I might add.

"Just answer the question." *Riedar Gi'Jhym* holding a needle full of anti-toxin. No truth serums just inject your ass with *Beigelipis*, Myie don't mess around when it comes to their own security.

"The injection wasn't necessary I've told you everything," Colde beginning to get extremely angry and Myie or not you don't piss off a Dwaelioc.

"You are here because you had proof the slave *Gildyn Aswic* is a Myie," Riedar pacing in front of Colde as if taunting him with the anti-toxin, egotistically holding death by the strings directly above the Dwaelioc.

"Do you have the proof-" "You've already asked that and I gave you my answer," Colde's unwavering eyes moving up and down as if sizing Riedar up. Could he take him, probably not?

"It would be easier to kill you and the woman." "Leave her out of this, I brought her here under false pretenses she knows nothing-" Colde interrupting Riedar.

"Don't lie on my account," the captain cut him off as she steps through the door being escorted by a woman in a military uniform.

"What are you-" "Their stories match," the female officer speaking above Colde's whisper.

Riedar didn't look too pleased either way but in good faith and gratitude for rescuing Gildyn Aswic he let them go, although he was surprised when Colde asked if he could talk with him later. A good host wouldn't turn down the request, so he didn't.

Almost forgetting the anti-toxin Colde happy upon finding out it wasn't Beigelipis but a simple shot of UJ-6 (equivalent to vitamin B12.). On the down side he does not like to be lied to, especially when it pertains to his life. UJ is short for *Umieceus Jie* English translation vitamin supplement. 6 the number of double protein strands present in the vitamin.

Not allowed to walk freely amongst the tunnels Colde and the Captain are confined to minimum-security quarters, Colde is bothered by this. The captain can see why and so can Colde but he isn't accustomed to waiting, she is.

"Relax at least we're alive." The captain sitting back in a cot legs partly open inviting, welcoming, and calling to him as if saying we have found time to explore the possibilities.

"Captain your apparent lackadaisical attitude fails to realize the validity of the situation," Colde looking over the innuendo and ignoring the possibilities; cold even for Colde.

"Both of us felt that chill up our spine standing in that corridor, a very hot corridor I might add," the captain looking up at an over anxious Colde.

What does that mean? They have bonded or something, yeah right, try telling that to Riedar.

Colde didn't say nothing only turned away as if not wanting to face the possibilities, much less explore them.

She wasn't going to give up she made her decision all ready and would try until she felt she tired hard enough.

Colde pacing ranting to himself is suddenly stopped by the captain, who is standing behind him with a firm grasp around his upper chest.

"Woman, there is no time for this," Colde fighting as hard as he can to try and ignore the boiling kettle of his loins and the seductive passions of the Captain.

"And I say there is." She whispers ever so lightly in his ear, teasing his senses with her alluring tone.

Colde trying to push her away, but not really, "you're making this very hard."

"Oh is that his name, this." She chuckles probing her hand up his leg toward his low center of gravity.

Quickly he grabs her hand stopping her advancements her impetuous desires, what he believes are dictated by the moment and not by how she really feels. Is he trying to protect her from himself?

"You're not going to make this easy?" She smiles and swiftly moves around her prey stalking with her fingers moving vicariously over his body, lightly rubbing against him with her shirt all ready open.

Colde just realizing is in awe at the spectacle before him soft yet firmly in place and well rounded perky attentive nipples eager to be explored by his touch.

"Captain, I'm not adapted to seeing you like this." Colde not sure how to react is a swift kick in the nuts coming, or what?

Taking a hold of Colde's hand she caresses the rough palm side and then the backside.

"My hands are rough-" "Shh," she lightly covers his mouth. "I want them here," she moves his hand onto her right breast and slowly across her nipple, as if she were a puppet master pulling his strings.

"Captain is this really a good idea," his tone now much lighter as if giving in.

"Captain is so informal," she looks deep into his eyes and through his soul.

Colde unable to help himself has now fallen under the category of 'seduced.' Only a woman who knows herself well is capable of seducing him and she obviously knows who she is, and what she wants.

Colde placing his other hand upon her breast he is now moving on his own and her hands are free to reach for something she knows is of an admirable quality something she has longed for since she reached womanhood, a man that will truly love her. Is it ironic that she believes this man is Colde, of all people?

She pressed against him as he moved his hands down the sides of her breasts rubbing his thumbs over her perky stiff nipples then onto her well rounded cheeks squeezing them lifting her legs around his waist. Their lips meet and tongues connect, she pulls back biting his bottom lip then his chin down to his neck, the salty skin yet to her it's sweet.

Her skin to him was every bit as sweet and both wondered at the same time; "is this love?"

He moved her toward the cot but she shook her head. "No," she softly replied undoing her not so lose fitting pants, while still wrapped around his waist.

She wraps her arms around his neck, loosening her grip around his waist just enough for the clothing to drop around his ankles. He takes a couple steps and is now exposed to the full extent, without the burden of being bound at the ankles.

She keeps her legs around his waist and slowly slides down him rubbing his manhood across her breasts, and kissing the tip as her knees touch the ground.

Colde caressing her face looks within her eyes seeing the same fire he felt in his heart. She kissed the tip again and worked her tongue down the shaft and around the sac, lightly kissing her way back up to the tip. Colde caressing her hair and lightly rubbing the back of her head he tilts his head back as she engorges his manhood down to the base and slowly comes up applying 'pressure' to the nodes of pleasure, as she slowly goes down again. Colde releasing tension and anxiety slightly buckles and wonders what she is doing that other women didn't do. It feels so good and he didn't want her to stop, not in the least bit.

As he wished and hoped she remained vigilant and moaned as if she enjoys it as much as Colde, he couldn't wait for his turn. He would show her the same enthusiasm.

She goes down again feeling the tip in her throat as she delves deeper into her soft wet love canal, growing out of control she is no longer able to engorge as she tilts her head back, stroking his manhood.

Colde looking down admiring her uninhibited actions, she rubs his shaft and begins to go down on it once again. Colde growing out of control himself wants her so bad he is trying to pull her up attempting to take what she so enjoyed out of her warm mouth.

"No," her tone soft yet firm and adamant as she engorged his manhood unlike any other man she had ever been with.

Colde slams his hand against the rock wall again as he releases a lifetime of defensiveness and buried feelings.

She has never acted this way before why is she so out of control, or is she for once in her life free from the restrictions of her own defenses the very thing that wouldn't allow her to act so impulsive and unconstrained.

At this time Colde is still stiff as an *Ungallian Bull* observing her act of wanton erotic sexual pleasure.

Her fingers back in her pink wet palace of pleasure she is beckoning to Colde spreading her legs and laying on her back, running her foot up his leg.

Colde laying above her his hands on the ground beside her head holding himself up as he meets her lips then down to her neck, a mouthful of nipple and tit he too feels this candid desire to let it all out.

She feels turned on even more as he moves down to her stomach with his tongue directing his movements, knowing what is there she knows he doesn't mind.

Probing her inner thigh with his lips he teasingly moves closer and briefly licks the door to her pleasure palace, as if initializing the portcullis to let him in. She spreads her legs wider and rubs the top of his head trying to direct him back to the pinkness of her glove where her drawbridge is down and yearning for his entrance into her palace, she moans as if signaling him from atop her tower waving to him a warm welcome to a wary traveler.

His lips met her lips and she pushed him into her entrance, forced by the reigns of desire. He is now in the main hall of her palace and is probing his tongue all around enjoying the flavor of her fine food. She responds by rubbing it in his face, working her hips to the rhythm of his wild tongue.

She moans a bit louder and verbally expresses the pleasure she is feeling. "Yes," she says once and then twice, and then a third time.

Moving further into the depths of her palace, she is climbing to ecstatic pleasure as he makes contact with the "G"arden spot located behind her wall defenses, a catapult of pleasure as she lets out a scream of pleasure looking down at Colde who is very busy and engrossed in what he is doing. Why did it not feel this good with other men? She tilts her head and arches her back in this pleasure that felt so good it hurts when he stops but she wants him in her, now.

She is trying to pull him up, "I want you in me," she pleasurably demanded.

Colde did not listen maintaining his oral position in her palace, as the natural rivers of her palace begin to rise above her shores.

"Don't stop," pleading with pleasure, insistency told through her tone as well as her eyes.

She releases a little more of her sweet juices then licked her own fingers, this turned Colde on even more.

His erection so stiff it hurt, he can wait no longer.

Their lips meet and Colde on top of her as she wraps her legs around his waist

"Put it in," she demanded with a firm and seductive tone.

Colde gazing into her eyes lightly placed the head inside her as if taunting her or wanting her to work a little more for it. She responded by thrusting her hips upward, which is exactly what she should have done because the stiff shaft penetrated the surface and rubbed against the wall of her inner palace.

She smiled with an enormous amount of pleasure behind those eyes, revealing something hidden amongst the fires of her wild burning passion.

Colde began by working it slowly yet thoroughly deciphering the code of their symmetry, and rhythm.

On her back she is so turned on that she continues to rub her self, on fire by the burning passion of the moment she is all too eager to indulge in such erotic pleasures.

Colde working the room of her palace like a champ steadily increases the rhythm. She is breathing heavily and almost whimpering from the pleasure ensued by Colde's thrusts, lifting her leg up he slowly turns her body to the side and picks up his pace just a little bit.

She tilts her head upward and gazes deeply in his eyes letting out a series of small screams just loud enough so that no one else could hear, but, Colde has no problems and climbs even higher with her approval of his methods of pleasure. She opens her legs letting out another series of impassioned screams but this time they are louder.

Colde continuing to work the avenue of pleasure he closes her legs and turns her on her stomach Colde is now lifting her up as he stands with knees bent thrusting harder than before, her boiling passion nears the rim of her sexual cauldron.

Colde on his knees behind her leans her forward and increases the rhythm, raising the level of arousal even more arching her back in the process as he pulls her toward him with every thrust...

A constant moan has now turned into a constant yet subtle series of pleasurable screams.

Colde moving her back around is suddenly stopped when she pushes him backward and ends up on top of him. Colde begins rubbing her breasts then probing around to run his fingers down her back.

She can feel his shaft nestled firmly inside of her as she rocks to a rhythm of which he found very pleasing; soon both would erupt in orgasmic pleasure.

Colde at such a heightened state of arousal is speechless as she continues to let out screams of pleasure riding his manhood that seemed to tap her spot every time their thrusts met, her valve running steadily she is beginning to move even faster.

A shrill of a scream is followed by a shivering of her body as she tightens up all over and comes to a complete stop. Colde equally as tired, breathing heavily, that was amazing!

Laying there in the serenity of the moment time seemed to freeze and wrap the two up in a blanket of mutuality comprised of common interest and the differences that bind, at this moment these two are closer to anyone they have ever been in their lives. Neither says a word only stare at each other tired but not wanting to close their eyes, in doing so maybe both feel the moment will never end; or maybe looking away is denying what just happened and how they feel.

Perhaps both are in shock from the over flow of emotions and pleasure but both can agree that neither had done anything so extreme with anyone else. Will the next time be so free and open? Will there even be a next time?

Colde staring at her, something suddenly occurred to him; in all the passion and ecstasy he forgot one little detail.

"What's your name?"

Both laughing at the same time, the captain just a bit louder having thought the same thing right before he asked, is followed by a moment of silence.

For some odd reason everything seemed to slow down the captain not getting out the first letter before the door to the room abruptly opens revealing two guards holding raised weapons startled upon the sight of two naked bodies on the floor, looking away quickly asking; "I guess no one's been in here."

"Does it look like it," Colde grabbing up articles of clothing so she could cover herself before him.

The two guards turning to leave are interrupted by Colde's curiosity.

"What's going on?"

"Gildyn Aswic is an imposter," the guard to the right speaking in hurried tones quickly shutting the door and activating the magnetic locking system.

"Wait," Colde yelling out to them as the door shuts dropping the article of clothing that covers his front side. "Ain't that a bitch," Colde turning around to face the captain. Damn it, he didn't want to think of her and only know such an informal name as 'Captain.'

73

Before either could get a word in the ground shook, and violently I might add. This means only one thing the imposter has accessed sensitive areas and relayed the location of this place to the bug heads; this whole thing from the beginning was a set-up.

"Captain I think its time to go," Colde getting dressed as fast as he can.

She followed suit and both were now standing by the door forcing open the panel that housed the locking system, which wasn't very easy to do.

The ground shaking again a lot more violent this time causes a small cave-in at the backside of the room, great not again. They know that this whole area is collapsing and the Myie will quickly abandon the tunnels. They must have another safe location to go to for such an occurrence.

The lock not being cooperative Colde is wishing for his weapon, abruptly, the door opened.

"Good job." The captain replied as the door opened.

"I didn't do anything," Colde glancing back at her.

Making sure it's safe, Colde leads them out the door and down the way they took when escorted here; got to track down Riedar Gi'Jhym.

The tunnels beginning to break apart and drop chunks from the ceiling Colde knows this place won't last much longer have to get clear of the impact zone but remain hidden from the aerial bombardment.

The door leading to Riedar's office is completely covered in rock and the tunnel seems to be empty has everyone gone and left them behind, that's' not very nice now is it.

"Hey!" A voice calling out from behind them, it's the one that brought them here.

"Sorry I'm late the tunnels have been shut off from all sides I had to blow my way thru to get to you." His uniform covered in dust.

"The others," Colde asking in somewhat grim tones, as if knowing the answer all ready.

"Most have made it out except Riedar," the special operative motioning them to follow him.

Heading to a more secure location, if that is possible with their cover being blown, Colde and the captain close behind the special operative. The tunnel beginning to collapse directly behind them as if following them advertently aimed at destroying the three, the dust and debris enveloping their position as the collapsing tunnel comes down around them.

Dust and smoke bellowing from underneath, above ground is completely decimated with large blast holes and rubbles of rock. The wind blown dust fluttering into the air as something that once was but is no more, is finally crushed as the entire area collapses covering one mile with nothing but dust and black smoke. It is painfully obvious that even if they did get far enough from the impact zone the after shock will have gotten any stray survivors. If any did survive they will never find their way out of that nightmare, Myie or not.

"Captain," Colde calling out standing over piles of downed rock large boulders and trace amounts of technology, crushed by the cave-in.

"Damn it," the special operative stepping in the open from behind a larger pile of rocks holding his MPFS that is permanently busted; crushed by the fall and the rocks.

"You wouldn't happen to have another one of those?" Colde calling out to him about ten paces away, as he hears him throw the MPFS at the ground cursing the bug heads and how hard it was to acquire such sensitive equipment.

"I feel for you but I can't find the Captain and I'm going to need your help," Colde snapping the Myie back to reality with the sternness of his voice.

Colde moves cautiously through the rubble toward the Myie and the larger pile of rocks beside the soldier very concerned calling for the Captain. She has to be in that pile it's the closest to them, looking up and realizing they have fallen into another tunnel or corridor beneath the tunnels they once occupied.

"What is this place?" Colde beginning to take the larger rocks off the pile calling for her again but getting no answer, this doesn't look good for the Captain.

"It was built beneath us to accommodate such things as aerial bombardments." The Myie beginning to pull a rock off the pile is suddenly stopped by Colde's urgent tone.

"What is it?" The Myie startled to a stop, sounding some what annoyed.

"I found her," Colde driven by something powerful seeing as he found her in virtually pitch-black conditions.

"Hold on- I just remembered something," the Myie feeling his way around the wall of the cave.

Colde just barely able to see silhouettes he knows there has to be a light source coming from somewhere, a faint light blue catching his eyes above a small ledge, a series of lights about six-feet apart; *such ingenuity* Colde thinking to himself. Where has the special operative taken off to and why isn't he back yet, looking but mostly feeling for what he believes to be the captain's ankle underneath the pile of small but chunky rock? Wonder if this special operative is one of the famously feared Miscreant Scouts? Not bad people, as a whole the Miscreant earned their respect and people liked them.

Abruptly a beam of light crosses the front of the pile closest to Colde then to the top following it back to the bottom; the rocks bigger at the base but the pile mainly consist of small chunks. Now beside Colde having walked and investigated in unison, both have a good idea of how to deal with the situation. Small chunks however have a habit of creating pockets so if one is moved it could cause shifts and even collapse the whole pile toppling onto the captain causing more damage, one thing Colde will not let happen.

Beginning to dig her out, the secret room a.k.a. bomb shelter has grown suddenly bleak, Colde unable to seen any silhouettes only where direct light is present.

"It's gotten darker," Colde looking around unable to see even the top of the rock pile standing right next to it, hesitant he does not want to keep pulling away rock.

The Myie initially distracted is now looking around and vehemently moving the light around the ceiling and the trap door they went through that ultimately buckled under the weight of the collapsing corridor along with a good size section of the bomb shelters ceiling, which filled the shelters floor with the rubble beneath their feet and the pile on top of the captain.

"This isn't right," the Myie slowly backing away.

"What you doing-we got to get her out." Colde slowly moving around the pile, which he couldn't see, tries to take the flashlight.

"She will be all right," looking at the pile using the light in unison widening the beam, but not for too long.

"Besides she's better off than we are right now."

"What are you trying to say?"

"Those safety lights along the edge aren't supposed to cut off they have their own independent system built into the lights themselves."

Colde kind of blank and expressionless, at first, suddenly realizes what is going on.

"Are you saying there are Scaedrein soldiers directly above us," Colde still apprehensive he will not leave her side.

"I'm not sure how they could have achieved this but that's what my instincts are telling me."

Now Myie instincts aren't always right but who can argue with eight-five percent, the average of how many times their instincts lead them in the right direction.

Colde still wouldn't have it taking a few steps back he hides by the rock pile. The Myie continues to step back toward the south wall to get out of plain view.

How could the Scaedrein's have gotten through the tons and tons of rock above them so quickly?

What has happened to the imposter Gildyn Aswic-where is the real Gildyn Aswic?

The captain's face and laugh echoing within his mind torturing him with visions of her death and how much he would miss her and more importantly-a lump in his throat a sudden emptiness in his heart as he realizes at this moment and for as long as he lives that he loves her more than his own life, and that he would rather die knowing that he at least tried to save her. At that instant Colde stands up.

The Myie now stopped is holding the light down and cannot see Colde or even knows Colde has stood up, his instincts tugging at his shoulder pulling him further back; the bug heads are close. Colde and the captain in the range of his instincts, figuratively speaking, he knows they are okay and out of harms way. Wait, something is here? The Myie slightly tilting his head as if 'listening' yet he expects to hear no sound, what ever this something is it seems abstract yet an outline is there. Colde is standing by the rock pile there seems to be a heavy concentration of fast moving molecules around his position creating a faint glow around the outside of his entire body, yet this glowing effect seems to be a separate entity of the darkness around it because there are no shadows being thrown.

Colde no longer cared about those Scaedreins and everything now seemed so small and trite the only thing that matters now is the captain's personal well being, moving the rocks from the pile as if the chunks were mere balls of paper. He is buzzing all over and never once has he ever felt such power in his life and it wasn't from money; it wasn't from revenge; it wasn't from killing; it wasn't from manipulating people or discovering some other angle or con. He has so many other feelings behind this newfound salvation that he will use even if she does not make it out alive; she showed him that.

The Myie watching the rock pile dwindle is not befuddled by the events unfolding before him, how he is able to see this 'miracle' at such an in-depth level is what has him stunted. Sure their culture is no stranger to the spiritual side of life but who has ever really comprehended any part of a miracle, how come it just happened to him? A 'new' something has triggered within him opening his eyes to a back drop behind the web of not just life but the grand scheme of things; a greater aspect of everything. This has been there for a long time yet he seems to have discovered a deeper root? A better understanding of their belief that none have ever seen? Is he experiencing a moment of instantaneous realization so powerful it could be conceived as a miracle as well? One thing he knows for sure spiritual text have no documented event of what happened to him.

Have two miracles happened in the same room?

The last rock to move bigger than all the rest is still easily thrown to the side opening up enough room for her to be lifted out and Colde did, quickly.

The Myie taking quick notice of Colde's success, instinct grabs his secondary weapon and centers it directly on God knows what because he's not using the light and it's completely dark. Again, instinct reacts and pulls the trigger. Abruptly a figure falls from the darkness slamming face first against the rubble covering the ground, a lone Scaedrein must have got lucky found a way in and was scouting ahead upon telling the others. Great that just means more are coming. As quick as they went out the safety lights are back on there is no one else above them to trip the sensor that deactivated the light, in the first place. Maybe that's a good sign?

The thud of the dead body faint Colde is completely focused on the captain and to be honest the blaster didn't seem too loud either. There's blood on the left side of her forehead her beautiful bottom lip gashed covered in blood Colde seeing the damage as if highlighted throughout her body two cracked ribs; a concussion; a broken arm and leg; two places on the leg. He did not seem worried as he ran his hand over her body starting at the head, steadily working his way down. Could it be that another miracle is taking place? This is miracle three and counting maybe four if you account for them even being alive?

Dust kicked up around the body as it hit and settled back to the ground fluttering in an area virtually void of wind. The Myie seeing Colde as if it were daylight and his clothes and hair ruffling in what could be misconstrued as wind but he has an idea of what and how this 'wind' effect is created, not just spiritual it is all so molecular and how one can learn to manipulate these molecules and become a sort of medium for channeling the mystical powers of a greater aspect thru not just the soul but the kinetic energies of life itself plays a role in the part, as well.

Colde has not said a word the whole time not even to him self, as a matter of fact it doesn't seem like he's even thinking. Is this the power of his soul doing the work he can't do in the flesh? It feels as though he's just watching yet he is aware of all his movements, and in control of them. Does being directed by instinct feels like this? Is this what Myie feel like when their instincts kick in? Can the Myie even see him? Colde can't see anything beyond the captain it is all pitch black, even darker than before when he couldn't see. Colde watching as his hands continue to move down stopping momentarily on right rib number five, then moving over her stomach and abruptly stopping at her upper legs, abruptly as the power surge started it ended in the same fashion.

A light groaning is heard as Colde smiles and suddenly becomes very tired. "Captain," his tone dragging but relief is prevalent and taken with equal kindness.

Colde collapsing on the ground beside her is glad to see her alive, and although very weak she simply replies "Eve." Colde smiling as a tear runs down his cheek her name is Eve, what a beautiful name, his last thoughts before passing out from exhaustion.

The Myie running over to Colde and the captain: *Eve*, a voice seemed to echo off ancient winds being pushed by the 'now' and finally catching up to the future. Is this a residual from the moment? Is it something the captain had reserved great power to release and in doing so he is capable of obtaining her name without having a clue of what it is? Is this the strength of intent? He feels tired as well what them two are doing sounds real good about now, sleeping. Question is how safe of an option is that? His instincts no longer tugging at him feeling suddenly relaxed, almost involuntarily he sits down against the wall and falls asleep without concern for what is happening around him. Myie are not often lackadaisical during a catastrophe of such magnitude.

The Scaedrein once leading the man hunt investigation is missing and so is the Scientist, both were once the leading figure heads of a growing 'chain of influence' that rivaled a long time 'strong house' within the Scaedrein political infrastructure, the two nearly toppled the house and claimed a position held by the same members and their offspring for a record twenty years. Their political ventures were black balled and they were kicked from their chairs, of course this was all done by the rival but legally I might add, which in turn landed them at the positions they held for five years leading them to their current status of M.I.A. What the two do not know is that the manhunt; the destruction of the *'Jid'* post, and even the clone are part of a bigger picture that only a few other Scaedrein know about.

The discovery of this underground network of Myie is unsettling but suspected; the clone's behavior modification worked well beyond expectations and is still on the loose, a few Scaedrein's know this; not to mention additional support from the *Tarsuon*-class vessel above the planet. The known reputation of the captain and first officer; one of the few remaining survivors from the battle of *Cly'ruk* which in fifteen minutes produced an astronomical amount of Scaedrein casualties; the reason behind their presence is more than coincidence. The clone directed by implants and tracked since starting what he was originally designed to do infiltrate, sabotage, and relay his location. The infestation should be neutralized in a matter of hours, if not sooner. The size of the infestation estimated somewhere between twenty and two-hundred Myie, although two hundred isn't likely, these projections are there to help damage control teams be better prepared and organized. These conspirators have their bases covered no other Scaedrein knows the truth about these 'cave dwellers.' The cover story will be a group of escaped prisoners during a revolt from years passed, whose bodies were never found, will be the scapegoats for this scenario. This well concocted and covered conspiracy seems solid or as the Scaedreins say, *cie'koo*. The ironic thing is these prisoners were actually picked up by the Myie a short time after the escape and have remained alive to this day.

An eerie dismal backdrop accompanied with an almost oozing haze *Djri'gee'din* city and its oddly shaped monstrosities that are supposed to be buildings but how these 'buildings' manage to maintain any stability is beyond reason. Because, and brace yourself, these buildings look as though some giant person took an enormous size dump and instead of working with gravity it laded on it's end and managed to support itself, years later it hardened and created what is known as *Djri'gee'din* city. The streets barren and there is a stench reminiscent of what this giant person has left laying around, a silence a stillness of the moment imbruing an apprehensive group of all so silent 'directors' within one of the many unlabeled 'buildings', who seem effected by this night despite the fact they are inside. The source of this silence is a question not one in the room can answer. "What has happened at or to a *Jid* post that has lasted for more than twenty-years?" The commander of the post seems to be unavailable for comment this makes them uneasy not because they feel he is acting deceitful instead its for his MPC (Mass Population Count) number, for every Scaedrein lost the ruling directors are held liable and accountable by striking years from how long their members and family can maintain a 'strong house.' Directors a human translation Scaedreins refer to them as *Gr 'K' lee'my* and they can smell something too but its not the city, it's trouble giving off that odor and every passing second puts the leaders in a bad position driving them off the edge. The only thing left to do is send a gaggle of soldiers directly from their department to the *Jid* post hopefully there will be a good explanation, opposed to total annihilation.

Oh-oh guess its too late for that the commander of the post one of the conspirators has a plan of his own that will discredit the current *Gr 'K' lee'my* and credit him for the discovery and destruction of the Myie-oh I mean escaped prisoners from years back who were thought to be dead, which upon the destruction of these immigrants he will make the truth known at least his version of it.

A laugh that could be misconstrued as a hissing buzz erupts from the Scaedrein now standing on the bridge of the Tarsuon-class vessel staring out a opening about two feet wider and taller than him sealed by a force field, despite the field protecting him from the elements of space it still feels as though he's out there floating in some sort of Scaedrein heaven. What a rush breaking such a sacred law it makes him feel even better to know that his acts will go unbeknownst to most of his own kind. Them fools will take his story like those accursed humans take candy from one of their hideously atrocious atrocities they call babies, his peers eating out of his hand as he takes the *Gr 'K' lee'my* of old and replaces it with himself as the lead 'director.' No other will oppose him or the reputable captain, and the first officer, when the times comes to make a 'power play' while the directing-house scrambles to support political implications they know nothing about and are too busy dealing with disputes and accusations from the other houses trying to activate their power play. The post commander will make sure the others houses get falsified casualty reports heightening their anger with the current directors. What he has done is concealed a group of Scaedreins before the post was destroyed. Upon destroying the post the Jid-commander will claim it was over run by a militia suspected to be escaped slaves and prisoners trying to leave the planet, and here is where it gets good; one of the human soldiers supposable tips them off about Myie being in some caves in the north-east and south-west sectors of the now wiped out *Jid* post. He is conveniently stacking the deck in his favor giving a reason behind whipping out the post with such magnitude and being so secretive about it, if word got out that even one Myie was still around after all these years the rest of the humans might begin to doubt the validity of the Scaedrein ability to really mess somebody up.

The other Scaedreins will again take the story as the truth, without a doubt. If Myie are involved and it can be verified the others will accept with open arms, you see, Myie know there one weakness and have always known it because they were the one's responsible for the existence of the Scaedreins. Another story that sort of turns the major powers and some of the other smaller systems against the Myie and eventually on the side lines as their own creations wipe the creator out, showing no mercy. By now most are not very fond of the Myie blaming them for the Scaedreins take over as much as the other galactic super powers, which still have done nothing about this 'bug' infestation. The post commander wondering briefly if it would be time to start the next part of his other plans, not just yet. A noise behind him stirs his attention nervous perhaps paranoid he turns around; it's the first officer. He says that the captain wishes to see him there may be a problem. The post commander aged with experience the lead strategist during the planning of the destruction of the Myie, now moving along side the first officer heading rather quickly to the bridge of the Tarsuon-class vessel.

The ship much like *Djri'gee'din* makes one wonder why that particular *Jid* post looked so organized and geometrically sound. Remember that Colde and the captain noticed areas under construction; is that post the first of many upgrades? If so that could indicate a change in perspective, are the bug heads moving further away from their roots; an evolutionary revolution?

The post commander moving thru construction on the ship walking by working human slaves, stupid humans wish he didn't have to be around them, nudging the first officer and then vicariously knocking one of the slaves to the ground. The non-essential piece of plasmic poop to small to even see with the naked eye hits the 'metal' flooring face first an electrical board being crushed under the weight of the impact, as well as the humans nose. If he is dead, who cares? There is one thing you must know about the Scaedrein's not all look completely the same, they go through changes and hibernate within cocoons to complete each transformation. Two earth years is what it takes a Scaedrein to reach young adulthood during this time a young male may go through two or three cycles and each one evolves with their strengths thus having larger mandibles or a bigger *'Nythillic Spear.'* A Nythillic Spear is a long sharp exoskeleton protruding from the left or right appendage beneath the Scaedrein equivalent to a hand. Some of the Scaedreins on this vessel have hands, strange these Scaedrein's do have almost unnoticeable differences. The hands are small but present, as well as being a bit more bi-pedal than the others. Perhaps there is a Scaedrein equivalent to a freak of nature all species have them so why shouldn't they? If so, it's obvious they intend no harm and wish the best for all Scaedrein kind.

The bridge completely over hauled is organized and complete with steps and not ramps. Every Scaedrein on the bridge at a different stage of neo-revolution a new breed of Scaedrein smarter, better trained, and superior to the others? Just when you think the plot is really beginning to expose itself another interesting discovery adds more mystery and hazes any concrete facts discovered earlier in the investigation, expanding a broadened conspiracy that stretches around the galaxy and threatens to wipe out every human or until the last Scaedrein is dead, which ever comes first. If any of the non-human species take up arms they too will fall to this neo-order of Scaedrein kind, their numbers growing they are not labeled with legitimate MPC numbers. The Scaedrein equivalent to the men in black which yes they are dealing with a alien species, at least to them, and attempting to cover the fact. Around seven or eight hundred on board you can bet there are more else where hidden from the prying eyes of their own kind awaiting the day they will be accepted by other Scaedreins and be allowed to walk amongst their own, a civil rights movement.

The captain of the vessel standing proudly on the second level observation deck rubbing his own ego as he notices his old friend approaching with the first officer beside him glad to see the post commander, their team work is the reason behind the battle of *cly'ruk* (Instant death.). A firm handshake is followed by a hug, almost human looking these Scaedreins are, facial expressions clearer and more prominently defined features. A year ago they did not look like this, and since cocooning days are long gone, it doesn't seem possible. The others were born that way freaks of nature, an ugly duckling, and like the story they have grown into something greater than any ordinary Scaedrein. The question still remains what is responsible for the captain the first officer and the post commander's sudden change?

Back to why the captain believes there is somewhat of a problem the *Gr 'K' lee'my* is sending three drop ships to inspect with two in reserve three grids from the now bruised north east coast line, if you put into consideration that it looks like a week old battle field. The early reports will be devastating to the credibility of the current directors beginning the domino effect described a few paragraphs ago about the 'power plays' and regardless of the opposing drop ships it is too late to stop what is beginning to unfold; a

fabricated war fueled by deception, political paranoia, and misinformation an almost perfect crime. There is however one little hole.

Eyelids extended touching one another, fluttering momentarily, the real *Gildyn Aswic* suspended in a cryogenic type freeze as a trophy piece in the center of the captain's private chambers. No one is allowed in and if caught in the act the penalty is instant false death where you merely live to maintain MPC, and do nothing else. *Gildyn Aswic* has been frozen for seventeen years. The clone, well clones, is the last of two that were created at different times. The first one lived to fifteen and was cloned again in order to continue with the project, an attempt to draw out any living Myie that survived that crash landing eighteen years ago.

The post commander's mentor died just recently and headed the earlier stages of the project with the captain's mentor, who died just recently as well by natural causes. Not many Scaedreins do that, at least not at this point in time, this may be a changing fact between the old and the neo; I don't say new because they are not a different generation per say, they're the gifted ones of their generation. Smarter and stronger hidden by a neo-face beneath the top wrung of a new evolutionary jump, a glimpse of what is to come in the development of a new generation. The old fogies dropping like flies means a series of new elections that will bring out candidates within these houses in order to maintain their comfortable stature, unfortunately this has been accounted for as well and is not going to work. This plan stands to incriminate and deteriorate several smaller houses affiliated with the *Gr 'K' lee'my* that will do their best as well to support the directors during this crisis, perfect, this is exactly what the three conspirators are counting on. Now in the captain's quarters admiring the frozen artwork the hissing/buzz sound of their laughter as the post commander indicates the scare to be superficial, at best. How have these directors held office for so long? The laughter continuing the three all ready celebrating success; there is one thing you should know Scaedreins don't laugh. Is this part of the neo-drein, yeah, not to mention the fact they can experience joy at such levels. Scaedreins can and do experience joy but not enough to make them laugh; happy is about as far as they go.

His eyes popped open and he jumped back the uniformed Myie quickly looking around suddenly becoming aware of his surroundings, temporarily forgetting where he is. *What a strange dream,* lackadaisically to himself still a little out of it, must have been tired. The captain and Eve still sleeping they must have been really tired. Eve, what a strange name yet there is a certain power to it he can't put his finger on. Despite the fact that he knows her name he will not use that knowledge out of respect for her privacy. The dream, a still drawn image motionless in his mind, one second of a moment an echo in a drop of water, the image now disrupted by the intervening of consciousness slowly dissipating leaving only a dry bed of emotion to decipher the subconscious pictures created by the aware mind while the host sleeps.

A light rustling is heard breaking the Myie's train of thought, knowing it to be Colde and the captain he's glad that he didn't have to wake them. Hope the captain is able to travel?

Eve is the first one sitting up straight and on her feet in no time, guess that answers his question; she looks invigoratingly fresh and ready to take on the galaxy. Colde on the other hand is groggy longer and stays quiet. She walks away Colde doesn't seem to mind. Abruptly he holds out his hand she stops and turns; but walks off again? What the h-wait.

There are faint sounds just beneath the stagnant air, an indication of stillness, a residual a reverberating resonance bouncing *thwatts* off the slow moving molecules within the *Kinetic Web of Creation*, not life but the essence of all things around us. Imagine playing connect the dots with every tree with every strand of grass and even stationary points for living things because on this web rests your web, woven right into the grand scheme of things. This faint sound tickling a strand on this massive web as if it moved with great power and truth; a divinity of love that transcends even the soul; that the truest examples of such passion are two webs and although dissimilar were intertwined at the moment the emotion occurred bridging a gap between the flesh the soul and this Kinetic Web of Creation (KWC.). The faint sound is mumbles of some sort a realization hitting him like a ton of rock, been there done that, the two are still connected even hours after the powerful and moving experience—The reason they need not speak, literally hearing one another's direct intent.

A *thwatt* is a residual of mental energy, loosely defined as intent that bounces off near by strands and sort of strengthens the effect of the thwatt, if it matches the base 'frequency' of the KWC and only then will such an act occur.

The two still distant pulled out of reality, caught in the splendor of a moment that has suspended them in the realization that they will love each other for all time, and there isn't anything that can stop that. Love will find a way because it goes even deeper than life itself because without love you wouldn't have life, and it all started when the first 'single' cell organism formed.

The Myie still observing the two as they maintain a distance apart approaching them ready to go, but at the same time the two are wondering if he knows his fly is open. The first clear thought he heard from the mumbles of their thwatts, intent has a lot to do with it, curiously to himself he wonders if one can clear up undirected thought or decipher the actual meaning behind someone else's false statement? Saying not one word he turns away from them as if looking around, shinning the light all over the south wall, casually going unnoticed as he buttons his fly.

"There should be a narrow access point that leads to a larger tunnel somewhere at the base of the south wall." The Myie stopping on the left side of the south wall, quickly finding the concealed entrance to the crawl space leading to a tunnel that continues south but cuts a degree or two west after a mile or so.

The Myie knowing this tunnel in particular very well acting as though he didn't, hiding this knowledge, either out of habit or a lack of trust for the two outsiders? The body! The Scaedrein he shot a few hours ago still lies in the center of the room; might find something useful on the body?

Well then again maybe not. Gaining access to the secret tunnel took no time and all three are heading southwest toward a secondary safe spot opposed to a primary safe spot, which are now labeled hot spots. Some distance between them they're not out of the water yet, along with the other surrounding networks that are dated back from when they first began over eighteen years ago. These tunnels are the secondary I speak of; there is however another final resort, caves to the west about eight grids from their current position. There is one flaw to this most if not all travel is done above ground with a number of stops in near by caves, if necessary, being so deep behind enemy lines eight miles may as well be eighty so cover spots are mapped into the course for a good reason. All traveling is done at night with *Miscreant Scouts* equipped with heat and refracted light goggles taking point two hundred *mils* (yards.) ahead of any group of non-combat personnel, and around the group is any number of active personnel readily available at the time to serve as escorts and protectors. The tunnel heading southwest seems to be a tad more dank and a hell of a lot darker than even one hundred yards back up the corridor; are they closer to the center or top of the rock shelf?

Only one source of light to navigate with isn't so bad unless it's the light Colde and Eve jimmied together hours ago it's not a light designed for penetrating darkness at such an extreme degree, its getting dimmer and dimmer as the minutes pass.

"This light of yours is fading fast and we still have a good ways to go, we're not going to make it unless," the Myie hesitant to suggest but he must. "Let me go ahead by myself, alone I think I can get to a cache of supplies about a half a mile up."

"If it's anything like the other cave light you had then we're shit out of luck," Colde not very happy about a light that is of such intensity it burns the bulb out in about two or three hours.

"Do not worry we are no more than five miles from the nearest power source." The Myie trying to reassure the two by showing he does not want to leave them here either but it has to be done; there is no other option. He knows how treacherous the last part of the tunnel is and knows they need better light if all three are going to traverse the tunnel.

"What happens if something happens to you?" Eve not wanting to sit in pitch-black conditions; who does?

"We're wasting time. I can assure you there will be people looking for us, if not now then soon. This is the safest spot you can be because even the Tarsuon-class vessel can't penetrate this rock shelf with its sensors," the Myie throwing out another assurance.

Colde and Eve know he is right and accept the circumstance for what it is the last option.

"There is one thing I must know before you go," Eve taking the Myie by the hand that holds the light shinning the light upon his face, indirectly. "What is the name of the one who risks his life by coming back to get us?"

"The name is *Kelmu Cw'jur*, and going back to get you was and is my job," walking off without a word when from the darkness a voice replied, "your welcome."

Eve and Colde no longer able to see the light and he has just walked off can't be more than ten-feet away.

"Hope he doesn't take too long?"

Eve pulled him toward her, "we'll just have to occupy ourselves."

"It's dark so we're all ready half way there."

Eve giggles like a teenager as does Colde, the laughter slowly fading as passion takes its place.

Kelmu half the distance all ready and the light is still going, however he is stopped and the light is on the ground at his feet. Perhaps he has found this cache of supplies?

"I have them sitting in the dark about two-hundred mils (yards) behind me. They believe I am looking for a supply cache." "No," *Kelmu* responding to a voice over his short-range communicator, "I haven't activated any tunnel lights." "Orders received, bringing them in." The okay to activate guide lights makes his job easier and he all ready feels a lot safer.

Hope the two aren't sore for being left in the dark, twice.

When finished and fully clothed *Kelmu* returns answering all the questions pertaining to the lights and where they're going, things seem to be rolling their way for once. They have no reservations about Kelmu acting as he did they would do the same, these last remaining Myie are in dire straits and another breech in security isn't what they need.

"Kelmu what an interesting name; what does it mean?" Eve standing before the uniformed man, quite attractive.

"The importance of my name is *Cw'jur* it means neutral or unbiased," Kelmu turning to guide them the rest of the way in a low light equivalent to say a torch.

Interesting, Eve and Colde exchanging glances then follow the Myie down the southwest corridor toward what they are not sure? A bit of reluctance is all too prevalent standing at the threshold of a risky venture; both parties are making a tremendous leap of trust and courage. The knowledge Colde and Eve attain can and may easily get them killed not to mention the lives of all the other surviving Myie in these tunnels, this Underground Resistance Network (URN.). Colde at one time when the Myie were still around wanted so bad to gain entrance into one of these networks and now that he's getting his chance he wants nothing more than to turn around and find another way of getting off the planet, but this is the only option where they actually stand a chance. Eve around 32 has never had such an urge and she doesn't at the moment, either. One thing has changed her perspective, these Myie are not your usual humanoids.

Colde is feeling an urge to go around the main areas of the URN avoiding the whole visual and social experience, cold feet. He can't back out now he has to keep going facing the new danger ahead by channeling his fear productively and wisely.

Eve almost happy go lucky is just glad to be alive and taking it as obstacles occur she's as ready as she'll ever be, bring it on.

The oval reception area ground zero in the southwest network houses many joining tunnels most are dead ends rigged with traps, only a few actually lead to sensitive areas. Colde and Eve surrounded by armed personnel receiving their reception; an interrogation is more like it.

"I will not ask again," a young officer in training standing firmly before Colde with stern tones.

"We have all ready gone through this back at the other tunnels," Colde becoming frustrated.

"Well since you two have entered the picture we have lost a good commander," the young would-be officer smug inflated with a cosmetic level of authority.

"The clone Aswic Gildyn is responsible for that," Colde defending Eve and himself.

"What if you two are clones and conspiring with him?"

Colde shaking his head at this kid who obviously is over paranoid, not saying anything.

"In light of the events unfolding around you and what you stand accused of we have no choice but to execute you for treason."

Several barrels pointing in their direction quickly calm down an outraged Colde holding back an even more infuriated Eve. "Where is Kelmu?" Colde knowing the high-ranking Miscreant Scout can put a stop to this non-sense.

Abruptly the circle of guards break as one Kelmu Cw'jur walks through and approaches the officer in training, he doesn't look happy.

"What is the meaning of this?" Kelmu motioning around the reception area, "You were ordered to conduct a low-level security check and not threaten possible allies with execution," Kelmu stopping momentarily, looking over at Colde and Eve.

"These two are my personal friends and if I ever see you abusing your power in such a way again your going to have one mean mad miscreant on your hands, now get out of my sight before I change my mind and decide to have you ejected from active duty and nullify your officer training." Kelmu humiliating the lad in front of everyone including, and especially, the lower ranked Miscreant Scouts forced to take orders from such a schmuck.

The assistant to the assistant C/O, this would-be officer runs off with tail between his legs; dignity and ego badly bruised. The guards exiting as well leaving the three alone in the reception area; now what?

The Clone Aswic Gildyn has created one hell of a security breech paranoia is heightened and morale is dropping, but will the events be detrimental to the entire project or just a few individual networks?

One thing the reader of this story must know is that Colde and Eve have found themselves in the middle of not one but two conspiracies spanning an eighteen-year gap conducted by both the Myie and these neo-drein; question is who is more prepared and who exactly has the upper hand? Up to now you may think that Colde and Eve are the main characters, which they are but in the secondary sense, but the major characters are Aswic Gildyn and Kelmu Cw'jur. Colde and Eve are the triggers of the story their previous actions are what brings about the final stages of the *Scaedrein Infiltration* conducted by the Myie, and all this time I thought the book was called Scaedrein Infiltration because Colde and Eve infiltrate the Scaedrein home world; guess there are times when even the one who tells the story is left in the dark.

In conference with a number of delegates from connecting networks Kelmu is being debriefed, Colde and Eve are part of this as well. The topic of conversation at the moment is the location of the clone impostor and why isn't one of the lead Miscreants doing his job? Threats of dereliction of duty and not following a direct order from a senior officer have all ready been used; Kelmu seems to be taking some heat as well. Strange this is, it feels like there is something else going on behind the curtain of this whole scenario; has a smaller conspiracy spawned off two larger ones? Why is this more important than the threat of annihilation? These Myie should be packing up and heading for the hills not wrapped up in military politics. Is another impostor amongst these Myie?

Kelmu standing up to address the delegates hopes he has a remedy for all the accusations, and paranoia.

"The search for this clone is currently underway I have a technical team on it as we speak eliminating and projecting possibilities."

"And where is this team?" The western delegate briefly interrupting Kelmu.

"Due to the current crisis I must use my oath of silence-" "And why is that?" Kelmu interrupted once again this time by the northeast delegate somewhat tense having been in the tunnels that were destroyed, he has good reason to be on edge.

"I will maintain my oath because I believe there is another imposter amongst us who is using this to hide his identity; Aswic Gildyn is the only link to this other impostor. If we chase him down now the larger fish is going to get away."

The delegates know what Kelmu wants to do, use the clone as bait.

"Are you suggesting we give this clone free roaming of the network, why don't we just open the door for the Scaedrein's-." "It's too late for that." Kelmu doing the cutting this time, the western delegate looking appalled.

"The bug heads could have all ready been in here months ago, probably years ago; who knows? We came here over eighteen years ago knowing our home planet would be destroyed and we have waited for the time to exact vengeance because we know the one fatal weakness of our enemy and the time has come to show ourselves to the Scaedreins for the last time before we wipe that wretched disease we created so many years ago off the face of the galaxy, only then will we gain our respect back and be accepted by the other systems." Kelmu stopping briefly, "If you choose to sit by and let procedure dictate our survival then let the Scaedrein's kill me because right now I'm not very proud to be Myie," Kelmu sitting back down to a completely quiet room.

Colde and Eve pat Kelmu on the back for a formidable defense that was informative, quick, and to the point.

The delegates briefly looking at each other then call a fifteen-minute recess they must have heard enough.

The three walked out the room trying to ignore the uncertainty they still feel despite Kelmu's decisive defense. If Kelmu is right about this other impostor he or she could very well be exposed by the delegate's *reighning* decision, that is if this imposter has influence over the other delegate's but without them knowing he/she is a spy. The door opened up ending a quick fifteen minutes that was more like five this isn't a good sign.

"Kelmu Cw'jur and company," the western delegate looking over at them from his bench seat, his eyes unrevealing without the slightest bit of intent. "You have been found not guilty and there will be no further inquiries into this matter, this conference is adjourned," the western delegate slamming a gavel against a small wooden block quickly standing up as if in a hurry.

Kelmu eyeing the delegate did not like the vibe he was giving off he's hiding something.

"Colde," Kelmu lightly speaking over the sound of exiting delegates. "You and Eve follow him," Kelmu motioning with a light tilting of his head toward the western delegate. "I'm going to check on the progress of my technical team," Kelmu walking out the door ahead of Colde and Eve.

The western delegate exited through the back door that leads out into a tunnel heading toward the living quarters; perhaps he's going home? A stout fellow with dark graying hair and a handle bar mustache he will be easy to follow.

Colde and Eve file out the front door and go left, away from the delegates exiting right, heading for the end of the tunnel that only cuts one way and that is left.

Standing at a 'T' intersection in the tunnels that make up the living quarters Colde and Eve seen the western delegate go right but that's it. The tunnel reaches to a dead end so it's obvious he has entered one of the rooms, this right corridor houses six doors and one emergency ceiling hatch could the delegate have used the hatch before the two seen it; not likely.

"Can I help you two with something?" A voice from behind them sounding awfully familiar sounds just like.

The western delegate! How-what-who-when?

"You two are supposed to be in the conference room," the western delegate looking quite puzzled.

"We've all ready attended that meeting," Colde looking equally puzzled.

"That's impossible all delegates must be present I wasn't there," the western delegate now completely lost.

A sudden realization flashes into Colde's mind, Eve must have had the same realization because she has the same look on her face. It's the ever-popular oh-shit face.

"I was running late-."

"Listen to me," Colde cutting him off. "Go back down the corridor and find Kelmu and tell him to get down here quick," Colde practically pushing the delegate back down the tunnel.

Colde acting as quick as possible pulls Eve down the right tunnel, stopping at the dead-end.

Eve trying not to be caught in the moment can't help but wonder why Colde is at the dead-end instead of five-feet from their original position, peeking around the corner looking down opposed to up.

Abruptly one of the six doors open, second one on what would be their right. A young man steps into the open looking down to Colde and Eve then casually walking off exiting left heading out of the living area.

Eve quickly makes a break for the end of the corridor, while Colde stops to investigate the door. Colde seeing signs of a struggle toward the middle of the room promptly glances up the corridor at Eve, whom is now peering around the corner back down the tunnel they used to get here. Colde making a dash for Eve's location as she begins moving up the corridor after the one they suspect to be the clone, a clone that appears to have an identity shifting ability.

A concept that is supported by augmenting and implementing all ready present muscle tissue so that one can tighten or loosen the muscles in the face and conceivably change their appearance, but you see the trick is that this sort of manipulation is done at a genetic level before the clone is actually conceived, all the things Aswic has done since his 'genetic program' initiated has ran through his sub-conscience mind from the day he was created.

The suspected clone impostor drops out of view behind a slight curve in the tunnel, as Eve steps around the corner to follow.

"No wait," Colde stopping her, "give him a second."

"Who-?" Eve suddenly stopping her question when she notices the suspect walking toward her, Kelmu close behind holding him at gun-point.

"I see you found our friend."

Kelmu saying nothing it looks like he wants to pull the trigger; the impostor now adorning a hood, Eve reaching to remove it.

"Don't do that," Kelmu stopping her in mid-motion. "He's breaking down at a genetic level this clone has done what he was programmed to do, you don't want to look at him."

"How do we know if you aren't the clone?" Eve becoming defensive but ever so briefly, looking into the unwavering eyes of Kelmu.

"That's definitely you in there," Eve replying with a smile.

"I'm going to show him to the visiting delegates before he dies so they can see the proof, my word is good but it seems my skills have been put under scrutiny since this mission started and this will silence that criticism and doubt."

"I'll go with you," Eve eagerly walking off with Kelmu.

"I'll check the room," Colde watching her walk off feeling a bit jealous can't have love without the other. He knows he has nothing to worry about but why is she suddenly so curious about the Myie? Not to mention her giddy schoolgirl tone. "I'll go with you," what the hells that about? Colde thinking his own thoughts foolish setting them aside for the more important things like investigating the room, someone is either hurt or dead. Damn, should have got Kelmu's com-link so he could report while investigating.

The room isn't that messed up but Colde can see the struggle started in the middle of the room and ended with the real occupant against the wall by the collapsible bed a drop of blood on the floor at the base of the wall is the indicator, no other traces of blood are present. It's a small room with a bed, table, and one closet type indention against the back wall closed off by a red drape. Colde pulling the drape back revealing the occupants dead body slumped over long ways across the floor of the closet the delegates aren't going to like this, finding no other evidence he will report the body to the delegates or section chief who ever he finds first.

Kelmu standing before the delegates with the long tunic in his hands the only thing left of the clone the delegates not happy reluctantly take his word, but their reluctance soon fades as Colde comes thru the door informing them of the body he discovered killed by the clone Aswic Gildyn. A forensics team dispatched immediately they will give the place a thorough once or twice over. The council ready to convene is abruptly stopped by a commission of guards entering the room.

"What is the meaning of this?" The real western delegate the first to protest.

Kelmu standing between the guards, which are all Miscreant Scouts, arms crossed ready to distribute his own authority to these delegates.

"This is not over yet one of you is a traitor that is how the clone was able to infiltrate so fast," Kelmu accusing each and every delegate without hesitation or reluctance, for he has true authority dictated by seniority and experience. He is the only Miscreant scout that has reached the status of Colonel.

"You can't do this," the southeast delegate testing Kelmu's authority.

"I can't. This comes straight down from the head director of all the Networks. None of you are exempt from this order and I will uphold it as directed by the senior officer," Kelmu didn't even flinch much less budge.

Eve and the Captain standing beside Kelmu fully supporting the effort by drawing holstered secondary weapons on the Miscreants beside them, they didn't mind at all.

"I want your hands up now," Kelmu pointing his weapon at the delegates implying deadly force if necessary, "one at a time step into the center of the room."

The delegates putting their hands up each showing they have nothing to hide, politicians are great actors.

Kelmu watched each one step into the center of the room not getting one obvious tug from his instincts, but something is there. This plant is deeply rooted and has been established for at least two years, a sudden memory flash of an incident called *Knuwock Ravine* has him slowly recalling the details from the botched mission and the once non-essential details that now seem to make sense when connecting the traitor to this incident. The missing soldier when the shit hit the fan then the return of this missing soldier during their unseen retreat, and sometime after that a network was forced to move upon the discovery of a Scaedrein patrol in the sector well after the incident. Yes it all makes sense now. The only one present that was in that particular mission other than him self is; the door behind them opens redirecting everyone's attention.

"We got drop ships coming over our position," a young lieutenant frantic and worried; is the enemy aware of every network hidden underneath this rock shelf on the northeastern continent?

"They can't know we're here," Kelmu confident that his instincts would have picked up on it.

Kelmu's eye's back on the delegates is thoroughly convinced that: "It's a trick. The bug heads want us to think they know our location so that when we move we incriminate our position." Kelmu scanning the delegates very carefully as he throws out the accusation, not one reacted suspiciously. What are his instincts trying to tell him?

"Your right," the lieutenant quite surprised at how clear Kelmu's instinct's are. "The drop ships are off short range sensors and long range has them heading east," the lieutenant impressed with how clearly Kelmu interprets instinct and the great connection.

The great connection is a term used to loosely describe what Kelmu has all ready discovered and what no other Myie knows; the Kinetic Web of Creation.

If the delegates had been allowed to leave the impostor would have been able to transmit this location and those drop ships would have been the first of many, but now that's over and although Kelmu isn't sure who the traitor is he knows they are safe from the above ground threat.; at least for now.

Kelmu's technical team is now coming through the door each have a DNA scanner in their hand, these scanners are designed to detect synthetic manipulations performed on a genetic level. The impostor may not know he is an impostor, as with the Aswic clone.

"What are they doing here?" The eastern delegate now aggravated enough to verbally protest.

"This here gadget is going to tell us which one of you is the impostor," Kelmu motioning the guards to accompany the technicians as they take samples and perform the tests.

Kelmu of course taking point will observe them all from a closer position while the remaining guards maintain their initial standing point, directly by the door. Eve and Colde move off a few paces to watch the door and the guards, so no one can surprise them.

The entire test came back negative and no one is a clone. The impostor must be a traitor, and all Myie know what to do with a treasonous bastard-Kelmu narrowing his eyes, deadly force slowly becoming necessary.

"Who's the traitor?" Kelmu drawing his side arm holding a delegate at gunpoint.

The eastern delegate staring into the eyes of Kelmu as if daring him because he is no traitor, he would die before doing such an act.

Kelmu releasing the eastern delegate has eliminated one of six possibilities, immediately grabbing the next in line.

"Is it you?" Kelmu's firm grip on the collar of the western delegate suddenly loosens as he directs his weapon at the face of the southwestern diplomat, "How about you?"

By this time it's clear that none of these delegates are traitors but Kelmu remains persistent, he is beginning to act irrationally.

"No one leaves this room until-" His words are stopped by Eve's gentle touch against his right shoulder, he turns to look at her and there is some kind of 'grounding' effect that centers his focus and settles the 'tapping' of his instincts, like turning a switch to the off position.

The representatives slowly filed out the room followed by the guards leaving Eve, Colde, and Kelmu alone in the small meeting hall.

"What happened?" Colde having no idea why Kelmu was acting so vicious.

Eve has an idea but keeps it to herself. "I'm not exactly sure." She looks over to Colde then back to Kelmu who is wired on adrenaline and in need of rest, they can all use a little rest.

The cots feel like a cloud having slept on nothing but the ground for a very long four days, seems more like four months.

The calm before the storm a lull in climactic action a time where strategically placed pieces make their final move and then strike, the boiling brew in the cauldron of action is right at the edge of the brim about to bubble over. The drums of war are beginning to beat and the tension mounts with the introduction of cymbals lightly crashing barely heard over the all so faint beating drums. A triangle introduces a wave of thought that tickles the strings of the sub-conscience linking to consciousness a genetic memory over four-million years old, a vision of the past that induces inspiration to one particular individual.

Kelmu stands before war torn terrain on a planet he has never seen, faded images like thoughts after afterthoughts the echo of an echo drawing soldiers in different types of crude body armor and ancient weapons that haven't been used in conventional warfare for millions of year's bows and arrows, axes, and swords. There are a variety of different beings on this battlefield but the ones that seem to stick out the most are the bestial looking ones, they look piggish and are big and green. A symbol of some sort seems to be forming from a swirling mist at the center of this field of battle, two lines intersecting at an apex above what looks to be-a hideously wretched face abruptly erupts from the swirling mist barreling toward Kelmu opening it's mouth exposing a wickedly wretched tongue and piercing fangs, the jaws growing larger now directly in front of Kelmu as if trying to swallow him whole. He suddenly opens his eyes and finds himself standing beside his cot, a more than curious Colde and Eve watching him since he stood up within the last minute or two.

"Are you okay?" Colde walking toward Kelmu, whom seemed to be a bit out of it still.

Kelmu doesn't say a word he just rushes out the room, not even taking time to close the door. Eve and Colde exchange a puzzled glance then quickly run out the door to try and catch Kelmu. Colde and Eve heading into unfamiliar tunnels toward areas where Myie conduct their religious ceremonies, closer to the non-combat personnel (NCP), or Myie still too young or too old to be considered active duty. Colde and Eve know this because Kelmu gave them a general lay-out of the network; they just haven't actually seen it.

Midway down the corridor they pass the open doors of the ceremonial chambers briefly looking in abruptly stopping, Kelmu is talking with the company chaplain. Eve and Colde step back and begin to walk away, but Kelmu stops them. "My friends please come in," he says eagerly extending his hand motioning to them. Eve and Colde step into the featureless cathedral, the Myie will leave no traces of their heritage lying around to incriminate their presence.

"What's going on?" Colde stops in front of Kelmu nodding at the chaplain.

Eve coming up behind Colde wrapping her arms around him, giddy she is. "Why don't we get married," Eve sounding somewhat out of character; is she joking around?

Colde turning his head to the side then back the other way as she seductively slithers around the other side of him. "Don't tempt me; I'm liable to take you up on that offer." Colde joking back but is serious about marrying her; just not right now.

Eve smiling back knows that as soon as this is over Colde will ask for her hand and she will accept, no questions asked.

"We are currently devising a plan to evacuate all non-essential personnel from this network and I think you two can help in escorting them while I tie up the loose ends here."

"Wait, whose gonnah help you? If the Scaedreins decide to bust in you're going to need all the help you can get," Colde interrupting the flow momentarily wanting to be a part of the action.

"By the time you leave we'll be right behind you," Kelmu implying there will be no defensive fire on the Myie's part; a clean getaway.

"You must make a stand," Colde looking at Kelmu and the chaplain, "if not now when?"

Kelmu taking this advice as concern places his hands on the shoulders of his now trusted friends Colde and Eve, who were obviously very different people before they ended up on Scaedrei.

"Your concern is taken by an ear that listens but we have our bases covered," Kelmu patting them on the shoulder. "It would be an honor to fight side by side with both of you on the field of battle," Kelmu motioning them forward.

The chaplain following behind he's going to gather up all the NCP's and ready them for escort.

The retreat under way Myie moral is plummeting and most feel as Colde do; a stand must be made. The NCP's are even protesting the retreat; for once the populace wants conflict. Kelmu and the other senior officers know this base is not a good place to start an offensive that encompasses such a wide parameter, the extinction of the Scaedrein race.

Kelmu turned right down the corridor back toward the command center. Eve, Colde and the chaplain turn left heading toward the NCP dorms deeper into network but closer to the rear exit for evacuations like this one in particular. Kelmu rounds a corner coming into the reception area running directly into the western delegate, that's odd, what's he doing here shouldn't he be gone by now? Kelmu shaking off the aftershock of the small collision, the delegate doing the same, there's something weird in the air.

"You should have left hours ago," Kelmu suddenly defensive toward the delegate who seems as though he's hiding something, but he's not sure what it is.

"I was in a private meeting."

"Oh, a private meeting," Kelmu beginning to walk off satisfied with the answer; suddenly he whips back around quickly drawing his side arm pointing it at the western delegate.

Where'd he go? Oh shit! Kelmu stumbling tripping over his own feet falls on his back, dropping his weapon during the impact. The gun not going very far may as well be eighty feet away because there's no way he can reach it in time. The western delegate on the ceiling above him clearly takes him off the human list and places him under giganticus insectus, translation Scaedrein. There is no way the western delegate could have passed the DNA scan, how and where did this one come about?

The bug turned its head a complete one-hundred and eighty degrees looking directly at Kelmu's downed position, preparing to terminate his designated target.

Kelmu blinking the instant death pounced down from above never seen the southwestern delegate blowing the bug in half with a condensed version of a MPFS called a FMPB (Focused Mult-Phasic Blast), which propel a smaller concentration of particles called *Deiro* particles. Deiro meaning disrupt is the name for the altered state of these molecules they come from Cleivorro particles, which perform the opposite, but when re-sequenced what helps support life at a molecular level can be made to destroy it as well.

The southwestern delegate helps a thankful Kelmu off the floor, whom is now pledging the Miscreant oath of secret guard, the southwestern delegate turning down a very high honor showing his modesty. Kelmu wouldn't have it and practically gave the delegate a military order so that he couldn't turn it down.

"Where'd this Scaedrein come from, one so young shouldn't be out so far?" The southwestern delegate looking at the Scaedrein's severed torso.

"It was disguised as the western delegate," Kelmu's words splaying a look upon the delegate's face. "What?" Kelmu feeling a sudden surge of dread reading the face of the diplomat standing before him.

"We better get to the northeastern delegates temporary quarters I seen the western delegate leaving the room," the southwest delegate putting words to the face he just made.

Both take off running toward the room in question located in the tunnel the delegate just came out of.

Meanwhile on the western side of the network the C/O sits calmly in his office having been there for the last hour since his return from the southwest tunnels, he smiles but the source of this smile is not as obvious as one may think.

Kelmu rushed through the door with weapon in hand, a startled northeast delegate jumping to draw his weapon as well.

"Hold it!" Kelmu looking equally startled thinking he should have discovered the delegate's dead body. What the hell is going on here?

The delegate refusing to put the weapon down demands the exact opposite, but not for long.

The southwestern representative steps in and easily sways the northeast elect to put the weapon down.

"Explain to me how you are still alive if the western delegate just left this room and he turned out to be a Scaedrein impostor."

The northeast envoy says nothing only dives at the two blocking his exit, all for not.

The southwest delegate easily pulls the trigger of his FMPB and cuts the delegate in half, both pieces dropping to the ground making a thud-squirt sound. A white fluid seems to be coming from his body, pouring from the upper torso by the lower spine.

"What is that?" Kelmu directing the southwest delegate toward the white bile like substance.

"I don't know but maybe we can take a sample and find out later when we have the time," the delegate stepping out the door to check the corridor for any other bug infestations.

The area secure both are ready to go and should be the only one's left in the base everyone else is well on their way to the southern network, at least they hope so.

The *Gr'K' lee'my* not pleased to hear the reports made by his drop ship pilots and troop commanders they will send a commission to find the Jid commander, and all who choose to consort with him. The lead directors know something is going on they will prepare for the political mess in every way possible. An attempt is being made to discredit them and the proof is the remnants of a battle that seems to have never happened; all evidence on the battlefield is inconclusive. This Jid commander better be dead because if he isn't they will make it happen, and quickly.

Meanwhile above the planet in space the Jid commander the captain and first officer sit calmly in the captain's chambers, aboard the 'phased-out' Tarsuon-class vessel. A phased out ship is different than a cloaked ship for the simple fact it's shield technology however any ship using the shield technology has to lower their shields in order to fire, which is one reason why phasic-shielding isn't as popular as originally estimated. The dual conjunctive dampeners are supposed to filter the power outlet in a way that would appear as natural space particles but the sequencers often misalign even after light use of the dampeners, which is a heavy strike against the technologies usefulness. Colde had problems with his conjunctive dampeners during the moon incident earlier on when they were hiding in the crater, biding their time. The captain of the Tarsuon-class vessel isn't worried about his dampeners failing because unlike all the other ships in the Scaedrein army his technology is new and improved, thanks to his crack crew of 'Scaedrein' engineers.

You see despite a rumored two-zillion Scaedreins the rest of the galaxy isn't all that worried about a bunch of half-evolved bugs if they knew these neo-drein existed it would be a different story, soon they will know and find a new expression of terror for the rulers of the galaxy.

The suspended life of Aswic Gildyn high-lighted in the darkness with one single low-intensity blue light, the frozen chamber hardly noticeable it looks as though the Myie is suspended in a pocket of air iced by the captain's hatred for their creators. A frozen pre-death purgatory a state of limbo while still in the realm of the living; is the mind capable of dealing with it for eighteen-years? How long can someone maintain balance on the edge of death before teetering into that great beyond?

The mystery of the northeast delegate is unsettling as it opens the hand of yet another addition to this ever twisting plot another type of clone but not of Scaedrein technology, is it the same person using different means of sabotage to hinder any attempts of investigation? The white substance pouring from the body is actually *Bio-mantic* fluid, which is actually used to stabilize a pre-clone embryo the northeast pretender's blood was this fluid; how can that be and why did it impersonate the northeast delegate? This brings them back to the western delegate being the suspect or even the southern envoy? One thing is for sure this other hand is responsible for tampering with the Scaedrein's DNA after the Myie abandoned their creation, which they no longer needed. The first on this list of suspects is of course the *Kybans.* Is the western or southern delegate a pretender as well, spawning other pretenders to bring about the destruction of every network by leading the Scaedreins right to them?

The dual assault is not a good idea but they must go through with it to make it look as though they suspect nothing, lulling this conspirator into a false sense of security only then can this breech in security be identified.

URN soldiers from every network established over the last eighteen years have gathered in two places but have separated into fours with a ten-mile gap between each of the two groups or, companies. In this case with the Myie being so few a company varies between sixteen and twenty-two combat ready soldiers, as much as ten or twelve more NCP's two to five command crewmembers and one to three NCO's. Non combat Officers are usually specialized technicians that earn rank on how well they excel in the job they usually starts with an equivalent to a Lieutenant in the Marine Corps, oh-rah. An additional note on the number of combat ready soldiers includes any Miscreant Scouts or other special operatives amongst the company of grunts. Group one will consists of two companies a half-mile apart forming an offensive line about three miles from the city. Group two has two companies in it as well and both are a mile apart steadily moving toward the rear of the southern city. The second group however has a twist an insertion team that will enter the southern city and begin the initial stages of bug eradication; why here, and how they plan to do this has not been revealed only one person knows and he isn't the talking type.

This insertion team is none other than Kelmu, Colde, Eve, and the Chaplain a former miscreant out of action due to injuries a few years back. On a not so small note the Chaplain was an assistant to the head of the genetic research center responsible for the creation of the Scaedreins, another reason why he's a chaplain to maintain a low and inconspicuous profile. His name is *Exle Widjrue,* which means wild fire.

Group one is going to make it look like they are trying to enter the city but will be purposely discovered and intercepted, the Scaedreins will think this is the offensive front that is when group two comes in and announces their presence a mere mile from the rear of the city. The bug heads will be prepared for this but by then the insertion team will have all ready made it into the city, the stupid insects will never realize both groups are distractions and by the time a large number of soldiers reach either point both will have retreated back into the comfort of their tunnels. The insertion team will have a clear path for several minutes this should be more than enough time to complete the mission, getting out is another story; too many unforeseen obstacles to be fully prepared. In any event the first part of the mission will be complete and after that it won't matter because the bugs will be well on their way toward extinction; so they hope.

Okay now comes the reason why the southern city on this continent is the center of focus and why the Myie have set this plan into effect five years prematurely. One; the city is a gathering point for the swarm that is held every five years, during this time virtually every Scaedrein will pass through this city that is similar in appearance to *Djri'gee'din* except larger and built specifically for the *swarm*. The city structures are pod like and vary in size from one to nine stories high, but most average around two and four levels high. Two; the current events have opened too many avenues to maintain even a minimum level of security and moving and/or building another network is not worth a five year wait, which could very well be their downfall.

The southern city covers a forty-seven mile radius and is about six miles from the southwestern coastline; shrouded by heavy trees on all sides the city has only limited ground access for being so big.

"The insertion team will enter *Jumere* through an alley at this point," Kelmu pointing at two buildings on the ocean side of the city midway down the southwest side. "It's a high-risk mission and companies three and four will be the deciding factor, your presence on the surface will allow the insertion team to submerge from the coastline tunnel a mere two-miles from the city, while you engage the enemy the insertion team will have a small window of opportunity during the fire-fight to enter the city. Your job is to hold the enemies for twelve-minutes, after twelve is up begin falling back to grid coordinates *Yuma*-6." (Yuma-equivalent to the Greeks alpha.).

Kelmu looking over to companies one and two. "You will engage the enemy until three and four signals the retreat, understand that the order to retreat is initiated by the units engaging hostiles at the perimeter of the city."

Kelmu taking a few steps to gather his thoughts, "The insertion team will procure transportation when leaving the city and head for Yuma-6, be ready to lend support upon our arrival." Kelmu pointing at a series of bushes, "I want three men here." He then points to another set of bushes on the north edge of a clearing they will use for a landing zone, "perch men up in the trees on the east side of the clearing five minutes before we arrive, our estimated time will be no more than thirty-minutes after you have retreated. There is no doubt the area will be crawling with Scaedreins and some may not come back but remember this we represent something that even two-zillion enemies couldn't eradicate," Kelmu briefly stopping.

"And even if we fail the galaxy will see these hidden actions and hear our courage from within the silence of their own screaming conscience but if we are triumphant even at the cost of all our lives the galaxy will remember us has the one's who freed them from Scaedrein oppression we will win back our respect either way. My friends, my brothers it is time to rise above the ashes of our people's destruction it is time to correct the mistakes of the past and regain the respect and stature of our once thriving culture. My fellow Myie follow me on this path of rejuvenation look into the light of hope once again and share with me a prosperous vision of our salvation, the first sanctuary of freedom amongst the controlling and domineering hand of Scaedrein rule. When the enemy pushes us down what do we do?"

"Get back up!" Every soldier replying in unison.

"And what do we do when the lines been crossed," Kelmu pointing at a private in the front row of the second company, everyone becomes suddenly quiet waiting to see how the new recruit responds.

The private stands motionless for a second, "these immoral bastards will burn 'neath the hammer of morality," the 'Boot' replies with rapid tones aggressively drawing his weapon. A cheer of approval erupts from everyone Colde and Eve exchanging glances knowing for once in their life they are part of something truly great that stems from others instead of themselves.

They have found common ground in a cause and a bridge of mutuality spanning the gap between their love for each other; Colde and Eve now holding hands an expression in the reciprocated emotions of love.

Companies one and two will head northwest upon emerging from a southwest tunnel marked as an emergency exit for the now abandoned southwest network, the last time this tunnel will be used. Companies three and four will head north then cut southwest upon emerging from the western tunnel labeled as an emergency entrance for the southwest network, the last time this tunnel will be used.

The Miscreant scouts from companies one and two are the first to emerge, separating to initiate the one-mile gap between both groups. The first one-hundred mils (yards) is traversed before the others slowly file out of the tunnel in groups of three keeping a short distance between one another as they move across the landscape to avoid bunching up, each group of three is fifteen to thirty-feet away from one another. The same applies for companies three and four, this will mask their numbers and it'll be hard to tell if there are fifty or five soldiers.

Group one is moving along steadily but anticipating confrontation over every hill behind every group of trees on top of every ravine and high spot in an area of two miles, an intruder would be hard pressed to get through these nets unnoticed.

The insertion team led by Kelmu are making their way through the tunnels that head toward the coastline moving at an open rate of speed anticipating but not expecting any unfriendly encounter until they reach the surface, the beach will not be an easy place to remain hidden when traversing the shores.

The *Gr 'K' lee'my* is under enormous amounts of pressure with the coming *swarm* this whole area will be covered with Scaedreins that will see the damaged landscape while taking part in the swarm, starting the accusations and rumors the perfect political weapon when trying to discredit a rival 'house.' The lead director's credibility will start to buckle as with their support when they can't supply answers to the burning questions of who, why, and when.

The swarm is a type of ritual to celebrate one Scaedrein that's the equivalent to the inventor of the wheel; he brought the bugs into a new realization and put them on the path that has made them rulers of the galaxy.

The swarm is the single most important thing in a Scaedrein's life, other than reproduction. The ritual takes about two-minutes and ends with them drinking from a well located in a building dead center of Jumere city the water is said to be the purest in the entire galaxy, and the blessing from the descendants of this one famous Scaedrein ensures long life and/or an honorable death.

These descendants are actually above the lead directors in some ways they have their own strong house as well but it is taboo for them to sit on the counsel of directors, at least the whole house, now an individual descendant may try for such a position but it's better to come in as support backed by an entire house opposed to independently stepping in. In some cases autonomous collaboration works, the ancestor of these descendants proved that. Now, if only I knew his name. In any case he swore no allegiance with one but with all and established the strong house policies to improve the living conditions of every Scaedrein, reasons with more in-depth meaning. If these descendants knew of the Jid commander's deceitfulness they would remedy the problem real quick then kick out the current directors, who let this happen, and begin elections for a new house to hold the chairs while they sit as temporary delegates acting as administrators during the political process; this is the only time the house of descendants can legally occupy the director's seat. There is one thing that the descendants have in common with this Jid commander; both have a certain amount of dislike for the current directors. The thing is these Scaedreins wouldn't kill each other over it, unless they could get away with it, which is the last resort or the harder way out. If the descendants were to kill a Scaedrein it would be easier for them to cover it up, but even the implication of such and act would lessen their respectable reputation.

Scaedreins from all over the galaxy are now heading for *Scaedrei* convergent lanes are popping up all over the sector a horde of ships now massing in the space above the planet, good thing the Tarsuon-class vessel modified 1/C has moved to the back side of the system behind a heavy concentration of *Cilloetheim*.

Cil-loe-the'im; a inert gas that is otherwise harmless unless a charged wave of particles moves through the Cilloetheim but even then it has to be a balanced mixture, if the circumstances are right these two gasses will produce electro-chemical storms called *Cielo* storms. The name Cielo (silo) is given because of the gasses form a funnel like effect and if large enough can create a field of gravity strong enough to pull a small moon into its whirlpool currents, this of course is not likely to occur naturally but it could be done by the hands of men.

The modified 1/C vessel close to becoming the first 1/D was the first 1/C modified as well, and now there are three other 1/C Tarsuon-class vessels in the neo-drein armada. The captain and first officer staring at a large screen watching as all these Scaedrein ships mass above the planet some are permitted to stay other lower class ships have to drop off then leave the system to keep the clutter down, then return to pick up and drop off more continuing the process until every crewmember participates in the swarm. The Captain and first officer haven't attended a swarm in several years, and don't feel the urge to. The Jid commander attended them up until nineteen years ago when he first accepted the neo-drein and respected them for who they are, about the same time the Myie ship crashed on Scaedrei. The Jid commander is around thirty-eight years old by human standards. The captain and first officer are around thirty-five; in both cases it's fairly young for Scaedreins.

The current lead director is estimated at around seventy-eight human years and he seems active and aware. As age limit goes the Scaedrein aren't real sure they've been in existence for about eighty-five years but most of that was spent fighting amongst each other, the last forty-years or so went into population growth then the destruction of the Myie and for the remaining eighteen years they have ruled the galaxy unchallenged by all.

The Myie never took the Scaedrein mental evolution into account and they paid for that mistake, it came back on them two-zillion times over. The first Scaedrein was bug like and didn't have what we would consider a brain now they do but how this has come about is another question; the neo-drein could be somehow connected to this mystery? Perhaps a dormant gene activated upon the spawning of the first neo-drein and then somehow spread to all the other Scaedreins; but how? Are these neo-drein by-products of an experiment in genetic manipulation conducted by some outsider because at the time of this mysterious burst of evolution Scaedreins weren't smart enough to achieve such leaps of logic, makes one wonder if the destruction of the Myie was a plan concocted by a larger hand using the Scaedreins as a weapon to protect the true identity of the one's responsible for the destruction of a population? Interfering with evolution is not a good thing and if there is a group of people out there who have done this then their mistake shall come back on them two-zillion times, not to mention some extremely angry Myie.

The sun sinking under a shroud of darkness as companies one and two get into position behind a series of protruding rocks, underneath the cover of a partially thick tree-line. A clearing lies before them followed by several groves and finally the heavy jungle around the city of Jumere, seems too quiet in that direction. If this is the swarm where are the Scaedrein transports and drop ships? There should be all sorts of aerial activity-Wait, there's one now. Here comes another transport behind that followed by a bunch of drop ships, the swarm is starting. They have seen scout ships throughout the entire day but none have came within a mile of the route used in getting here, and now it seems they have fallen out of the Scaedrein's search perimeter. There has to be some kind of mix up because if every Scaedrein on this planet even suspected the presence of Myie there would be troops and security post covering a twenty-mile radius, especially during the swarm.

Boot crouched roughly twenty-paces behind the point man is wondering if the others are feeling as uneasy as he is at the moment; he looks behind him at ground level then up through an opening in the shroud of trees above him. The Myie behind *Boot* is doing the same thing, something isn't right.

"Stay sharp," a voice over Boot's ear piece indicates that radio silence has been officially broken the others are feeling this uneasiness; well they wanted to be discovered this is better than trying to purposely reveal their location.

The insertion team is now about a half-mile from companies three and four moving swiftly through the thick forest on the west side of Jumere, the motives of the insertion team have not been clearly defined until now.

The swarm ceremony ends with the drinking of water from a well, this well has been previously contaminated with a toxin that not only kills the Scaedrein but all so wipes out their reproductive capabilities. The toxin odorless and colorless will eradicate most of them quickly some may live a little while but the toxin will ultimately eat away their insides like an acid eating away metal bit by bit until there is nothing left, the toxin designed specifically for Scaedrein DNA is harmless to everyone else. It will be necessary to add more of the toxin to the cities water supply.

Kelmu's group are infiltrating to keep the focus off the well by planting a series of charges in the city to make it look as though the attacks instill terror instead of motive, plus when the charges detonate this will add as a distraction for retreating units and delay any reinforcements from the city. The explosions will be near the well and the ignorant insects will believe the sacred water is in harms way but they won't think it's contaminated only that it may have been a potential target during the enemies botched mission; exactly what the Myie want the Scaedrein to think. Kelmu now holding a short conversation with the company's field commander is relaying pertinent details that couldn't be covered during the briefing back at base. The insertion team slightly augmenting their approach upon seeing the exact layout deciding that fifty-yards south of the initial insertion point accommodates the attacking soldiers right flank better, in the event the insertion team is forced to fire on the enemy while entering the city because the offensive is overwhelmed by opposition. The bug heads will be caught in a crossfire encompassing almost seventy-five yards if worse comes to worse.

Boot is last seen hitting the deck watching his fellow soldiers behind him being cut down by enemy fire from a scout ship hovering above the trees, behind that a drop ship filled with a gaggle of Scaedreins are firing into the darkness before being dropped off. Company one and two aware of the threat have turned to engage the enemy behind them, the scout ship buzzing the tree line before circling back around pummeling the ground with laser fire putting a hole in the Myie's rear flank so the bug heads can march right up the center. *Boot* the only one in position to do anything about it will not let this happen, scrambling to load his CGL located beneath the barrel of his FMPB. (Concussion Grenade Launcher.).

"Boot you still back there?" The field commander's voice abruptly cuts out that could mean only one thing, communications blackout. *Don't worry commander I'll stop them,* Boot raising his weapon waiting for the Scaedreins to break the top of the hill before firing.

The area entirely green through night vision technology the bug heads show up as light green, indicated by the bugs own body temperature. Humans and human like species show up as yellow, and there is a special color for Myie soldiers a light blue. The NVT display is like a HUD and is cast over the eyes of the wearer upon initiating the apparatus that connects to the soldier's helmet, when needed.

Boot forced out of his position when the scout ship opened fire, almost forgot about the speeder type ship as it opened fire toward the front of the two companies hitting the large rocks they hide behind and the trees above them. The whole front of the offensive is covered in smoke dust and small bits of rubble; Boot is just outside of the impact zone watching as the scout ship banks left to make another circle.

The first Scaedrein has breeched the rear flank and he's now motioning for the others to follow, and follow they do.

The first concussion grenade hits dead center of the Scaedrein's line the explosion killing at least five while piercing high velocity shrapnel cuts down another three, all this with one shot. The beauty of CGL is the load once and shoots twice capability. The second grenade hit a little further down the line increasing the frazzled chaos from the first explosion, every Scaedrein scrambling to find the nearest cover.

Boot ejecting the old clip quickly grabs another loading it into an alternate magazine slot swiftly cocking the launcher, a practiced routine done over and over again something he could do in his sleep and blindfolded. He knows he hasn't much time before Scaedrein air support swoops down the center of their line from the left possibly causing a lot more damage than the first two sweeps; why haven't the others moved to avoid this, must be pinned down from the front as well? Unable to move as well he is nestled in a bush line about thirty to fifty yards from the back side of the forward line, any movement will draw the foot soldiers to his position he has to break the oppositions rear offensive before he can move.

The Scaedrein offensive mustering their composure has found shelter, right back where they started. Out of nowhere another explosion rocks the ground from behind them, throwing a number of them back over the hill several feet in the air flailing dead before slamming to the ground. The once aggressive opposition spreading further apart, believing the enemy is all around them. The second explosion hit the right side of the hill just behind the 'lead' Scaedrein and his command staff, knocking them out of commission.

The smoke cleared over the hill and Boot to his surprise seen no Scaedrein advancing over the hill. He knows there is still some alive but they will not be coming over that hill for a minute or so, which gives him ample opportunity to leave his pinned down position behind the bush line.

The multiple explosions heard by those on the front line know that Boot has done his job, and the field commander would show his appreciation if he wasn't dead. A chunk of rock from the scout ships second pass penetrated his head when the impact of the explosion blew the commander's helmet off.

Boot crouched and running has spotted the scout ship preparing to swoop down and open fire. "Spread apart," he barks out but gets no response, not even movement.

Boot briefly stopping realizes they're dead and quickly takes off again to avoid the speeder's rapid laser fire cutting directly through the path where Boot stood a second before, throwing chucks of ground up in the air leaving potholes to imbrue the mark of destruction upon Scaedrein soil. Boot is now up to the front lines and can see that air support has scattered their offensive capabilities, and how they are taking a beating by opposition coming from the direction of the city. What the hell are companies three and four doing?

Meanwhile on the western side of the city communications have been jammed for the last three-minutes, and two drop ships have been seen heading toward the area that company's one and two occupy. Just as the soldiers get edgy the first Scaedrein patrols are spotted exiting the west side of Jumere, picked off quickly as the bug heads take their first steps into the heavy wooded forest.

A few brief moments later companies three and four are engaging a number of Scaedrein forces filing out of the city, some taking cover at the tops of the buildings while others peer through transom like openings in these buildings.

The insertion team steadily making their way toward the new entry point takes a few short seconds to open fire down the left side of the Scaedreins advancing from the city, the crossfire proving effective as the enemy's front line scrambles for cover. The units coming out of the city behind the front line are momentarily held up by the crossfire effect, not sure how many or exactly where the left side fire is coming from. The situation partially under control the insertion is underway.

Companies three and four spread throughout the bush makes it more difficult for the adversary to center on exact position and number of soldiers attacking the city the Scaedreins aren't going to walk blindly into the battlefield, and the Myie know this.

The battle on the east side taking a turn for the worse has yielded no survivors, on the Scaedrein side. The few remaining Myie making it passed the initial attack but only twelve remain the other sixteen have fallen, but one obstacle still remains.

The scout ship still making passes has the remaining twelve; now lead by *Boot*, trapped on the front side of the rocks. The Myie forced to do so because of resistance coming from the rear flank that Boot knew about and took the necessary precautions, in doing so he was able to temporarily save the life of twelve men; not bad for a boot-new recruit that is.

The pilot of the scout ship coming back around won't give up until every one is dead, but he will not call in anymore support as ordered by the captain. The participants of the swarm must not learn of these attacks and they won't, if he has anything to do with it.

"We can't retreat it's too early," a lieutenant uttering his last words as his body falls limp and lifeless.

Boot suddenly becoming angry and fed up will not let anymore of these men die around this rock.

"Private," Boot looking over at the closest soldier. "You said you seen the anti-air projectile?" "Yeah but it's no longer operational," the private reminding his new senior officer.

"Go get it," Boot being completely serious, the private looking at him like he's crazy.

"Oh and while your at it find me a CGL round," Boot stopping the private before he walks off.

"I all ready have one," the private turning around to hand him the concussion grenade knowing full and well what Boot plans to do and it might work.

Boot can tell the private is not happy with going out to look for busted ordinance, but if it works they will be rid of this annoying flying pest. Good thing the Scaedreins can't fly without a ship, an option the Myie didn't follow through with when creating the Scaedreins so many years ago.

The private making his way around the backside of the rocks as the ship above swoops down and fires on him pelting the ground just behind the running private, before he takes temporary refuge behind a very small pile of rubble avoiding the laser fire. Boot and the other ten laying out suppression fire but they know that even a MPFS couldn't penetrate the shields much less the armor of a ship, as with any other small and medium weapons.

The scout ship waiting for the last second to pull up trying to get off as many shots as possible, before making another complete circle; the pilot knows they have no defense against his ship they need heavy weapons or anti-air, both have been destroyed.

The heavy weapon specialist fell during the initial onslaught while Boot dealt with the rear flank problem, heavy support ceased rendering the Mini-blast cannon useless in the aftermath of Keele (Keel) the support gunner's death. The commander went down shortly after, which is about the time Boot showed up.

The speeder type ship got so close he wind whipped Boot and the other ten, a very hot wind I might add.

The private maintaining his persistence is on the move again if he can get around to the other side he will be temporarily out of harms way, with plenty of time to retrieve the anti-air rocket no more than thirty feet away from his central turning point. He makes it around as the ship dives back in and commences to fire all along the front of the large protruding rocks, Boot and the other ten scrambling to get away separate to avoid being an easy target. The private moving steadily along the protected side of the rock barrier is coming up on the place he seen the anti-air mini-rocket; hope it hasn't been damaged or destroyed?

The private's anxiousness coming to a sudden halt as he sees the undamaged ordinance lying there beside the body of the field commander who tried to use it against the ship seconds before his death the launcher destroyed along with the rocket that was in it the one he holds now is the only left of three destroyed mini-missiles; this one covered in soot may be useless as well?

Boot on his stomach in a patch of trees fiendishly ripping into the concussion grenade to remove its insides, the circling vulture above readying for another low altitude lunge except this birds beak is two blaster cannons built into its narrow fixed wing span. Boot taking a quick look around to make sure the other ten are out of sight, three aren't. What are they doing, they're just standing there? Wait, taking his attention off the grenade, the private is coming around the rock barrier and the MM6 is in his hand; good job soldier! The three are out in the open to draw the pilot's fire, and attention. Boot pulling himself off the ground drawing his weapon up walking out from the cover of trees behind him, stern he stands his ground and deactivates his NVT apparatus aiming his weapon at the right wing of the ship. He has never tried leading a ship with small arms up until now but he feels this confidence, and he knows he can do it. The ship has opened fire and the three in front of him about thirty paces away have successfully avoided the laser spray, but Boot hasn't even flinched. He suddenly pulls the trigger the bolt humming through the air on a direct course for the air below the wing; he missed. Oh shit!

A diving body from Boot's left side pushed him out of harms way sending both men to the ground inches from impacting laser fire.

"You saved my life soldier," Boot still on the ground below his savior.

"Think nothing of it," she said holding him rather tightly.

Boot can feel her trembling both are equally scared, in that moment eye contact is made and yes even on the field of battle love will find a way to show itself, back to the action.

She and Boot are both off the ground in no time and running to meet the private. The other nine are gathering to further distract the circling pilot by shooting straight over the protruding rocks in the opposite direction of the three at the other end, while Boot attempts to place a MM6 charge in a CGL round so he can dispense of this aerial pest. All this noise yet no other Scaedrein reinforcements have arrived? If the Myie can see the ships hovering over the city dropping off Scaedreins then why can't the hovering ships see this scout speeders destructive laser light show?

The scout as suspected changes his heading to compensate for the direction of the oppositions laser fire, perfect that means the bug head will see the actual weapon of his destruction right before it blows his ship to bits. He opens fire early eager to destroy his target.

The nine spread apart and dive avoiding the path of laser fire a couple is knocked down and out from the impact, fortunately they are not dead. The pilot making another circle is approaching from behind the group this time.

Boot getting the last part of the jimmied contraption together using the explosive putty itself to adhere the detonator to the inside of the concussion grenade, as ready as he'll ever be Boot can't miss this is the only option they have. The one that saved him doesn't seem to think it'll work; women always want to criticize at the most inopportune times.

"Can you do better?" Boot holding out the modified grenade as if handing it to her.

"No that's okay I don't want it to blow up in my face, I'll just stand over here," she steps back being serious about her doubt in Boot's handy work.

Boot wasting no more time raises his weapon with no doubt about it not working.

"Extreme times," Boot loading the shell into a clip, "call for extreme measures." He then inserts the clip pulling the cocking mechanism directly after, "and the chaos around this rock stops here," Boot drawing up his weapon and taking aim at the scout speeder's right side as it approaches the other nine Myie. "This tiny little bug is about to be exterminated," Boot pulling the trigger sending the modified grenade in an arch just in front of the lunging ship.

The Scaedrein pilot heard the early warning system; by then it was too late. The whole front half of the speeder was blown off before the remaining part of the ship began a downward spiral blowing up as it hit the ground, the twelve remaining Myie cheering Boot's success. The female soldier who saved him is the first to congratulate him and firmly I might add, as if releasing all her fears in the arms of this man she has only known for a short while; in saving his life was she in fact saving her own? She begins to slowly let go as their eye's meet similarities they find highlighting differences that bind, both captured in the moment like a motionless shooting star halted during the peak of its brightest burn by the stopping of time itself; this bright burning star a symbol of how their love for each other would burn for lifetimes to come.

The two besieged by this mesmerizing effect briefly touch lips in the moment of vulnerability feeling suddenly embarrassed by the inappropriate action they break apart, but neither will admit they liked it.

The other nine running up to congratulate Boot they can't help but feel the awkward energies bouncing about the air, like those *Thwatts* I spoke of earlier.

"Activate secondary communications tune to the alternate frequency of 47 point 3," Boot trying to hide these tongue-tied thwatts with the more important issues like sounding the retreat.

"Sir the radio was damaged during-." "Let me guess," Boot cutting in, "destroyed during the initial attack." Shouldn't have even asked the question, half the offensive and everything else they needed was whipped out so why not the radio too.

"Looks like we'll have to do it the old fashioned way," Boot yanking a couple concussion grenade clips from the remaining nine. "You men get to Yuma-6. You're coming with me," Boot looking at the bravest woman in the galaxy doing the work that most men wouldn't do, even if you paid them.

"Where are you two going?" all nine curious as to what their new commander plans to do.

"About two miles west from here I'll send up a few of these concussion grenades and hope the western units realize this is our signal. Let's move out."

Myie women are very agile and can defend themselves but over ninety percent wouldn't take the path she has chosen it doesn't mean they can't handle the boundaries of battle they don't have to prove anything she doesn't either, believing this is her calling in this lifetime.

Meanwhile on the west side companies three and four are holding their own against the city defenses, but *Puderium* mortars are now screaming through the air sounding its voice of destruction shaking the ground throwing brittle and chunks of debris getting closer to their mark with every passing shot. A few of the Myie beginning to move to avoid being centered on by mortar fire, are clearing a path for the others so they can begin to move as well.

This militia has delayed Scaedrein return fire by not giving them a target to shoot at they hide themselves well. Their firing patterns appear concise yet precise and they are organized; there is something more to these so-called escaped prisoners and slaves? The warbled MPFS bolts hitting everything except the moving humanoid soldiers, the lead Scaedrein of this defensive front is feeling ill prepared because there is something the directors have kept from him. These humanoids have kept his soldiers pinned down since the firefight started, and now it seems the mortar fire is all so proving to be ineffective as well. Why won't command send in more reinforcements, especially with the swarm taking place?

The Scaedrein return fire starting to turn with the shifting front line as a volley of concussion grenades impact in front of the Scaedrein's fire line, momentarily stopping about sixty-percent of the return fire. The lead Scaedrein's sergeant taken out in the barrage of explosions, as the opposition concentrates their fire on the right side of the Scaedrein line. The right side ducking and diving behind cover to avoid the sheeting effect of warbled and standard bolts like sideways rain in a typhoon, a few falling to their deaths but most manage to avoid being totally maimed. The left side of the Scaedreins line has started back up but the multiple explosions took out most on that side; the return fire is minimal and unfocused too scattered to do any real damage to a shifting opposition. There is another factor as well, the Scaedreins haven't really been able to center on where and how many enemies there are. The lead directors should know by now that their armies work better with more instead of less and it's obvious these Scaedreins need more; they are out-classed a victim to superior strategy. A few more short range *Puderium* mortars scream through the air but are even further off target than before as they explode closer to the advancing Scaedreins on the left, than the enemies on the right.

The Myie spreading their offensive fire to keep the Scaedrein defensive pinned down. This spot was chosen because there is a minimal amount of natural cover for the enemy to get behind, and the edges of the city are just a bit too far away from the Myie's offensive line. The scaedreins forced to hide behind small trees and low bushes crouched or laying down while engaging an enemy, not a preferred posture for bulky bug like beings.

Company four taking notice to the Scaedreins on the left advancing across a small semi-circular clearing to try and out flank the offensive, redirect their fire on these wide open targets. There's a slue of bolts that scour the approaching Scaedreins, about fifteen or twenty of them, now behind the haze of impacting laser fire. One half of company four redirects its fire back to the right side, the other half reloads or recharges.

Company three maintaining a heavy fire/suppression status while company four deals with the left side threat, cut their firing rate by half to reload as well. Half of group four now ready turns back to the right side and supports one half of company three, while the other half of four is now raising their weapons at the clearing smoke. Enemy fire is beginning to increase. What's this, Scaedreins trying to make their way out of the city and up to the defensive line? A few bolts in their direction will cease their effort real quick, the other half of company three now ready turns to fire at this new threat.

The smoke clears from that small section on the left side and not one Scaedrein emerges from the aftermath of that mini-chaos, a gratification that adds to their all ready elite morale the energy to keep going.

This new threat is moving and firing as the other half of group three raise their weapons-Out of nowhere the scream of a mortar is heard followed by a violent explosion directly beside this other half, ripping three of nine soldiers apart upon impact. The other four are out of commission or dead from the exploding mortar, not one is moving. The explosion rattling others close enough to a halt, namely the intact half of group three, company four is now firing on this new threat and the Scaedrein defensive line moving further left as well. The scream of another mortar hits on the far side of the still rattled half of company three knocking most of them out of commission, the commander has fallen. Company four is now on their own, but they will not leave any wounded behind. The scream of another mortar is followed by one more both impacting at virtually the same time directly on top of group three, thwarting any attempts at retrieving wounded. Group four now changing direction to avoid mortar fire and to initiate the retreat waiting for the eastern group is no longer an option, they must have fallen to the enemy.

Company four isn't on the move for too long before Scaedrein drop ships come in from behind them and light the woods up with laser fire, the Myie not caught by surprise quickly duck for cover avoiding the hailing laser spray.

The first to react is the company commander swiftly loading a concussion grenade clip into the alternate slot, raising his weapon and firing. The round arched and hit the top of the now hovering drop ship doing little damage, but damn if it didn't shake up the pilot. Another round followed from a corporal on the adjacent side of the commander it hit the second drop ship dead on and hit the protective glass again having little effect, but it's enough to create an avenue of escape. The scaedreins from the defensive line now on the move will not catch the retreating Myie in time and the drop ships will be unable to detect them after they move, thanks to independent sensor jamming technology.

Now on the move company four is breaking up into smaller groups and spreading apart, leaving the same way they came. The same way as in the method used to cover one another while moving through the bush. Abruptly, a faint explosion in the sky is seen about two miles east of their position. Company four taking it as a signal is glad to see that there are survivors from the eastern group and know why it took so long to sound the retreat; the concussion grenade would have never been seen from the eastern group's original coordinates. They will all meet at Yuma-6 in about thirty-minutes the bug heads will never find them there, despite the fact that it's about six-grids from where the eastern assault started. The western assault is close to ten-grids from the rendezvous point.

The cities defensive units converged on the former front lines of the opposition's offensive knowing that no survivors are present; they approach unwary and unaware of the danger left behind. The Scaedreins moving in a zigzag type line across the clearing between the once hot firing lines encounter the first three enemy bodies left behind checking them very carefully just incase the dead are rigged with explosives; don't want to find out the hard way. The enemy looks healthy and unscarred, not the appearance of a typical prisoner or slave, even if they had escaped ten years ago there would still be permanent marks and signs of sickness because the Scaedreins always keep their slaves and prisoners infected with deadly toxins and given anti-toxins on a weekly basis, in the event they escape and are not recaptured. He didn't want to be part of this defense against this group of humanoids because the whole concept of escaped prisoners still living after five or ten years and then conducting an assault is highly unlikely, and their uniforms and gear are top of the line custom made with parts from Scaedrein technology but put together differently.

By this time the drop ships that once hovered above have left the area and now search for possible escape routes trying to find the surviving soldiers of this assault, quietly, without drawing any attention to them. Other ships moved over the land sides north, east and south dropping off the next participants in the swarm then picking up those that have finished their swarming ceremonies. You see the west side of the city is close to six grids from the heaviest concentration of Scaedreins, while the edges of the eastern side are over six grids from the heaviest concentration of Scaedreins within the city at the moment. This is important to the neo-drein and the Myie because the activity in the city produces so much noise that anything beyond the center of the city goes unheard and even the vibrations of the ground when mortars and bombs go off are not felt by even someone on the outer edges, yes the center of the city creates so much of buzz that it's felt throughout Jumere.

The new lead Scaedrein picks up a helmet in fair shape from the scattered remnants of body parts and mortar holes. The rest of the Scaedreins spread out a bit but move slowly through the bush; a group of six stay within a twenty pace radius of the leader, fanning out in front of him. The helmet is padded on the inside with a thin liner over the padding quickly noticing the liner can be removed, he does so. The padding is gray and of medium thickness, at least by human standards, he rips the foam out knowing what lies beneath it. The Scaedrein quickly noticing a small patch of sticker thin electrical circuitry, beside that a small blinking button.

A few of the other Scaedreins discovered more bodies with virtually identical uniforms, none rigged with explosives. The six closer to the leader have seen nothing else beyond a fifteen-foot perimeter and have turned their attention toward the captain's right, facing the city. A set of legs protruding out the bushes draws the attention of one of the six; it looked as though the leg slowly moved.

The blinking red button suspected to be some kind of triggering device for a bomb but why so obvious? The lead Scaedrein noticing a small electrical slot located underneath the front edge of the helmet, some kind of exterior device plugs into the slot. Night vision or Optical Terrain Scanners can be run through similar looking receptacles; this militia is better equipped than some of the larger armies the Scaedreins have encountered over the past few years. He orders the others to take one body for a further analysis of this enemy to have a better perspective on dealing with this new threat, taking another look inside the helmet at the flashing button, abruptly something self-activates the helmet.

A small group of Myie sitting amongst the bush about six grids out observing the actions of the Scaedrein now looking into the helmet, using the camera in another helmet purposely hid to do exactly what the three Myie are doing now; observing the Scaedrein from afar.

The lead Scaedrein startled expecting the helmet to explode drops the headgear but is ultimately relieved when the helmet doesn't detonate. A voice is coming from the helmet a message of some sort, the lead Scaedrein kicking the helmet over hearing the voice more clearly. The volume of the voice draws the attention of the surrounding Scaedreins finishing up the investigation on that side leaving all the bodies but one, now walking toward the lead Scaedrein.

The lead Scaedrein listening intensely to try and distinguish the words spoken in a common tongue and is saying the same thing over and over; the leader motioning the others to back off. G-go-goo-good-b-by-. The lead Scaedrein suddenly realizing the implications throws the helmet to his left as far as he can and begins to laugh, he has out-witted these humanoids. Taking a few steps back he is still laughing raising his arms up to the air calling it a blessing from the swarm abruptly he trips over something sticking out of the ground, a root or something? He looks down and sees before him; the entire perimeter of the assault swallowed by a chain of claymore like napalm sticking and burning everything in a line about sixty-mils (yards) long, the entire defensive taken out by four of these planted *Hythilidium* charges. *Puderium* tweaked with charged and re-sequenced *Cilloetheim.*

The once observing Myie on the move only hear the explosion but know that it will attract attention and bring in more reinforcements from *Jumere,* that's okay they still have plenty of time to make it to Yuma-6 without drawing attention or being spotted. The insertion team should be on their way out of the city preparing to detonate the charges they set in Jumere, the distraction would ensure the retreating units make it safely to the rendezvous point. The majority of group four is more than half way to the shrouded north tunnel all so known as Yuma-6, a man made tunnel that leads to other unnaturally occurring tunnels that go in the direction of an underground labyrinth; this labyrinth a maze of many possibilities with only one right answer. The one's who have chosen to stay behind are safe for the time being there has been no sign or even trace of a Scaedrein presence, the three commando's will make good time under the cover of this semi-heavy jungle. Initiating a fifteen-step spear the three have secured a radius of about thirty-six feet increasing their rate of speed, and chances of survival.

Yuma-6 a heavily covered area at the north end of a ten grid rock ledge; the south end heavily damaged over time due to natural causes, way before the Myie were here, is virtually barren and broken. The break in this large raised rock shelf looks like a massive gouge on the southern tip and one quarter of that is on the verge of peeling away from the ledge like a slab of dead skin from a healing sore, a condemned area where no Myie goes.

Boot and the female soldier now within the tunnels beneath Yuma-6 are taking a few moments to rest and prepare for the next part of the operation, still together and feeling awkward both wonder why they haven't separated to avoid the uncomfortable silence that happens every time the talking stops. Boot can't stop thinking about the kiss and how much it warmed his spirit and the attempt to cover this fact is creating an 'innocent' allure of deceit on his part, not that he is lying but hiding instead. The funny thing is he doesn't even know her name and for some reason he feels this fear toward that particular question; is he ready to ask it?

"If we are successful what do you plan to do afterward?" Boot glad to start another conversation with her, but how long can he keep it going?

"That still seems so far away sitting here in this tunnel on this God forsaken planet, it's hard to believe that all this is actually happening now. It's like," she stops. "Like being in a dream or something," Boot finishing her sentence making and maintaining eye contact for the first time since the accidental kiss.

She turned away from him but did not walk away. Boot lightly touching her arm trying to easily turn her around but she is resisting him, not wanting to let down her defenses.

"Hey, what's the matter?" Boot with a low concerning voice.

"There's nothing wrong. I have to go," she begins to walk away without a second glance.

Boot will put a stop to this running around her and stopping in front of her, "don't walk away," his voice even lower than before still she would not look at him. "Will you please say something to me? These last few hours can't end like this," Boot firmly grabbing her arms lowering his head to try and look upon her face.

"And why does this matter at this point in time," she lifts her head up, "there are more important things to worry about." She pulls away from his firm grasp, looking into the eyes of this man whose name she didn't know but feels this fear toward that particular question.

"Yeah I guess your right," Boot shaking her hand walking off in the opposite direction deeper into the tunnel. He didn't want to know her name anyhow.

The female soldier stands there for a second, ultimately walking toward the tunnel entrance away from him. *"Don't walk away,"* his last words running through her mind; is she really walking away or delaying something she has no control over? There is one thing for certain she has never felt so secure in the arms of a man before. She preferring the company of her own gender and has for about a year now with a NCO who has two young children, whom lost her husband in a collapsing tunnel three years back. The female grunt loves her very much but their relationship has been deteriorating for the last month or so; is he the one she needs? She is now outside the tunnel talking with some soldiers from group one in an attempt to keep her mind on the job at hand, which turns out to be easy after the first few words.

Boot emerges from the tunnel a few minutes later walking away from the other soldiers heading to where the western group will enter Yuma-6, feeling no urge to talk to her at the moment. Besides, if this works out both will more than likely be stationed miles or worlds apart and never see each other again. If this operation doesn't work out they will all be dead with no hopes of rebuilding their culture and they will be but a distant memory eventually forgotten, unless there is some other group of Myie hidden elsewhere?

Colde and Eve, almost forgot about them huh, moving behind Kelmu with Exle Widjrue taking the rear are well on their way out of city leaving the same way they entered, having heard the explosion the *Hythilidium* explosions know it is safe to exit the city and they don't have much time before the enemy blankets the area with reinforcements. Double-time, move it! The exit entirely too easy not that any of them are complaining but there should have been more on the way by now, it's obvious that not all the Scaedreins knew about the assaults. Clear of the city they don't even take the time to look at the war torn terrain, run is the only thing on their mind. The timers on each detonation device are linked by what is called Multi-Target Timing (MTT.); this means that the first timer isn't activated until the last explosive is set. The jungle is thick but they maintain a somewhat constant speed, initiating a fifteen-step spear upon entering the bush. Colde and Eve are both tired but not worn down this running over the past six hours is something they are not accustomed to, but the medium pace is actually keeping down the fatigue factor.

One mile outside the city they slow their pace for a few hundred yards more then stop, pacing in a small area to keep from cramping while they momentarily rest. Kelmu seeing there is only four minutes left on the timer wishing they could have procured a mode of transportation as originally planned but upon seeing the exact layout of the city it was in their best interest to leave on foot maintaining zero presence; that's enough rest.

The three spearing back out beginning a light pace that will eventually build to a medium after about thirty-mils, from then on quick short bursts every other mile until Yuma-6 is reached.

Boot meeting the remnants of the western assault pleased to see survivors but can see they lost half of their numbers, as well. Three commanders fell during the assaults and two were versed in Miscreant training and techniques, and well respected. The commander that survived, a decorated officer who was the fourteen-year-old son of the captain who got them into Scaedrein space, the captain dying shortly after they arrived on the planet approximately eighteen years eleven months and one week up to the day the assaults started. Boot having a minimal conversation with company four's commander as the fatigued group enters the protection of the tunnel to rest for the next fifteen to thirty-minutes, before the next part of the operation starts. The insertion team will more than likely be under fire when reaching Yuma-6 and Kelmu will need the energy of all the remaining units because of the high casualty counts during the assault. Boot is now walking toward group one he will be leading them and sitting on the southwest side in the surrounding canopy of trees, while group four will take the east side near the wall of the large rock shelf. The insertion team will come in on the same path used by company four, except they will be either flying a ship or using an anti-grav sled. Group one is all ready getting into position being extra quiet listening for the electrical whine of the ship or sled, Boot crouched behind a line of trees ten-feet from the nearest soldier on either side of him. The rest of company one is set up along the same line as Boot but some are a few feet back to disguise their numbers and the exact location of the front line, in the event Scaedrein drop ships come swarming in trying to land or get close enough to drop off foot soldiers. If opposing sleds are following the insertion team the enemy will be meat before they ever reach the clearing, and the only other way to get through this thick jungle is the western path and eastern path. If the Scaedrein forces wanted to attack in any other direction than west and east they would be forced to cut through or just blow the greenery to bits, but the Scaedreins have evolved passed the point of scouring every green leaf they see.

Scaedrei used to look very different thirty-years ago, a barren wasteland covered with dead trees and sand. Since then Scaedrein kind has evolved and found respect for their planet saving it from its sterile fate, now it flourishes as a living representation of all Scaedreins. A conservation act was passed by the previous generation of the current *Gr 'K' lee'my* and it became a law that a controlled amount of resources would come from the planet to ensure the longevity of the home world's existence. All this happened before *Jumere* or *Djri-gee-din* was even built and most Scaedreins lived in cities dug out of rock walls and canyons, this act was a new beginning for all Scaedrein kind a renaissance age.

She sat there in a crouch position twenty-feet from him and could not stop looking in his direction, the blue outline of his form through her night vision stirring her lustful wiles from deep within her oceans of passion; the flicker of a fantasy blinking her eyes slapping her back into reality. She shakes her head wondering why of all times she is feeling so—hot and bothered; is it him or is it the fact she misses *Gyldrea* her lover? She looks away from him and toward the western entrance of the virtually sealed off clearing, then to the sky. The entire clearing is void of unnatural sounds, and this is with company four now exiting the tunnel and getting into position on the east side near an extended but lower rock ledge connected to the higher protrusion called *Nielouwithia* translated into English as rocks of great age.

Nielouwithia is actually a term in Myie used to describe a rock formation that is over six billion years old. This ledge used to be a lot bigger but it has been dwindling down for the last two-hundred and seventy million years. It has been theorized that *Nielouwithia* was actually the end of the larger canyon like shelf that rests beside the area where the eastern assault took place, but it's uncertain exactly how long the rock extends underground after going passed the northern tip. The Myie have dug a little in that area but not very far they know there is rock directly beneath the surface of the broken tip, and the dirt above has merely accumulated over the past sixty million years or so.

She is beginning to feel a certain weight a boiling tension one that is making her wary and dizzy at the same time, a grinding of the teeth a scratching on the boards of her mental endurance, the waters of uneasiness beginning to roll over the rim of her equilibrium. The pressure is a growing uncertainty, doubt, is she beginning to have reservations about walking away from what she didn't think was real at the time? Gyldrea has never left her mind once, yet, this man is running through her entire body like his very presence has become a drug that she needs. Now she is slamming her head against the tree, not literally you know inside, she loves her true soul mate. Her thoughts come to an abrupt halt as a light blue form registers on her night vision and emerging from the western entrance, some of her fellow comrades have all ready started their approach toward what has to be a Myie. Remember, only Myie show up as blue on night vision. There should be four why can she see only one, did something happen? Is that Exle or Kelmu?

She is making her way toward the western entrance still under the cover of trees; as is the rest of group one. Group four is maintaining position watching the back door in case any Scaedreins are sneaking up behind or above them. She is guessing the get away vehicle was a failure or an unnecessary risk determined upon entering the city into an unforeseen obstacle, something that couldn't be accounted for when using dry information to plan an infiltration. What I mean by dry information is estimations and a few satellite photos from eight years ago acquired through technology they can no longer use; another story that ends with them almost being discovered, which is why the technology was deactivated and pulled out of every computer system in all the networks.

You see there is something else the Myie know about Scaedrein technology, it is bought from the *Kybans* in exchange for large quantities of natural resources. The satellites above the home world as with every other satellite are Kyban technology, which is why the idea of tapping into it wasn't such a good idea in the first place. If the rest of the galaxy knew of the Kybans consorting with the Scaedreins in such a manner they would not be in such high respects with their fellow galactic powerhouses, whom don't sell or even deal with Scaedreins. The Kyban could lose support in the business world of intergalactic exchange markets; perhaps have a decrease in outgoing materials because of this deceitful endeavor. The other powerhouses of the galaxy gladly substituting Kyban grade steel for D'neirie, it's just as good, this act alone could cause a serious drop in the Kyban systems galactic markets.

She stops thirty paces out behind him, noticing Exle is crouched in the tree line talking with the commander of group four.

"There's something not right here this entire area should be covered with Scaedreins. We have reason to believe that Scaedrein intelligence is onto our little mission and the leak can only be one person," Exle relaying information the four discussed on the way to Yuma-6.

The commander of group four a thirty-one year old Miscreant is part of Kelmu's honor guard and is good friends with both, as well. His name is *Dielan*. A name that seems to have no known translation it's a word that has been in the Myie language far longer than any other word, you can say it was the first spoken word of their dialect during an age predating any prehistoric history from the past four or five million years. He is the only Myie with this name, but not even his mother knew how or where she came up with the name.

"Who could have leaked this information the clone was destroyed."

"Yeah but something happened after the clone was destroyed and the only one around was the western delegate," Exle cutting in and then elaborating, "Kelmu killed a young Scaedrein inside the southern complex after seeing it leave from the direction of the western delegate. If this Scaedrein lashed out at Kelmu revealing its true form then why did it not kill the western delegate?" Exle stopping to see if Dielan has put two and two together.

"The western delegate used quick cloning technology to make a host for a Scaedrein to grow in; when the time came the bug just peeled its host like a *lablur*." (Banana.). Dielan filling in the obvious gap, overcome by the full realization of the damage this potential leak can cause.

"Get these men out of here, take the tunnels and head due east as far as you can go. Leave the tunnels when you reach the end and don't look back," Exle saying what may be his last words to a dear friend.

"If I don't see you again," Dielan stopping Exle, "it's been an honor and a privilege to serve beside the best." Dielan finishes letting Exle leave he doesn't want to know where the four are going its better that way.

A quick wave of Dielan's arm and everyone makes a break for the tunnels running along side the edges of the clearing; their route requires them to take the condemned east tunnel used only for evacuations. The tunnel is their because it leads to the only place the Myie could drill an exit far enough away and by a sufficient amount of cover, but not too much cover, leading to an area where one can hide a large group of people. The tunnel is considered condemned because it has never been used and is a last ditch effort after all countermeasures have failed. The Myie standing on the outside edge of their existence looking into the void that lies beneath the spiraling black currents drawing the Myie closer to it every passing second. The Scaedreins *Poo'shawng,* the one the swarm is held in honor of, pushes the all ready heavily teetering Myie more and more off balance until the final nudge sends them over the edge; an elapsed existence a way of life forgotten by most and lost in the cosmic currents of time. The stakes have been raised but the obstacle expected has the Myie up with the game, not ahead, but there is one advantage that can very well increase the odds of survival. The condemned eastern tunnel is something only a few know about and the western delegate isn't one of them, the north east and east sides were mainly responsible and applied a need to know basis to ensure the last line of defense maintained a high level of anonymity.

Back in the tunnel Dielan is leading the twelve left from company one and the sixteen left from company four through a now opened hole about one-hundred mils further down from the eastern tunnel, quickly waving the twenty-seven soldiers through the once hidden entrance. Company four's remaining numbers include the commander.

Through the opening one after another continuing straight, never stopping or even slowing until the tunnel comes to a abrupt end about two miles down. The tunnels are narrow so they all stand in a straight line some thirty-mils (yards) from the dead-end, waiting for Dielan to find the entrance into the next series of tunnels or an exit to the surface. The Miscreant stands there for a few moments shining a light around the corridor this doesn't look good.

"We'll have to cut through," Dielan speaking in low tones making sure the sound of his voice doesn't cause a cave-in. "Assemble the laser, everyone else back off," Dielan maintaining a low voice motioning with his arm so the others in back can see what they can't hear.

It didn't take long to cut through but it caused a series of shakes that brought down pieces of the corridors low ceiling but no damage was done. Now moving through this newly cut hole the laser managed to burn through about two-hundred yards of solid rock in less than thirty-minutes, luckily what is being cut through is a lot more stable than what is behind them. Beginning to cut at an upward angle because the layers of rock are starting to thin an exit will have to be made within the next half mile or so, if that. The troops tiring and the surface is no place to rest they decide to cut a small room for them to rest and finish the tunnel through the remainder of the night and surface tomorrow after the sun sets, cutting the exit hole itself right before they leave the tunnel. Once leaving the escape tunnel the effort to cover it won't be hindered by daylight.

The fashioned room is about seventy-five by seventy-five and gives thirty people five feet of cubic space, but a few have chosen to set up and rest in the two-hundred mil corridor just freshly dug out by the cutting laser. The other tunnel now sealed back off covering the passageway they currently occupy.

Boot the furthest one out and closest to the collapsed hole is just within earshot from the rest of the soldiers. The last thing on his mind is tomorrow's task, right now he wants to think about nothing so he can go to sleep. He removes the padding from his helmet and sets it on a near-by rock, laying his head back and looking up at the ceiling of the low corridor. The padding not sufficient he takes off the jacket of his uniform and places it underneath the padding, once again he is staring at the ceiling. The light scrapping of a boot across the rock floor of the corridor stirs his attention turning his head to the right, looking down the corridor.

"What is it?" Boot seeing that it's her is remaining professional, "Do you have something to report?" Boot sitting up.

"No," she replies.

"Then why aren't you resting up, you're going to need it," Boot sounding somewhat bitter laying back down.

She studies him for a second then turns to walk away, only to turn back around.

"Don't be like that," she takes a couple steps closer.

Boot sitting back up, "don't be like what?"

"There is something you should know about me," she sits down beside him, "I have been with someone for almost a year and to walk away from that is far worse than walking away from you."

"Good for you but why are you telling me this," Boot must have missed something; did she not walk away from him.

"It's just that," she hesitates, "I'm not what you would call a lover of men. I mean I have, with the exception of this past year."

"What is the point you are trying to make here?" Boot missing the point of her indirect statement.

"Let's just say that I love her very much."

"Oh I see," Boot taken aback but not grossed out; love happens in different ways for everybody and if she's truly in love then it doesn't matter.

"I'm sorry I didn't think that would be the reason for your lack of interest in me."

"No, that's okay you didn't know and how could you. But you are wrong about one thing," she stands up and begins to walk away.

"What's that?" Boot looking up at her as she turns her head to look back at him.

"I do find you interesting," she replies and turns back to face forward starting back down the corridor.

Boot suddenly remembering something he wants to ask her jumps up and stops her. "Wait," he says, "what's your name?"

She smiles at him lightly replying, "Arianna."

What a sensuous name translated in Myie as the beauty within a dream. "I am Boot," extending his hand, "a pleasure to meet you."

She shakes his hand and walks off with a hidden smile, what a strong name. Boot sounds pretty plain to us, but in Myie it actually means *one of enduring relentlessness a leader of men*. Is she wavering from her sexual standpoint again, is she finding this man more appealing than *Gyldrea*? She finds that hard to believe at the moment Gyldrea is an amazing lover but is her opinion all ready changing, is the crossing thought her sub-conscience questioning her feelings?

Boot smiles glad another woman had not rejected his advances and offered up a sorry excuse, although he's never heard that one; at least it's the truth. He briefly wonders about how he would react if he seen the two making out or making love? Not a minute later Boot is out like a busted light, sound asleep.

Boot is now walking through a thick and sharp smelling gray smoke that tumbles through a warm breeze over the terrain of a place

134

never seen before; a stench of archaic death whipping within these wind currents adding to this gray a barreling black smoke. The source of this heavy black smoke unseen as he continues to move forward the land seems familiar and the distinct feeling of having been here before is overwhelming him, stopping to catch a breath. The black smoke is becoming thicker and he can now see casualties of a war a great conflict of epic proportions spanning hundreds of years fighting the oppression of a Hoarde rule; a sense of pride, achievement and hope fills him as if recharging his soul. Yes indeed the humans that died fighting this battle stood for something true and moral. Now standing at the source of this black smoke a line of burning wooden weaponry never seen before, even in their oldest records, but he knows the large wooden weaponry represents oppression and hate. He knows now that these ancient human soldiers died advancing on the enemy's artillery, a sudden overwhelming sorrow has him envisioning segments of the battle how horrifying and hopeless it seemed. The exploding artillery ten-times more intense than twenty puderium mortars producing sound waves that can be heard from three-miles away, antiquated yet powerful weapons. An ancient deeply rooted fear pulls him from this battlefield vision and redirects attention behind him quickly noticing some human forms emerging from the gray smoke, the guns and black smoke behind him are suddenly sucked away like an after-thought and further behind him but he hasn't moved. The intensity of his focus warping him from place to place within the unbounded world of dreams, the sub-conscious answer to traveling above the limitations of time, the power of thought. The forms are still fuzzy but he can clearly see three humans breaking the haze of gray smoke but they're not wearing the same type of clothes as those on the battleground, they're dressed in modern clothing like him. A sudden feeling of completion settles within the very fabric of his soul, the joining of a circle the reunification of old beliefs once forgotten blended with the ideology of present time to bring about the beginnings of a new era soon to fill the galaxy with a breath of hope.

Boot is now able to distinguish one of the three approaching him, abruptly a nudge pulls him away and the conscience mind opens his eyes. Dielan is now standing above waking him up saying it's time to go; all ready? Boot is up and ready in a matter of seconds, but insist that he speak with Dielan alone before they go any further.

Boot goes on telling the commander about the dream and is taken by surprise when he learns from Dielan the Chaplain mentioned that Kelmu had a similar dream and that its meaning would be revealed from the outcome of current events, it is a dream that represents our fate. Boot stopping Dielan, "No you don't understand," he says looking directly into the eyes of the commander.

Dielan taken aback by Boot's asserting tone, how the girth of the knowledge he now possess has given new meaning and hope to this once wary soul.

"What have you seen?" Dielan serious and curiously concerned all in one moment.

"I have seen our fate," Boot's eyes staring through the soul of Dielan, splaying images in his mind of his trials and tribulations.

Dielan drawn in by the power of Boot's hypnotic gaze is suddenly standing beside him with the feeling this young soldier is and has been his friend for lifetime after lifetime, and is now participating in a shared vision of Boot's dream; the gray smoke; the battlefield; the three forms standing on the edge of this gray.

Dielan shakes his head and is standing across from Boot, "that was your dream; how'd you do that?"

"Did you see the strings of our fate?" Boot placing his hand on the commander's shoulder a fire burning in their eyes.

Boot suddenly takes off, Dielan running up behind is not sure what Boot is doing.

"My friends," Boot stopping in the middle of the rock room, the soldiers all turning to look.

"We have been standing on the precipice of our very existence staring down into the void, day by day we have lived on this planet beneath the noses of the one's responsible for our people's destruction over eighteen years ago. Yes we are few and our timetable has been pushed forward but this means we are one step closer to the commonality that unites us all and shows us the true calling of our existence. My friends, my comrades in arms, my brothers and sisters it is time to exact vengeance and place this hand on the girth of the entire galaxy and in one swoop we will eradicate the violators of free-will. If it takes a thousand years, two thousand years we will always fight for the betterment of all life. The destruction of the Scaedreins is but the beginning of our quest in life, we are here to maintain a balance and to fight anything that threatens this stability. In this hand," Boot extending his left hand, "is the hopes and dreams of every Myie living, dead, and reborn. In this hand," Boot extending his right hand, "is my defense against the tyrannies of oppression and the wanton neglect of those who stood by and watched as our culture was destroyed." Boot not finished just yet he turns around to face a group of Myie behind him.

"We have a long road ahead of us as we did eighteen years ago but we have survived and we will continue to thrive despite the opposition. Everyone will remember this moment for the rest of their lives and there will be stories of our heroism told well after this lifetime. We are the hope of tomorrow open your hands and light the way for the entire universe our voices will carry this light to every system every being because even the Scaedreins can't extinguish this light, and the strings of our fate has given me a message," Boot looking around to everyone, "it is time to reclaim our destiny so long subdued by the Scaedreins, the cosmic currents of life are awaiting our return to take our place as protectors of free-will and justice."

The whole room is quiet, Boot wondering if his speech did any good. An onslaught of cheers erupts throughout a newly raised morale within every soldier, the revitalized spirits of the Myie ready to face this immense obstacle.

"You heard'em line up," Dielan stepping in front of the newly cut tunnel leading to the still sealed off entrance.

The troop's line up facing the tunnel Dielan activating the rumble charges that quietly opens the exit leading to the surface, a ground level hole that required the cutters to ramp the exit. Boot is the first one up the ramp peering out the exit keeping his head down looking over the area through his night vision receptacle attached to the front of his helmet, the heavily shrouded area supported by a three-foot high ridge about four-hundred meters long and two-hundred meters wide. The back edge of this ravine is more south than east so they will exit left to maintain an easterly heading through the surrounding jungle, starting at a doughnut hole like clearing about forty-feet long. The area looks clear but Boot is feeling different, stopping to get a better look at the south side of the thick jungle. There seems to be movement about two hundred meters away, ducking his head a bit lower. No fluorescent green aura around this movement it can't be a Scaedrein, must be an animal. Boot turns his head to the left but quickly hit's the deck, looking straight ahead seeing a fluorescent green glob covering the southeast about one-hundred meters away. Boot slowly ducking back down into the tunnel turning to face Dielan.

"There's a large group of Scaedreins advancing from the southeast heading directly for us, three-hundred feet and closing."

Dielan and the others fully prepared to fight their way out but there is another solution, looking over at three of the closest soldiers and sizing them up. "We need a distraction," Dielan momentarily stopping pointing to a soldier from group four, "you go with these two and head south long enough to draw the enemy away meet up with us two-grids east of this position. We'll wait fifteen minutes at the rendezvous point giving you thirty minutes or more to get back," Dielan practically pushing the soldier out of the hole behind the other two.

The three grunts looking though night vision receptacles as well can see this bright green blob moving through the jungle, that's a lot of Scaedreins. All three firing on the advancing Scaedreins to grab the bug heads attention begin heading south.

The Scaedreins pick up the pursuit and begin returning fire following the three humans, wait some are staying behind and continuing their advance from the southeast. The green blob is beginning to separate as the enemy approaches the doughnut hole clearing, looks to be about twenty of them, Dielan looking back to signal the troops for a frontal assault.

The signal received the Myie readying their weapons and mentally preparing by remaining relaxed, yet focused. They watch Dielan's raised arm like hot-fuel muscle speeders waiting for the green to GO! The hand dropping as he runs out into the open at these half-surprised Scaedreins firing his MPFS, evaporating the first one he sees. A slue of Myie soldiers come running out behind Dielan firing at will toward the still startled Scaedreins, which are dropping like flies as each small group of Myie come barreling out of the tunnel firing as much as they can before ducking behind cover. The Scaedreins falling back to avoid being totally annihilated seek refuge behind the large hardwood trees. The last remaining groups of exiting Myie have made their way out and the last few shots in this small battle ring out as the only six remaining

Scaedreins attempt to retreat south leaving the cover of the trees they stood behind, the six dropped just as quick as the other fourteen, dumb Scaedrein's haven't learned a thing.

"Everyone get moving," Dielan motioning the Myie east.

The soldiers break up in groups of two and three setting a thirty-five pace circumference between each group, as they head east into who knows what?

Keep in mind that radio silence has not been broken they can use them now but that's not a good idea the Scaedreins are probably monitoring every radio frequency listening for human voices, would be nice to have a way of communicating over the radio without having to talk.

"I think we lost'em," one of the grunts behind a set of bushes in prone position, lying beside the other two Myie soldiers.

"We better get moving to the rendezvous point or we'll get left behind," the Myie pulling himself up keeping an eye on the surrounding area.

The three are soon heading toward the established meeting place about two and a half miles away, the Scaedreins no where in sight.

The three Myie grunts head deeper into the bush maintaining a fifteen-step spear the whole way through reaching the meeting point without one sign of a Scaedrein, of course half the mystery is cleared up when Dielan tells them of the quick firefight that ensued after the three left. The next question where is this other group of Scaedreins? Oh boy, or should I say oh alien they're not out of the bushes yet. This group of Scaedreins will have to be dealt with before even attempting to secure a good hiding spot, but all in due time.

Kelmu, Exle and their two newly established galactic allies haven't really been moving a lot to avoid being detected by the Scaedrein patrols, and the occasional scout ship. The operation has been altered a bit because of the western delegate's dissension but things are going better than expected due to the alarming amount of casualties, of course the 'western leak' made that happen. The bug heads had to know about the assault it's the only explanation for the amount of opposition companies three and four encountered during the initial strike, according to Dielan's field report during the rendezvous at Yuma-

6. Kelmu has been leading them in a small circle moving through the Jungle in an easterly direction; elliptical security net is the Myie military term.

There is an elliptical-advance, as well. Others have copied these strategies but none can touch the designers of this calculated technique, the Myie have patterned them step-by-steps over hundreds of terrain types but with the Myie the knowledge is there so learning it is only a matter of doing it. The Myie aren't big on textbooks in most areas in their life, unless one feels a need to use written text as a basis. The Myie usually discover their calling in life before the age of sixteen, a small percentage have gone as far as eighteen before honing in on their genetic calling. Genetically pre-disposed to certain abilities and attributes but in no domineering manner, it all depends on how the individual uses their talents.

"Well now what?" Colde crouching beside Kelmu. Eve and Exle are seventeen-steps apart on adjacent sides of the two now talking. The pace adapted to better accommodate the current terrain raised on the right a bit and a lot thinner than the left side the underbrush thinning all around them, a slight sign of a sooner than later geographical change.

Kelmu remaining quiet for a few seconds keeping a constant eye on the terrain around him the first nature to look and feel instead of talk has him doing both, focusing more on his senses.

"I'm not sure but I believe we are being followed by something bigger than a Scaedrein," Kelmu raising his arm signaling a convergence on his position.

"A night predator?" Colde not liking the fact that this suspected predator is small enough to hide, yet large or mean enough to attack humans. "Be very still," Kelmu becoming suddenly quiet slowly lifting his arm to slow Eve and Exle's approach, too late both are all ready here.

Exle stopping in mid-crouch realizing the presence of a near-by predator grabs hold of Eve's hand ceasing her movements as well, and then both slowly finish crouching.

"It's moving on the elliptical course behind us, we can carefully continue and more than likely go unnoticed because we are upwind." The wind suddenly shifting direction, "well maybe not," Kelmu grabbing Colde's arm; "Run!"

The large land eel is a by-product of Scaedrein science; it actually has legs like a lizard but leans more toward snake. You see the eel or *Lyoleedius* was the only thing close enough to a snake they could use that would maintain solidity with a giant water lizard or *Giecerius Thylim,* the generalized translation gigantic multi-terrain predator. At over twelve-feet long but only four-feet high it is all so capable of changing colors and its tail, when in water, can produce electric currents that will totally fry a human in about a sixth of a second. The land eel's top speed is around thirty miles an hour, which is good for its short legs, and it can swim at speeds up to and over sixty-miles an hour. There is a couple other things about this monstrous little creation not only can it feel the lightest vibrations it can see and hear, as well.

The massive head from this method of cruel destruction unleashed by the Scaedrein's turns to its right catching the first hint of prey upon the abrupt shifting of the wind, the animal's keen sense of smell picking up a hint of moisture in the air as well. The voice comes next the mammoth land eel's finely tuned ears honing in on the direction of the sound waves, a split second later the beast is running directly toward its meal.

Kelmu and the others have a considerable margin, about 1/8 of a mile to be exact, but these predators are what you could call a cut above the rest.

"We better split up," Kelmu grabbing Colde. "We'll meet back up in fifteen keep favoring the east," Kelmu finishing altering his course by half a degree.

Colde and Eve looking back at each other before going their separate ways both can see the urgency in how the Myie are moving but have no real idea of the threat this predator poses, they run entrusting in blind faith and these two well-decorated and experienced Miscreants.

From out of nowhere Exle and Eve come running up beside Colde that was quick.

"I think we're safe but let's keep moving," Kelmu slowing down but maintaining a steady jog.

This pace is maintained until they reach the edge of the thicker jungle standing about sixty-mils (yards) from a lesser-condensed grove with more small bushes than underbrush, not very good cover.

"We should go around," Kelmu not liking the layout of the grove it's too patchy the sixteen-and-a-half step radius will be harder to maintain and it would require them to split up.

Exle gazing along the south side edge, then to a ridge about one hundred mils from the southeast, "yeah I agree," Exle pointing out the ridge. "You can almost bet there are Scaedreins around that ridge. It'll add time to the route but heading north for about a mile will ensure our safety," Exle knowing at the moment they are safer in the field away from any of the other networks; but there is a problem.

You see the western delegate may have the women and children and those tunnels may be destroyed along with the east tunnels, at least the east tunnels were barren. The Scaedreins will not kill the NCP's (Non-combat personnel.) right away first they will use them to draw out the other hiding Myie. There is however one thing the Scaedreins haven't accounted for Kelmu, Exle, Colde and Eve. One thing's for sure when the genetic retro-toxin kicks in the safest place will be underground and away from the mass hysteria as these Scaedreins try and figure out why all of them are dying, which should start happening within the next day. The Scaedreins will be so busy with trying to preserve their kind that the Myie will no longer be of any concern, but the hostages will have to be found and extracted within the next sixteen-hours.

Kelmu is kicking himself in the ass for not seeing the possible western threat before sending the NCP's into what is now hostile territory but he feels confident that he can find and get them out before the bug heads start dropping; turning to the prisoners for answers they don't posses, then start executing them when the fiendish insects don't hear the answers they want. Kelmu is hoping the western delegate is a clone impostor because if the real delegate has betrayed his people the Miscreant chief might throw him in the middle of a Myie mob and let them rip the representative into pieces no that would be cruel and unusual, a bullet to the head will do just fine.

The clock is ticking and time is short, first they must establish a safe point. Secondly formulate and calculate a plan of attack, if this is even possible, the Scaedreins might have to come to the Myie? Kelmu beginning to frown upon the next thought entering his head looks like his nose hairs just caught the odor of something closely similar and comparable a corresponding equivalent to a non-combat engagement with the opposition, diplomacy. Kelmu hasn't even openly suggested negotiation and he's all ready thinking in double talk; wonder if the other three have any ideas?

The four are moving along the left side of this grove still at the edge of the jungle that leads further north wanting to maintain a certain anonymity they are moving in a straight line about twenty-paces apart this does narrow the secure radius variables but when it comes to moving down the edge of a tree-line sometimes it's best to cover less area, this must be one of those moments. Kelmu is on point and Exle is at the rear Colde is in front of Eve behind Kelmu. The edge of the jungle is starting to thin out it's time to change course, due east. Kelmu is beginning to think the worst of the situation the women and children are probably dead, and to risk exposure is to ensure the death of all remaining Myie and the complete extinction of their people.

Kelmu has seen the reports when the Scaedreins scoured the galaxy for Myie after the sentient insects attacked the planet Mieveodrin how they were able to track them down in the remotest of locations and destroy them, out of 90, 000 hidden Myie 90, 000 died. The links of the Scaedrein spy network stretch all the way across the known galaxy, but there is one place this network doesn't penetrate and that's *Scaedrei*. Kelmu's father used this avenue to get the early stages of this *Scaedrein Infiltration* off the ground, and into space. Kelmu's father had no real military influence at the time but his opinion was backed by a couple of 'big guns' in the armed services' chain of command.

The four manage to find a safe crossing point about half a grid north, which seriously hinders mission effectiveness and expedience, and then two grids east-southeast about a quarter-grid ahead of the grove they chose to avoid. This move will put the four about a quarter-grid from the ridge suspected of housing a Scaedrein ambush, which is exactly where they want to be, close enough to kiss the enemy before the Myie move in and mow the worthless, stupid, and poor excuses for bugs into small bits of gut-filled insect mulch.

The idea behind this assault is to procure a means of transportation but all enemies must be eliminated so it's harder for any reinforcements to track an escape route; that's if the Scaedreins used some other mode of transportation other than drop ships to reach this ridge? There is no doubt Scaedreins are around this ridge, how large of a group is the question.

The four are now stopped hiding near a large rock overgrowth, behind the only trees on the Southside, Kelmu peeking at the enemy through a rare and old pair of light-refracted night vision binoculars that allow the user to see images like you would during the day.

"Oh alien," Kelmu looking along the base of the ridge. "Looks like a garrison and not an ambush as we suspected," Kelmu turning back to face Exle then Colde and Eve.

"How is it every time we're wrong it always ends up being something worse than suspected?" Exle taking light of the moment frivolous in the face of adversity, looking toward the direction of the garrison with his night vision receptacle.

"It dates back as far as the first learned pattern in our genetic structure we are simple by nature but complex by our spiritual essence; what one may call a soul. We Myie stem from an adversity that constructed its own bridge within the building blocks of our creation before our DNA's evolutionary adaptation to the flesh," Kelmu's tone as distant as his current frame of mind the answer coming from deep within him as he stares off in a trance like state.

"What did you just say?" Exle re-directing his attention back to a now mumbling Kelmu.

"Hey you okay?" Exle lightly shaking Kelmu.

"What?" Kelmu not realizing that several seconds have passed.

Kelmu looking at Exle positively lost. "You need rest," Exle motioning to Colde and Eve who are a few feet from the two Myie missing the entire conversation.

Cold and Eve arrive seconds later to discover a sleeping Kelmu, another unscheduled stop.

All the Myie have been experiencing visions and strange occurrences within the last couple weeks, even before the destruction of the northeast tunnels, the Myie came into contact with a type of evolutionary vision quest induced by the tension of pre-emptive energies or sub-currents of intent projected by the *thwatt* of a coming disaster a warning and a sign from the deeper roots of life. Exle, upon seeing Kelmu collapse with fatigue, is now sure the powerful currents surrounding the Myie are responsible for the growing rate of spiritual experiences.

Kelmu out like a busted light the other three will start shooting out projections and eliminating obstacles to build a foundation for an assault that begins with a 7-1 ratio but they will have Kelmu build most of the plan his gift for strategy is above comparison, and to not access such an option would be foolish.

In less than an hour Kelmu is back up and full of vigor, ready to hear what the others have come up with.

"The perimeter stretches along the base of the ridge for about forty-mils, there are four temporary structures and I believe this is the back side of a larger security net that extends west and south beyond the ridge. We enter from the north side and separate Colde and I will move along the east side, Exle and Eve will take the west side along the base of the ridge. I want all enemies eliminated and a zero presence maintained the entire time." Kelmu putting up the binoculars and initializing his night vision receptacle, signaling the others to activate their NVR as well.

If this strike goes unnoticed by the other scout posts the four may have a back door to safely move the women and children through after extracting them from their estimated eastern location, although highly unlikely it's an option worth trying for.

The perimeter patrols dropped before the four started the northern assault on the main field command post, the four Scaedreins taken by surprise never got the first word out as each were eliminated simultaneously in one rapid and well-timed moment. The outer perimeter dealt with Exle and Eve are advancing down the west side for recon purposes, while Colde and Kelmu set up by the first two temporary structures on the east side waiting for Exle and Eve to get into position by the openings of the other two structures located on the west side. The Scaedreins don't seem to have any other patrols in the forty-mil compound; this may be easier than initial estimations?

Colde and Kelmu see the ready signal and prepare to clean house. The area is covered with a blinding white light, the four temporarily blinded from the flash don't see the Scaedreins coming around the south side of the ridge but Kelmu and his friends know that scout ships are responsible for the sudden flash of light. The four still unable to see are dragged across the ground thrown into a near-by drop ship the hard and cold metal floor is the next to last thing felt before the four are introduced to the butts of the enemy's MPFS then comes the abrupt black of unconsciousness.

The instant the four are captured the *Jid* commander, captain and first officer are informed and soon heading for the main hanger of the modified 1/C Tarsuon-class vessel to meet these foolish humanoids who dare to defy the rightful rulers of the galaxy. The shuttle transporting the prisoners touching down as the three enter the hanger, perfect timing.

Badly beaten and bludgeoned the four humans are thrown onto the deck of the hanger slamming against more hard and cold metal, and wait it gets better, the would-be lead directors get their kicks as well.

Meanwhile on the surface of the planet. Boot is surprisingly calm waiting for some kind of signal from the extraction team when he is rolled and tossed about overwhelmed with a horrifying and nauseous feeling like being confined facing an impending doom. This shouldn't be nothing new to him but this feeling seems focused and not one of the many random emotions mentally experienced in the wake of consciousness during the course of a day. The heart jumping maybe skipping a beat, the eyes wide focused on nothing. Boot is suddenly launched into the air moving through the cloud-break looking upward toward the stars breaking the atmosphere of Scaedrei and not to mention its gravity moving through space toward a reddish-green *Cilloetheim* cloud, there are ships everywhere around him because of the swarm but there is no vessel near the cloud. Boot knows Kelmu and the others are aboard a ship hidden within the small dense cloud, he can feel their presence because he can interpret and distinguish vibrations that shake the kinetic web of creation. All Myie have this ability but it's more passive not dominate like Boot, and Kelmu's intrinsic gifts. He feels safe and unafraid his soul bathing in celestial starlight still focused in on the cloud; there is something else amongst the more distant garbled vibrations moving across the webbed kinetic fabric? Boot is now feeling a tug at his leg followed by a low voice.

"Sir we got incoming scouts," a field promoted combat commander from company one, the private who retrieved the mini-missile during the eastern assault, is genuinely concerned and from his intent this threat is close.

Boot kind of upset for being disturbed during his soul's transcendent celestial journey but the reason is more than adequate and fully excuses the interruption he'll have to figure out this other distant presence later, if they survive for that long?

"Tell'em to stay within the dampening field and be sure that other external power sources are shut down," Boot dismissing the field commander gathering up his own gear as well leaving that area shortly after heading for the Miscreant Major Dielan. The short term is M.M. Dielan. Kelmu's is Miscreant Colonel or M.C.

"We got scouts above us-we'll be ready to go just as soon as the ships leave," Boot addressing Dielan.

A total of three scout ships speeder-class are buzzing a small grass covered rock shelf that looks more like a large hill about seventeen feet high, there is only a small amount of trees around one side of the rock hill. The scout ships blast a few holes in the side of the hill and maintain a circular course around the area, they know the Myie are in there.

"I don't think we'll be moving anytime soon," Dielan and the other twenty-seven soldiers crammed in the small cave.

"What about going under the hill," Boot reaching for the rock smelting drill. Dielan stopping him, "that's a negative the power output will key the Scaedreins right onto our position."

"We can't start an assault or establish a defensive perimeter around this barren area," Boot maintaining vigilance in the eye of adversity.

Dielan admiring Boot's gumption but there is no other choice the line starts here.

"Sir!" An urgent voice calling out from the front of the group, next to the entrance of the man made cave. "One of the ships is landing," a low hush waves through the group of soldiers followed by a series of low whines as each one takes their weapon off stand-by, ready to die for what they believe in.

Dielan squirms his way through the soldiers even after they made room, so you can imagine how tight it is inside this cave.

The ship and pilot just sit there for a few seconds before the amplified voice of a Scaedrein booms from the landed speeder-class ship. It's in Scaedrein it says something about having the Myie leaders and that terms of surrender have been negotiated; that's a crock of poop.

"If we make our move now we may be able to acquire that ship," Dielan utilizing every angle.

"No wait," Boot standing behind Dielan, "I have a better idea-We should surrender."

The whole group has this dumbfounded look all-staring at Boot. Battle Induced Trauma or BIT has bitten Boot's higher reasoning abilities; how could surrendering to the enemy not aggravate the situation?

"What do you have in mind?" Dielan anxious to hear Boot's idea.

"It's clearly obvious that these Scaedreins are not working with the other bug heads, they act alone." Boot looking back catching a glance of Arianna toward the middle of the group, "this may be our only edge against this oversized adversary."

"At the hands of our enemy without a weapon," one of the grunts interjecting.

Boot gazing into the eyes of this grunt, "you my friend are a weapon a genetically trained weapon with the power of ten-thousand sub-sonic cannons. I can offer no real assurance but I will say this we are meant to rise above this extinction and our opportunity will come when the time is right."

The words don't settle the soldiers but it does persuade Dielan to go with Boot's radical idea of surrender to bide time allowing this moment to present itself, it seems irrational to bank such an intuition on the fate of a race near extinction but for Myie intuition is their way of life and to subdue it now is to go against what they have believed in for millions of years.

Drop ships are now coming from the north and it looks to be about six of them, but they are empty. The empty drop ships touch down behind the scout ship as four more drop ships with a full compliment of Scaedreins and defensive weaponry; land just off to the side.

"Looks like they're waiting for us," Boot surprised the vengeful insects haven't started opening fire.

There seems to be some activity in one of the empty drop ships, an unarmed Scaedrein is stepping out the side of the ship and walking toward the cave. Fifty-mils from the cave the bug suddenly stops and waves its arm like appendage motioning to the Myie to exit the cave, this is unusual behavior for Scaedreins.

One by one the Myie carefully exit the cave a total of twenty-five are present but the Scaedreins know some are still unaccounted for; where are the leaders? Not one of these soldiers has a rank higher than Lieutenant where is the Miscreant commander?

Abruptly Dielan, Boot, and the young would-be field commander emerge from the cave and are instantly surrounded by Scaedrein soldiers. The lower ranked bug heads screeching at and taunting the three leaders taking notice to Dielan's rank insignia stitched into the left side of his uniform, a Major.

Dielan is quickly snatched up by one of the grunts and thrown about fifteen-feet then beaten to a pulp by a circle of kicks and very coarse *Nythillic spears* ripping his flesh. Kick after kick cut after cut he takes every hit for about two-minutes making sure most of the surrounding Scaedreins are no longer paying attention to the cave; he raises his arm.

"Hot drill!" Boot simply spits out, which is enough for the Myie they know what that means.

Instantly the Myie soldiers hit the deck.

An intense hot beam shoots straight out from the cave incinerating the ring of guards around the prone Myie going straight through the scout ship, and one of the six-drop ships behind it.

Both ships explode and take out several more Scaedreins still trying to catch up to the moment.

"Left to right at five degree increments in two-second intervals," Boot speaking into a verbal remote linked with the drill inside the cave.

The beam now fanning over the desired parameters has taken a few more Scaedreins but the explosion from two more drop ships is enough to pull the Scaedreins further apart dividing the unwise insectoids, as Myie soldiers begin pulling parts from their many hidden pockets to assemble their extra-light blasters.

The Scaedreins on the far right are the furthest from danger and the first to react firing at the Myie soldiers, although they are hard to hit because of the now dead ring of guards around them and a few other piled up insectoid carcasses.

"Deactivate then move right fifteen-degrees," the massive beam suddenly stopping, a beep is heard. "Activate," Boot yelling into the Voice Activated Remote Linking System (VARLS.).

The high-intensity laser easily going through the right side of the rock hill is now commanded to move five degrees left. The advancing Scaedreins from the right catch the full blast and over three-quarters of them are reduced to ash, the remaining survivors now running from the burning trees and smoke.

Not one second later the first Myie gets a shot off as a gust of wind blows the smoke directly over the prone Myie, temporarily concealing most of them.

What a perfect opportunity. "Deactivate," Boot shutting the hot drill down, "charge!"

The Myie come running out of the smoke weapons blazing the still scattered Scaedreins regrouping, or at least trying, as the screams of hope echo throughout the air currents. The Scaedreins have been forced outside the perimeter of the now remaining three of six-drop ships; two more were destroyed when the right side line was taken down.

Dielan is still just lying there he looks dead, Boot is moving toward the downed Miscreant's position with two soldiers laying down cover fire while he advances. *Dinneo 'V' naelou 'I' ohmera* Boot praying for Dielan's life.

The Scaedreins return fire increasing some Myie have assumed the prone position to avoid the barrage of warbled MPFS bolts, while others are continuing the advance.

Boot is now on top of Dielan's position and checking the body. *Thank the KWC he's still alive* Boot quickly picking up his commander as the other Myie now focus on covering Boot, who is now moving toward one of the remaining drop ships on the far left side.

The Scaedreins regrouped now favoring a north-west position exactly where the Myie want them, increasing the rate of fire they're attempting to draw the Scaedreins attention from Boot and Dielan. The Myie that continued to advance are now around the smoking remnants of the scout ship, twelve Myie soldiers to be exact. The smoke still blinding the opposition is as equally blinding to the Myie but who says you have to see something to hit it, senses are more reliable when directed through an individual who is focused and aware of all that is around them. A good example is how each and every Myie in the area knows that the remaining units in the now broken right side are about to open fire, four Scaedrein soldiers to be exact.

Arianna favoring the right side and still in prone position waiting for the moment to move is suddenly pointing her weapon directly beside her and pulling the trigger not once but three times and in three short increments each matching the trajectory of the three Scaedreins at her direct right, the fourth is taken by a fellow officer behind her and with that threat gone the Myie are now quickly getting up. The twelve around the scout ship are now increasing their rate of fire and preparing to advance, when the others clear the dissipating smoke.

Boot has pulled Dielan away from the action and is now looking down the backside of the empty undamaged drop ship directly at what looks to be thirty remaining Scaedreins; it's actually a pretty good view now all he needs is a sub-sonic grenade. Boot suddenly realizing the solution is directly beside him, but oh-oh I think the bug heads have noticed him. Four Scaedreins are attempting to cross open terrain and deal with this sneaky little Myie but are abruptly stopped when two are taken down by some of the Myie laying cover fire from behind the scout ship, the other two running back behind the trees and bushes for cover.

The Scaedreins can see the smoke is clearing and that some of the scout ship is now visible but twenty-mils beyond the smoke is still thick, at least by Scaedrein standards. The ones behind the decimated scout ship are now open targets and will be picked off soon enough. The Scaedreins open fire at the twelve and at the sneaky one, which is the Scaedreins direct right; they still can't see a majority of the Myie hidden in the smoke.

Whoa! That was close, Boot ducking behind the drop ship, that's okay because this is where he wants to be anyway. A few more laser blasts graze the rounded corner of the drop ship and a couple more whiz by as a few of the Scaedreins begin targeting the drop ship, Boot diving through the entrance of the cockpit as the mounted left wing engine explodes. The drop ship rattles shakes and bounces Boot thrown from one side to the other slamming to a halt against the co-pilots seat. The young Boot's ears ringing and he's seeing stars but that isn't stopping him, pulling him self up as quickly as he can.

Ten Scaedreins have their weapons directed on Boot's position and the other twenty are directed on the Myie behind the scout ship, both are about to become one with the stars.

The smoke that covered the majority of the Myie is now clearing exposing a hail of laser fire and a frontal assault, typical Myie tactics; ten of the twenty Scaedreins firing on the Myie behind the scout ship compensate directing their fire a touch to the left. The other ten focused on the sneaky one are about to finish off the drop ship when it abruptly lifts off the ground, the one engine heard only by those focused on it and they're raising weapons to compensate for the ships hovering position.

The bolts bouncing off the side of the ship don't even phase Boot as he turns the ship directly at the Scaedreins, more bolts striking the front of the ship in a vain effort to destroy it. Boot engages the engine pointing the nose down, the ten Scaedreins trying to warn the others but the frontal assault has them distracted. Boot bracing for impact with a vengeful smile on his face.

The Scaedreins firing at the advancing Myie notice the opposition has stopped their advance and are assuming the prone position, thinking they are the cause the bug heads have their last moment of happiness as the drop ship slides across the Scaedreins defensive line wiping out the tree line and every insectoid beneath it.

Boot now unconscious as the drop ship barrels through the trees clipping the right engine causing an explosion that flips the drop ship and sends it sliding the rest of the way on its roof stopping about thirty-mils beyond the now crushed Scaedreins; the ship on fire about to explode.

The Myie have no time to celebrate the decimation of these Scaedreins back-up is on the way, Boot and Dielan need help. The Myie separate in groups to check for survivors, on both sides, two go to get Dielan while Arianna runs to help Boot.

Through all the chaos one drop-ship remains undamaged and is quickly utilized by the Myie as they begin loading up and preparing for flight, none of the Myie have done this for over eighteen years.

Arianna is dragging Boot from the wreckage as the ship explodes and throws both of them a few feet, Arianna lifting her face from the dirt as the now procured drop ship hovers close by.

"Move out!" The field commander motioning to Arianna as two Myie step off the low hovering ship to get Boot.

The two are in the ship in no time and heading east why and to what they don't know; Kelmu said "you'll see it."

The Scaedrein back up arriving moments later from the south are a day late and a dollar short, only to see the aftermath left from the wake of destruction. These escaped prisoners and former slaves are a lot more dangerous than initial estimations, the scout ship pilot looking upon the destruction from above. The pilot then orders the other scout ship east, while he goes north.

"We gotta' set this bird down," the field commander piloting the drop ship pointing out a city directly in their path just over the horizon.

Boot paying more attention to Dielan turns to look through the transparent steel windshield, "yeah we better because that's our destination."

The field commander double-taking, "what?"

Boot looking rather amused by the captain's expression, "if we're leaving the planet that's the best place to secure a vessel."

"We are placing the fate of our families in the hands of our mortal enemies," the Captain obviously not pleased. "It would be better to save ourselves to ensure the continuation of our way of life-If that is so I choose to die with them instead of running away. What if we're destroyed trying to leave this accursed rock we'll be known as the one's who abandon their own children."

"Just hold up a second," Boot cutting the field promoted captain off.

"We all know the consequences and our families will die with pride despite the circumstances. We will be known as the Myie's last ditch effort at survival if we are destroyed leaving the planet, running away from such overwhelming circumstances is not the act of a coward."

"But to not even try and help," the captain interjecting.

Boot can see a sense of urgency on the captain's face, this private now holding the reigns of leadership wants to be personally responsible for the extraction of the captured NCP's.

"I want to save them too but there isn't any time and if we leave now we can return in a couple weeks to retrieve the bodies after the Scaedrein population has been decimated by the retro-toxin," Boot trying to alleviate the captain's conscience.

The captain trying to change course is an obvious act of deviance, Boot drawing his weapon stunting that idea quickly.

"I'm telling you this one time," Boot holding the blaster very close to the side of the captain's head.

"Land this ship right now and I won't have you tried for treason and shot when this is over," Boot dead serious staring through the soul of this inexperienced lad.

The drop ship touches down in an opening behind a large patch of trees about six grids from the city to the east. The Myie are quick and quiet exiting the ship creating a one-mile gap between them and the landing sight.

"I'm sorry sir," the captain-addressing Boot, "it's just that I feel so damn bad I can't think straight."

Boot looking at the captain with sympathetic eyes, "that's okay it shows you have character and values just learn to control them a little better."

"But how can we be sure this toxin works?" The captain not one to trust something that's still in the experimental stage because it has never been tested on a Scaedrein. The toxin may react differently when introduced to real Scaedrein physiology?

"We have been working on that toxin since before we landed on this rock eighteen years ago before you and I was born," Boot pointing out exactly how long the toxin has been studied and remodeled.

Just so you know these two Myie are seventeen years old, as with most of the soldiers that were killed in battle not to mention that a majority of the one's remaining are seventeen or eighteen as well. To make another point on the education process of Myie children when they reach fourteen they're able to take classes that teach the art of strategy, sorta like ROTC. The class picks apart documented and simulated conflicts examining the flaws and the reasoning behind the movements.

This class was very popular with the students at that age and most would take at least one year of the course. The *Mil- Tacs* the second year students do things like advanced camping; drills; simulated insertions and rescue operations where the Mil Tac students use laser-linking weaponry that beeps when you are hit. War games where strategies are developed or others are mimicked in real time sequences using factored equations that incorporate the laws of geometric configurations that in sound symmetrical strategy lay the avenue of opportunity. Boot and the now promoted captain were in Mil Tacs two years ago but most of their training was done behind enemy lines, no simulations here. Of course all Myie born in the last eighteen years have been specifically trained in military tactics, computer science, biology and anatomy, and arithmetic.

The time is ticking down and the remaining Myie have only seven hours to get off the planet before the Scaedreins start dropping like dominoes one after another; who knows maybe the Scaedreins will be too panicked to kill the Myie they have captured, probably not?

The plan is to procure the ship before the toxin takes effect and leave just as the chaos starts, using that as a cover.

Boot now on point with Arianna about three grids from the eastern city when the captain steps up behind them, Boot knowing the whole time doesn't even turn to look. "What is it?" Boot getting this *I've got an idea* feeling from the field commander knowing it involved the extraction.

"I'm not saying we should do this but since we are getting a ship maybe we can save them. What I mean to say is let's keep them in the equation and maybe we'll see the opportunity," the captain eager yet balanced.

"Very good suggestion," Boot placing his hand on the shoulder of the captain, "your hope could be the one thing that ensures their safety." Boot's words having an uplifting effect as the captain sneaks back to rejoin his team of three.

Arianna looks at Boot momentarily and lightly plants her dry yet soft lips lightly on his cheek.

"What's that for?" Boot positively puzzled.

"You have this amazing effect on people," she simply replies before scouting ahead leaving Boot with a half answered question, tying his tongue with half spoken words and broken sentences.

A boggled Boot bowled over by bewilderment; is she falling in love with him? Boot raising his arm signaling the others to spread out and begin advancing toward the city.

A two-man contingency is further back tending to Dielan, who seems to be feeling better and ready to move on his own. The injected nano-probes are repairing the Major Miscreant from the inside out and the one thing he can't do is walk until the probes are finished and no longer living, this ensures the healing process has been completed and nothing was missed. Bio-scanners do the same thing but it merely double checks the probes work and status these probes have been known to miss things, not very often if any, but it's always good to double check your work. At the moment Dielan is lying in a makeshift stretcher being pulled by one while the other scouts ahead but maintains a close distance and stops frequently.

Arianna and Boot are crouched behind the trees about one-mile from the city debating on how to approach and enter the city along with finding a docking bay without being detected. The sewers may be the safest place upon entering the city; now moving through them is another trick.

Boot raising his arm signaling to the closest group. One of the three in that group advances toward Boot but slowly because let us remember its daytime between four and five pm.

The captain moving within a line of trees that form a semi-circle curving outward toward the city, Boot and Arianna at the center of this arch shaped thicket.

"There is something I must say to you," Arianna apprehensive yet there is a sense of urgency in her tone.

"Yes," Boot turning his head toward her.

She pauses for a second then sorta loses the nerve, "I just want to thank you for letting me take point with you and that I was only a little upset when you passed me over for field commander but *Keele's* younger brother is who I would have picked."

Boot cracking a smile upon her statement that is not what she wanted to say. "Since Keele died during the initial assault it seemed the right thing to let the brother lead the rest of the field units," Boot sounding somewhat impersonal; disconnected.

"Your sterile modesty is a defense mechanism, have I upset you?"

Boot just wanting her to say what she is so afraid to admit. "No but what you said about being thankful is not what you wanted to say," Boot looking deeply into her eyes.

"Your sterile modesty is a-" Boot's words suddenly screech to a halt as she pulls him closer and roughly, at first, kisses his lips then mutual confirmation softens the touch and slows the process.

Their lips fueled by the fire of passion a desire that will stay the hand of this wild beast within Boot and start with a new path beside him, one like his own but with slight differences but not enough to keep the two paths apart. The differences that unite not untie. Abruptly, Boot stops.

Arianna not wanting to stop suddenly realizes why he has; the captain is coming. But wait how did Boot know that, must have heard the captain approaching? She could hear nothing but her pounding heart.

"Captain, we're going to fan out and approach the city from indirect-angles," Boot still feeling the pounding of his heart glad he felt the captain's presence before the captain walked up on anything unexpected or awkward.

The captain now crouched beside Boot looks across the terrain seeing how open and revealing it is. "Are we going to enter the city through the sewers?"

"We're trying to avoid that we need to enter through an alley located on the outskirts of the city where the hanger bays are more than likely located," Boot passing it on to the captain waiting for his ideas on the situation.

"With all the activity it should be easier to get in than get out," the captain suddenly stopping, "what if we never leave?"

"What?" Boot and Arianna say at the same time with the same bewildering look on their face.

"The sewer isn't a good idea if we try and travel through it, but if we hide there the bug heads will never find us and instead of returning in two-weeks we can return in hours after the population has been decimated by the retro-toxin."

"That's awfully risky but no more risky than trying to leave the planet; it may be a good idea." Boot looking over at Arianna to gauge her reaction, she doesn't seem too thrilled.

"We have all been dealing with the possible if not inevitable death of our families why are you so driven in wanting to save them," Arianna sounding a bit off the subject but she is dead-on.

"My grandfather is a retired colonel about two years back and is with the NCP's. He's unfit for combat because he lost his leg and he was forced to resign his commission because implications of his degrading memory were grossly exaggerated and learned through mis-information from his competitor."

"Your grandfather is that colonel, but isn't your last name Keele?" Boot surprised by this new information, suddenly something occurs to him. "But wait that would make his competitor-" Oh-no it can't be.

"The western delegate," Captain *Jyric* with almost leisure tones holding no grudge against the envoy for his actions.

"You don't have it out for the western delegate?" Arianna the first to ask the obvious question.

"At first I did then I see how good of a job he does and it doesn't seem to bother me anymore."

Fair enough, Boot and Arianna exchanging mutual glances.

"Where would be a good place to hide in the sewers?" Jyric popping out the next urgent question on his mind.

"An exchange near the main drain," an all too familiar voice replies from behind them.

Dielan!

The three positively relieved to see Dielan are all too eager to hear what he has to say.

"Probably located on the south side where the land slopes," Dielan elaborating on the location of the sewer entrance.

How can Dielan tell the land is sloping near the city?

"All the mountains favor the south and most of the rocks you see that have fallen over the years," Dielan pointing out a couple rocks that are covered with grass and vegetation, "have formed marks that reveal the grade of the topography and that it continues to slope beyond the south side of the city for about a quarter-grid."

The three are simply amazed I mean they're good at reading rocks and terrain but not that good. This is why Dielan's family so many years ago before the mass extinction were the Myie to see if you wanted to dig underground or do massive landscape readings for large cities or structures.

"Hiding in the sewers is a good idea," Dielan likes the idea of staying rather than leaving; "they'll never find us there."

"Besides if the Scaedreins would have killed our leaders they would have said so and not tried to negotiate surrender, something else is going on and I think Kelmu might have something to do with it."

"Conspiring with the enemy?" Jyric confused as to what Dielan is implying.

"Never in a million life times," Dielan glancing at Boot, "maybe he made a deal with a Scaedrein who has its own agenda and chooses to hide the fact that we are Myie from the other bug heads another reason why we have encountered so little resistance."

"What of the NCP's?" Arianna throwing in the major moral dilemma.

"Alive and well," Dielan more than confident about Kelmu's negotiation skills.

There is a moment of silence before the Myie are on the move and approaching the south east of the eastern city. In less than three hours all hell is going to break loose and hopefully by then Dielan and company will be safe in the sewers away from the dying population of Scaedreins.

Above the planet and for three systems the space is cluttered with all types of Scaedrein vessels supplied and manufactured by the Kybans over the last few years. The Scaedreins didn't have that many vessels twenty years ago then around the time of the Myie mass extinction their armada increased two-hundred percent in a mere two years that just doesn't add up unless the insectoids had help from some larger technologically advanced society that will deal with them, and the Kybans are the only one's who openly feed the Scaedrein war effort. The space around the Cilloetheim cloud is slowly filling with ships as the particles slowly begin to dissipate and the magnetic charges within the molecules can no longer hold its constituent parts together. The

Cilloetheim completely clears revealing empty space that is quickly filled by surrounding ships.

The modified 1/C Tarsuon rests at the backside of the planet just above the atmosphere using the planets gravity to maintain a steady orbit, still phased-out the ship is invisible even to the naked eye. Two smaller ships accompany the larger warship and are part of the Neo-drein civil rights movement. The human prisoners on the planet and the leaders in the detention block have been spared for the time being but the Captain and first officer disagree with the jid commander's decision and only wish to see the disgusting putrid and weaker human species wiped off the face of the galaxy; all in due time.

"You're a traitor," Exle lashing out at Kelmu.

Kelmu not taking too kindly to those words jumps at Exle. Colde staying in between them pushes Kelmu back but Kelmu spins with the push and is moving around Colde throwing a right hook at Exle's temple.

Exle taken by surprise takes a direct hit and drops to the ground without a sound, knocked out Cold, Kelmu stands above Exle.

"Who's the traitor," Kelmu pulling his leg back ready to kick the shit out of Exle.

Colde dives at Kelmu and tackles him to the ground attempting to reason with the riled Miscreant, but it doesn't seem to be working.

Exle still out like a busted light is being checked by Eve, who has had enough of the fighting, Exle is all right. She immediately bum rushes Colde knocking him off of Kelmu.

"If he wants to fight let'em," her voice loud and firm as she stands above Kelmu.

Colde wiping away the shock now against the door of the detention cell noticing an angry Eve about to go toe-to-toe with Kelmu.

"You Myie sit there and flaunt your egos like a banner for all to see nobility, decency, morality just look at yourself acting like a rabid Veareein at each others throat!" Eve stepping back some, "get up," she yells out at Kelmu balling up her fists.

"I don't want to fight; he's the one with the mouth!" Kelmu pulling him self up.

Eve pushing him down as he tries to get up. Kelmu roughly hitting the floor again, but no more, the Miscreant rolls away from Eve and is up in a flash slamming Eve against the door, directly beside Colde.

Colde has tried to remain reasonable toward Kelmu but now the Myie has gone and done it, made the biggest mistake of his life. Colde gets up off the floor even quicker than Kelmu and delivers a kidney punch yanking the mis-directed Miscreant and his anger across the room slamming him on the hard bench resting against the back wall.

"Kelmu any other time you could take me in a second but that's not gonnah happen here," Colde adding pressure pushing the face of the Miscreant chief against the bench, "if you ever do that to her again I will yank out your nervous system and feed it to you through your ass and pull it out of your nose and then cram it down your throat." Colde grabbing up Kelmu like a rag doll throwing him against one of the sidewalls.

Kelmu lying there for a moment is now hearing the door slide open, *perfect*, Kelmu hiding a smile as he still lies there.

Colde turning to see three Scaedreins standing at the open door is still acting pissed off practically ignoring the Scaedreins advancing toward Kelmu's downed position.

One of the Scaedreins steps in and grabs a hold of Colde stopping the humans advance toward the Myie leader; can't kill him yet they still need him.

Colde buckling in pain as a Nythillic spear lightly penetrates his shoulder, Eve reacting by kicking the insectoid in one of its lower leg joints only to be back handed by the second Scaedrein who just walked in. Eve flying back against the wall beside the door she slides down and slumps over, unconscious.

Colde screaming inside is doing a good job of pretending he doesn't care; as he slowly pulls him self off the floor. "Check all you want but he's dead," Colde still ignoring Eve looking right dead at the Scaedrein who is walking toward Kelmu's seemingly unconscious or dead body.

The third Scaedrein is still on the other side of the door standing in the corridor watching Exle's motionless body.

The second one who back handed Eve is now facing Colde with MPFS raised and ready to pull the trigger if the prisoner tries to escape. The first Scaedrein is now standing over Kelmu using the barrel of his gun to poke this supposed unconscious prisoner, momentarily stopping to order the door guard into the cell for added support.

Colde hiding a smile can't believe how accurately the two Myie predicted the events unfolding before them. Eve being knocked out doesn't hinder the plan seeing how it's designed for three or four, but four makes it a bit easier. You see the fourth man tackles the third guard who tries to fire on the three men who initiate the escape attempt from separate but close locations such as this, unless Eve is faking it this is going to be hard.

Exle moves a little bit to attract the attention of the guard slightly opening his eyes to see how the Scaedreins are set up turning his head and rolling over groaning, to keep up the act. He can see a triangle with one unequal side, the door guard now standing at the back corner of the cell needs to move up about a foot; can he somehow make this guard move closer?

Colde is standing before the second guard going unnoticed glancing over at Eve attempting to determine if she is actually knocked out, she slumps over more and falls on her side, this isn't a good sign.

The first guard is now nudging Kelmu with the gun in quicker increments to revive the human; nothing is happening he may be dead? The guard using the barrel of his weapon rolls the body over and pokes the stomach; Kelmu opening his eyes followed by the release of air. What the?

A kick in the abdomen by Kelmu sends the bug head stumbling back, initiating the escape plan.

The third guard moving closer, as the lead guard examined the body of Kelmu, tries to fire his weapon but is suddenly swept off his feet and staring at the ceiling dazed and confused. Colde quickly tackles the second guard as Exle pulls him self up and procures the dropped, Scaedrein sized, MPFS. Snug against his shoulder he fires the weapon.

The lead guard still stumbling back is defenseless as the warbled bolt evaporates his molecules.

Colde still wrestling with the second one is using every bit of his strength to try and disarm this Scaedrein, until a foot comes from beside Colde and hammers the head of the Scaedrein ending that struggle real quick.

Colde looking up to see an angel smiling at him.

"I'm glad-" A loud screech disrupts Colde as the third Scaedrein leaps to his feet, angry to say the least.

Exle quickly turning around triggers the weapon and the screech comes to an abrupt halt.

Colde looking back at Exle ever so briefly then back to Eve, "like I was saying I'm glad you're okay."

Exle peeking down the corridor down to the cells main station spying six more Scaedrein guards who are now getting ready to move down the corridor to investigate the screech, these six are in for a surprise.

Exle quickly closes the door crouching on the right side motioning for Colde to set up on the left side.

Kelmu kneeling beside the bench points the MPFS directly at the center of the door. Eve sits on the bench to the right of Kelmu. Three guards three weapons, four prisoners. Eve unable to handle the Scaedrein size weapon she doesn't mind not having one, hell Colde can barely hold up the bulk and mass of the weapon.

The six Scaedreins see the door is closed but they will not call the captain, they can handle this. Two of them move passed the door and further up the corridor. Two more nestle up beside the door. The last two stand against the back wall of the corridor adjacent to the door sentries.

The door slides open revealing a deceivingly harmless Eve just sitting there and an armed—The warbled bolt sizzles passed the two Scaedreins beside the door and separates the two standing at the back wall of the corridor, suppressing the oppositions forward firing capabilities. Colde and Exle firing down the corridor to stifle the two beside the door as the heated air from the bolt sizzles their face, and not to mention Exle's bolt that continues downward and startles the two at the opposite end of the corridor furthest from the home station.

Kelmu fires a couple more bolts through the opened doorway before Exle and Colde dive into the corridor opening fire down both sides.

The door sentries jumping back are the first to fall followed by one on Exle's side, which leaves one, and one of the now separated two by the back wall on Colde's side. Kelmu never leaving the cell approaches the doorway at an angle and can easily see the one remaining Scaedrein near the back wall, quickly triggering the MPFS that guard is no more.

Colde is now turning to cover Exle who is firing on the last of six D-block guards. The guards bolt hitting the floor in front of Exle temporarily blinding him. Colde firing the MPFS down the corridor the bolt whizzing passed the guards right shoulder.

The guard raising his weapon and advancing is about to open fire as Kelmu dives through the doorway firing down the corridor canceling out that attempt, literally.

Colde and Exle let out a tense breathe

"What you were worried or something," Kelmu getting up from the floor.

Eve who hasn't moved is still sitting on the bench, "what did something just happen?" Playing dumb as if complimenting the Myie's strategy and knowledge of their enemy, like she has nothing to worry about.

"Don't get cocky we're not out of this yet," Kelmu motioning Eve to get her moving.

"Indeed you are not," a familiar humanoid voice sounds out and he is coming down the corridor from the home station.

All four turn to see the western delegate or at least what is left of the western delegate; what the hell happened to him?

"What's the matter you look disgusted?" The western delegate wearing some type of bio-mechanical armor that has really done a number on his personal appearance; he's hideously hard to describe but from what they can tell the former delegate seems to have two extra bug legs and a human/bug torso with two smaller bug like appendages beneath his human arms, and even a Nythillic spear on the right appendage.

"You should try it," the traitorous envoys showing off like some kind of sick demented model.

"Ahhh!" Kelmu running toward the former delegate attempting to kill him, suddenly stops seeing a number of Scaedreins standing just inside and outside the door leading to the home station.

"I can see my old friends have swayed you," the western delegate looking deviously gratified at his accomplishments.

Kelmu and Exle puzzled, Colde and Eve lost completely.

"You should learn to be more considerate to the one that has kept all of you alive for eighteen years. Take them away and separate them to hinder any more attempts at escape."

"Where are the others?"

"They are alive and well, as you will remain, if you side with the Scaedreins."

"Don't even ask that because you all ready know that answer," Exle never taking his eyes off the altered delegate, even as they take him away Exle making the extra effort to keep looking back.

The delegate is left alone as the four are escorted to separate detention blocks located throughout the ship, he smiles and takes a moment to look around the corridor basking in his twisted and warped moment of glory.

Kelmu being roughly escorted to some detention block somewhere on this ship knows the well in *Djri'gee'din' din* was never contaminated and this *Scaedrein Infiltration* was a farce to begin with; but why have the Scaedreins waited so long it doesn't make any sense? The facts are hidden in the gloating words of the former western envoy. The clone Aswic Gildyn must have been his idea as with the Scaedrein disguised as the western delegate, which lead to the death of the eastern delegate and the mystery of the white like fluid pouring from the body of the dead eastern designate. Question is how long has the eastern political chain been compromised? Another disturbing question why hasn't he been asked about the remaining Myie still roaming the terrain of the northeastern continent?

Dielan and the others are about to enter the sewers when a scout ship buzzes the tree tops directly above them, all Myie hit the deck except for one.

"Jyric what are you doing?" Boot looking up at the field promoted captain momentarily before realizing what is going on.

"You don't need to worry about hiding I've lead them directly to us," Jyric pointing a weapon at Dielan and Boot.

Not one second later a light is cast on the Myie hiding around the outside entrance of the sewers, four scout ships hovering above and a bunch of Scaedrein foot soldiers converging on the Myie.

"Why?" Dielan confused and disgusted all at once.

"Is it really that hard to see," Jyric simply replies.

"How can you betray your own people?"

"The Myie quit being my family's people years ago even before the mass extinction, which I'm glad happened."

"Then you claim allegiance with the Scaedreins?"

"Yes and no. Yes the Scaedreins have helped us but others like me have made our own name," Jyric's eyes focused and filled with fire.

"You can call us the Khaedrin Nul," Jyric speaking with proud tones.

"You're sick you know that," Boot adds in knowing the Myie translation as *a great and divine presence.*

The others know this and feel the same way Boot does.

"Thank you," Jyric replies in kind. "Such a sentiment from my worst enemy is invigorating to say the least," Jyric motioning to the surrounding Scaedreins to take the Myie scum away.

Jyric has waited a long time for this moment ever since he was a toddler his father has prepared him and all of it has paid off. The *Khaedrin Nul* is well on their way to becoming the next galactic power house with the help of the Scaedreins, of course.

Kelmu looking back at Exle maybe for the last time is yanked by the arm and pulled through the exit/entrance of the detention block and into the adjacent corridor. He is to be moved and probably deeper into the ship because he's the only known military leader of the Myie. He's worried about his friends Eve and Colde; what will the Scaedreins do with them?

The one other thing weighing heavily on the story is what Jyric said about this secret organization called the Khaedrin Nul and how they have been working with the Scaedreins since the beginning; that can't be possible? The botched mission seven years ago seems to be the only plausible explanation unless this Khaedrin Nul was conducting missions directed by Colonel Keele? I still have trouble believing Colonel Keele made a deal with the Scaedreins; was it to ensure the survival of their secret society, and not the rest of the Myie, seems to be the next dot in the intergalactic cutthroat world of political and military espionage?

Thirteen levels later Kelmu is now being walked down a corridor; odd doesn't' look like a detention block? Abruptly the guards stop him in front of a sliding metal door that opens as they push him through it. Kelmu resisting a bit turns to slander the bug heads when he suddenly stops.

"What the hell is goin' on here?" Kelmu looking around the moderately furnished room equipped with all the bare necessities, including a bed.

The Myie soldiers captured near the eastern city have all been accounted for and are now being transported to the Neo-drein's vessel in orbit. The traitor Jyric is all ready talking with the western delegate about what to do if the Myie decide to turn down the only option they have, other than death. Kill them of course but how? In a cave with flesh eating *Mubai,* a bat like animal about a foot in length and about two pounds with almost transparent teeth. One isn't bad but they usually flock in the thousands and reside in large caves that can house up to ten thousand Mubai, the two gloating in the waves of pre-victory celebrations.

I say pre-victory because something tells me this isn't over yet. The transport ship docks within the main hanger of the 1/C Tarsuon before the larger vessel phases back out, going unnoticed amongst the clutter of ships on the front side of the planet.

The detainees are escorted to rooms and not cells, but still locked from the outside, all with the same question: "What the hell is goin' on here?"

Boot like most of the others refusing to even use the comforts are more concerned about the NCP's and sit on the floor of these lavishly decorated prison cells projecting scenarios for escape or a martyr to a dead society who's screams will never be heard or even known maybe they can take a few Scaedreins with them in the process, a little optimism never hurts. Boot is stifled by the turn of events and wonders if any of the other leaders had any knowledge of this Khaedrin Nul? A great and divine presence; how does betraying your own kind qualify one as being great? Boot stands up and kicks over a table located at the side of the bed; he needs to vent this anger.

Pacing the floor like a dreary mad man he's on the edge about to burst the pressure of these insurmountable odds broadening the gap between his better judgment and sheer desperation filling in its place, a menacing fear that builds a web of fibrous oblivion far worse than death. Boot will not cooperate with the enemy to ensure the survival of the NCP's or himself; all agree they will rather take death.

Another hour passes and it is now passed the deadline for the retro-toxin to take effect, clearly the plan was implemented but thwarted by these Myie who call them selves the Khaedrin Nul. He feels a sudden anger a resentment that has built up over the years one that has remained hidden until this time, a depth of hatred that he must face in order to maintain his sanity. How he reacts and responds to this anger may very well shift his outlook toward aggression or pacify this inner hatred?

The tides pull him under and rip at the fabric of his soul the water is black and thick like blood he moves through the rapidly descending currents toward a bottomless ravine of despair and hatred Boot gasping for air reaching for a hand that isn't there the soul fighting for its life; its purity.

The stream is almost like tar but not as thick and it reeks, standing on the edge looking down the stream to follow its path, this is a river of death and he stands before it but not as a representation more like an observer to even his own actions as if being persuaded by some other power. This lesson so deep that a passed life has awoken only to teach this one important aspect to his present lifetime, something forgotten or learned but never fully realized then lost again within the fabric of lifetimes only to be re-learned at this moment in time. Kelmu Cw'jur standing outside of himself as he watches himself watching himself standing before this black tar like river, an urge to dive in he's staring deeply into the rough swirling currents with waves as sharp as the devil's claw. He feels a hand against his back that abruptly pushes him into the ripping currents; he looks to see himself still standing on the shore.

Dielan stands before a precipice an abyss of condemned souls screaming from below horrible shrills of pain like a kinetic jackhammer being driven through the fabric of his being. He feels this as torment and rage daring to envelope his conscience in an attempt to destroy his well of morality. Dielan fights with every inch of his life on the line dangling on the edge of non-existence or a life without meaning. Will Dielan somehow find a purpose amongst this chaos and pass this test of his character a defining point amongst insignificance, a purpose?

Boot hangs on the edge of this massive black waterfall holding onto what looks to be a large dead vine from a tree, in essence this is the silver strand of web that connects who he is, if he lets go he will sacrifice the trueness of himself and the lie will manifest its own opinions and conquer the good spirit within.

Kelmu is captured by the very essence of this river of death and hate the black blood growing tentacles and needles to inject the black acidic substance into his body; Kelmu fights this threat off but is pulled back under.

Exle sits calmly in his room in deep meditation unaffected by these rivers but still observing the three amongst these independent but similar spiritual trials, and although he looks calm on the outside he is filled with fear because he knows he can't help his friends during this test of their divinity.

As if it can't get any worse the western delegate's new grotesque form appears on a monitor behind a retracting wall slot and only the Scaedreins can control it, as with most of the stuff in the room. Wonder what he's gonnah say, Arianna repulsed by the hideousness of the western envoy.

"I hope you find the rooms to your liking, if you wish to join the Scaedreins and the Nul your safety and comfort will be ensured. If not, then you will die when the room is filled with poison gas and become a martyr to a lost cause? I will wait one hour for your answer I don't want to kill any of you but I will if necessary, you must learn to forget the old way and join the Nul way." The monitor shutting off as the wall slides back in front of the screen.

Arianna throws the frail little table hitting the sliding wall, and then steps back. "I am and will always be Myie you'll never take that away from me!"

"Temper-temper," the western delegate's voice coming from behind her. She turns around but doesn't see anyone. He speaks again and it's obvious that he is using an intercom and the speaker is behind one of the vents in the upper right corner near the exhaust vents.

Exle only hearing mumbles has completely ignored the traitor and will gladly accept dying for what is believed to be a lost cause, in the eye's of this arrogant and ignorant little man of a politician. Exle beginning to feel some hostility toward this envoy channels his hate into something productive, like praying for the souls of his three friends in spiritual distress.

Dielan can hear a voice but it sounds nothing like the western delegate and it comes from the abyss below him a deep growling voice that eats hope and devours light but Dielan possess a shimmering beacon of hope the will of one-hundred men, and this despair will not claim his soul.

Kelmu toppling through the currents reaching for the shore that seems so close, yet so far, the rip tides pulling him under his extended fingers the only thing seen as he reaches for a hand that isn't there; the last moments of hope? Abruptly Kelmu's hand is grabbed and he is yanked out of the treacherous Black River, Dielan standing above him surrounded by a faint light. Kelmu shakes his head and realizes he is standing motionless in the middle of the room.

Boot still hangs from the vine of his true self but is losing grip, and fast. His strength giving out he looks above him searching for the strength within but his soul feels tired, and the fight has drained him considerably.

Abruptly a hand extends over the edge, "everyone needs a little help," Dielan now standing at the edge surrounded by an ominous light above Boot. "Let me be that help," Dielan's hand right beside Boot's hand.

Boot accepting Dielan's offered hand he is pulled back onto the ledge. Boot exhales noticing that he's standing in the middle of the room with fragmented emotions of his spiritual experience.

Exle abruptly opens his eyes aggressively the pupils bounce back and forth but the depth of his gaze is above and beyond the walls around him; someone is coming.

"You should really watch that temper," the traitors voice taunting Arianna.

"Why don't you come on down here and talk to me in person," her tone icy hot burning cold embers of vindication.

"Are you sure you want to die?" The western delegate remains quiet waiting for an answer.

"Ty'agnoome you can kiss my ass," Arianna really upset because she knows or at least thought she knew Ty'agnoome.

"Have it your way."

"How can you live with yourself what you've done makes you even lower than the Scaedreins," Arianna walking toward the vent in the upper right corner.

"If I tell you something will you at least please think about my proposal?"

Arianna crosses her arms and steps back some, "I know you have video and you can see me so just say what you want to say then leave me alone."

"Our people as you know lived in space for many years before Mieveodrin became our home. We lost most of our history during that time and soon forgot our origins upon establishing a civilization on our new home, I have re-discovered this knowledge."

Arianna showing a sarcastic form of enlightenment steps back even further, "this is why you betray your own kind this knowledge you posses of a history that we have forgotten?"

"Silence you impetuous bitch!" Ty'agnoome's riled voice echoing off the metal walls.

Arianna still taunting him with her body motion abruptly runs and jumps at the vent striking it with her fist.

"I've tried to reason with you and it's clear that you want no part of what I believe is the best solution for our people." The speaker goes dead with good reason Arianna using her boot to pound against the vent breaking the speaker behind it.

Arianna fumbling through her empty pockets hoping her captors over-looked something but only reassures her hopelessness, slipping her boot back on kneeling down to strap them on she begins to stare at the worn leather the aged hook and eye. Arianna remembering how they looked new and how the smell used to stir the desire she felt for men, all that seemed so long ago when actually it's not, she slumps down to the floor wrapping her arms around her legs putting her head down realizing the significance of her subconscious desires that the one she's in love with goes by the name of Boot. She may never see him again and will never know how much he means to her?

Boot not as anxious as before but he still paces around the room; there has to be a way out of this?

"Think all you like my young Miscreant," Ty'agnoome's voice filling the room.

Boot stops in his tracks and looks around the room.

"The Miscreant way is dead and you made sure of that," Boot still looking about the room waiting for a response from *Ty'ag*.

"It doesn't have to be that way."

"You should know by now that requires one of experience and that if anyone other than a field commander trains them, Miscreant's will be a mere shadow to what they were before."

"I will train you," Ty'ag a former Miscreant himself.

"No thanks," Boot declining now walking toward the rear of the room believing the voice is originating from a speaker in the left corner of the room.

"You can't throw away who you are because of me," Ty'ag using reverse psychology.

"Are you so blinded by your arrogance that you can't see you're the one who threw yourself and us away when you decided to work with the bug heads," Boot now standing in front of the speaker. Keep in mind that during his conversation on the monitor Boot was busy with his spiritual trial and didn't see what Ty'ag looks like, he doesn't have a clue.

"You are still young with much to learn let me be your mentor," Ty'ag maintaining a calm status.

"Are you hard of hearing or just stupid?" Boot now standing on the frail little table looking into a mesh covered slot beside an environmental vent.

"So you choose to die," Ty'agnoome remaining calm, "and then die you will." His last words before the speaker shut off.

Good. Boot having studied electronics and various systems knows about environmental vents and how big the back of the vents must be to incorporate the system into the environmental network, behind that vent is a shaft large and long enough to get him clear of this area all he has to do is follow it. He probably won't be able to access it because the front of the vent is only a quarter of the size and he doesn't have a cutting laser to fashion a twenty-eight inch hole in the wall. There's not enough time to yank out the housing assembly in front of the system itself much less getting though the template that protects the intricate boards behind it, sure the boards are easy to pull out but it's just a matter of where each board fastener is located. It must be a stroke of synchronization to be put in this room because the main system is located in but one room and all other vents in adjacent rooms are too small and more than likely wouldn't have been noticed if anyone other than him was in this room, much less accessing the thing without being noticed or triggering an alarm. Boot can see the potential of the idea and get passed the technology but that still doesn't give him a cutting laser; maybe he will be able to use this knowledge later? He uses his boot and a metal wedge, hidden within the heel of his shoe, to pry open the front of the quarter-inch metal mesh covering the small sound receptacle adapted to a transparent like fabric coated with a protective rubber layer. The speaker is very small and hooked to an even smaller thin square that houses the larger, but still tiny, chips and circuits.

The door to his room opens up breaking his concentration but not startling enough to where he loses his balance on the frail little table, legs bowing inward on the edge of collapsing, he looks back at the Scaedrein and lightly steps off the table. The door immediately closes afterward Boot looking around the room again but not for more vents, security cameras this time. He's beginning to lose focus the thoughts of Arianna emerging from the tidal wave of his efforts in trying to not think about her. The room has security cameras and the location must be ascertained, he needs to stay calm in order to maintain clarity.

A liaison to the new group of inducted Myie soldiers, which includes Jyric and himself, Ty'agnoome is underneath a very serious gun that doesn't take too kindly to someone that doesn't make good on a promise. Yes at the moment there are only two people in the Khaedrin Nul, the conniving traitor has told the Jid commander he has got twenty loyal members. None of the NCP's wants to join or surrender their children to the Nul order. He can probably get a couple of the soldiers to join but he's not holding his breath.

"Human your time runs short."

A voice from behind surprises and turns him around, standing almost eye-to-eye with the captain you can smell the burning embers of conflict fueled by their hatred of one another.

"The Nul will grow with or without the Myie," Ty'ag implying that he recruits another species of humanoid?

"No Myie no deal," the captain waving his roughly shaped hand through the air, the one with the course and piercing Nythillic spear protruding from it.

"I have other skills in the fields of science I can mass produce automatons until I perfect my sub-zero cloning experiments," Ty'ag knowing the captain is into science as well.

The captain still doesn't want to listen, Ty'ag persisting in order to save Jyric and his own life.

"Just listen for a second. I am so close but my only working experiment died but it only took a week and the clone grew to full size in less than four days."

"That technology worked only twice," the captain saying nothing more walks off.

Ty'agnoome must show the Scaedrein captain and not tell, he needs to act quickly time is running short. On his way to the lift he is seen injecting something in his neck; must be for the pain as his body adjusts to genetic manipulation and Biomechanical armor? A flinching wince indicates a slight pinching pain before the numbing sensation kicks in. It could be small doses of *Uthiex* an equivalent to what you earthlings call Morphine, except no side effects. The injection will last for several hours and moving at faster speeds is virtually painless.

Sub-zero cloning. The sample rapidly grows as the temperature rises to maintain some kind of sub-atomic solidity and because it has been in sub-zero for so long the living matter moves away from the heat and toward the still cool but not as cold center. This process is called Cold Matter Manipulation where the matter combines naturally clinging to its own survival therefore developing or building a working network of constituent parts that can support itself above sub-zero temperatures evolving with the varying temperatures until desired temperature is achieved, which in this case the average body temperature for a Myie is 97.6 degrees. The clone requires very little observation while it grows and doesn't eat until fully mature because it isn't awakened until then. Now when I say sub-zero I mean -50 degrees on an equivalent to our Celsius scale. The astonishing thing is watching the matter grow before it reaches a very small fetus stage about an inch in diameter. A protective shell like cocoon is around the clone until the day it breaks out of it, which is between four and five days. The white substance pouring from the dead eastern delegate impostor pumps throughout the body of most sub-zero clones. The shape shifting one was all so sub-zero cloning technology, but more time is required to produce a working sample and an extra three days is added to gestation.

The clone of Aswic Gildyn is Ty'agnoome's handy work but the Jid commander seen the plan through. Ty'ag created the memories for the clone so it would actually believe he wasn't a clone. Aswic is actually the best clone work he's ever done, the only, but the subject exceeded all simulations another reason why a second was created after the first one died in an accident. Then when Aswic exposed the location of the Myie, as if the Scaedrein conspirators didn't all ready know, that made the Myie believe the Scaedrein's had somehow discovered them and the clone was their doing. Ty'ag and his little distractions added to the confusion created from Aswic.

The Neo-drein's are fools this technology will put them above every race in the galaxy and more importantly put them above their own lower evolved kind. He needs to map an escape route if such a thing becomes necessary, which this may be the case because the Myie aren't going to budge. Jyric is only one level up; he must go and see him. If worse comes to worse he don't need the Neo-drein fools, besides the picture seems better with them away from it, as in out or not included or even erased.

"Jyric, I'm coming up to ya don't move."

"I'm all ready on my way to you we'll meet half way," Jyric responds.

Ty'ag quickly replaces his communicator and steps into a lift that only goes up and down one level.

The lift doors slide open and Jyric steps in. "Plans have been slightly altered," Ty'ag stepping over some as Jyric moves in close enough to trip the sensor that shuts the door.

"You will have to assume my duties I have another pressing matter that I must attend to," Ty'ag looking down at an unusually tense Jyric.

"May I inquire about this matter?" Jyric swallowing his fear trying to hide it from Ty'ag.

"It's a back up plan in case the first one fails. I just got done talking with the captain and it's Myie or nothing."

"What about cloning? I mean that's what the plan was from the start anyway secure the Myie and use their DNA to create the clones, and then put them in stasis to avoid any insurrections or unauthorized tampering of samples. Ty'ag we can't let the Scaedrein's get away with this," Jyric raising his voice.

Ty'agnoome from out of nowhere strikes Jyric with the back of his new left appendage, "fool Keep your voice down."

Jyric now on the floor looking up at Ty'ag as if he were a stranger that he no longer knows, his teacher; Ty'ag has never struck him with such force and magnitude.

Ty'ag helps him up but roughly pushes him through the now open lift doors, "keep trying to persuade the others to join; try the younger soldiers first," the door closing in front of Ty'ag leaving Jyric on the floor of the lower corridor.

Jyric is having trouble adapting to his mentors new look wondering why Ty'ag would do such a thing, and will he have to do the same thing? His genetic structure has been spliced with Scaedrein DNA and the bio-armor is a twisted addition to an all ready disturbing and terrifying image. Jyric is worrying about his safety in the presence of his mentor for the first time in his life; is Ty'ag going crazy and if so will his delusions declare Jyric a threat and kill him before all this is over? If Ty'ag could procure the captains precious trophy, A.K.A. the frozen and in stasis real Aswic Gildyn, you can bet Jyric would become an expendable commodity with one snap of his neck. Ty'agnoome could clone a hundred thousand Aswic Gildyn's in about a year mass producing close to twenty-thousand clones a week but one would need to build a massive facility to accommodate such a stock pile, regardless, without another DNA sample the task becomes increasingly difficult Ty'ag still needs him. What if the real Aswic Gildyn if pulled out of stasis and doesn't survive, or lives but doesn't adhere to Ty'agnoome's new order?

The next order of business how to persuade some of the younger Myie to join the Nul; who should he try to encourage first? The corridor has high ceilings and houses several rooms that are now acting as prison cells for the Myie soldiers, the NCP's are way on the other side near the front of the ship. He stops in front of the first door it slides open revealing a control booth for observing occupants in the adjacent rooms.

Monitors are set up in a half circle around a single seat console for easy viewing purposes. Jyric still a little shaken up from Ty'agnoome's behavior takes a second to gather his thoughts and mentally prepare for the task at hand.

Who should he try and persuade first someone his age, eighteen, or a younger soldier? There are a few that are seventeen and one that is sixteen. The sixteen year old is the least likely to be swayed, Jyric knows all about him.

The highest marks in Mil-Tacs in Myie history, well their known history, sharp shooter at age fourteen; minor demolitions; ATSAC training (All-Terrain Simulated Assault Calculations), most Miscreants don't start this type of training until their seventeen, this sixteen year old boy just finished the training about three months ago and it only took him a year and a half. He finished intermediate and advanced during the last year and a half, and no one's ever done that. The lads name is *Dwaejn* translation from Myie to English is *quadrilateral existence.*

Jyric clicks the switch beneath the small monitor linked to the camera to the room *Dwaejn* occupies; a larger view of the room appears on a separate screen beside the mini-monitors. This camera angle is centralized around Dwaejn and his movements, with zoom capabilities. Jyric knows this probably won't work but he's got to try; if he can coax the young prodigy then others may follow? The hour is almost up and if none of the prisoners comply with Nul policies the gas will be their fate.

Dwaejn is sitting up against the wall, on what is his left side, by the door and not in the center of the room as most we're. The room size is fifteen-feet wide and twenty-feet long Dwaejn learning this shortly after his arrival by walking around the room counting his paces and recalling his ATSAC training. The center of the room is five and a half long paces from width side to center and eight and half long paces from length side to center, since then he's done everything else to keep his mind busy to avoid going crazy in the last hour of his impending doom.

"Dwaejn," a voice sounding throughout the room pulls the young man to his feet as he looks around for the source.

"Don't be alarmed I wish to only speak with you."

"You needn't waste your time just gas me and get it over with," Dwaejn flying a finger around the room. For humans it's the middle finger but Myie use the first, or dominant finger.

"Your childish actions belittle the potential of your genius, such a waste how you choose to die when life is offered to you. If we work with the Scaedreins we can re-establish a population, safely I may add."

Dwaejn is now walking toward the backside of the room but suddenly turns to face the wall on his left side, "something tells me there was no real danger Ty'ag made sure of that about seven years ago."

"You were but nine years old how could of you known or even suspected such a thing?"

"Because even at nine I knew more about others and myself than you know now, so don't tell me what I'm wasting or what you think I don't know."

"So be it, you wish to die then your request shall be granted." The speaker cuts off as the young miscreant throws his boot at the hidden speaker having just found it, damn one second too late.

Jyric moving to the next young soldier can't help but wonder how Dwaejn connected the Scaedreins discovering the whereabouts of the Myie seven years ago and that he knew who was responsible, but does the lad know that it actually started eighteen years ago?

The next young soldier reacts the same way electing for the gas rather than side with the Nul or the Scaedreins. One-minute of hearing the same answer Jyric is checking Boot's room looking for a voice of reason amongst the soldiers.

Boot giving up on the camera idea is now sitting against the wall at the back side of the room, at least he won't have to see Ty'ag or Jyric for too long before the gas comes. He feels amazingly calm and at ease basking in the serenity of his last moments knowing that he tried as hard as he could for as long as he could before the end; wonder if the gas is odorless or colorless, will he see or know when it happens or will he just?

Kelmu, Exle, Eve, and Colde are somewhere near the middle of the ship between the NCP's and the NCO's (Non-combat officers.) near the front, and the soldiers near the rear. Kelmu and the other three are in actual cells spread amongst three different detention-blocks on three different levels. Scaedrein activity is ten-fold making sure no prisoners escape, the captain of the vessel not especially happy with the current arrangements is lashing out at Jyric for attempting to gas the prisoners without first informing him.

The Scaedrein Captain back handing Jyric sending the frail, weak, small, and insignificant humanoid across the main corridor of the observation level as an example to deter any future attempts at defiance.

Jyric's body slamming against the metal wall his head hitting one of the many small protrusions built into the walls of the corridor, and then face first onto the floor losing a couple teeth during impact.

"Take it easy I gave the order," Ty'ag coming down the corridor moving a bit faster than earlier with a degree of fluidity as well.

"The Scaedreins shall be responsible for destroying the last of the Myie," the captain moving his massive legs to turn his somewhat shorter torso raising up his side arm then pointing it at Ty'ag.

"Thought it didn't matter to you," Ty'agnoome filled with sarcasm, "as long as they die; but I'm beginning to feel you want to kill me as well?"

"The prisoners will remain unharmed for the time being we have our own plans for them," the captain holstering his side arm leaves the observation level without another word.

Ty'agnoome still not totally adapted to the bio-armor is still getting used to moving the extra limbs, the captain is very lucky in that aspect. He revives Jyric and helps the lad up, and then tells him to get cleaned up. Ty'ag now alone wonders if releasing the prisoners so he can escape in the commotion, along with Jyric, is an option worth looking into. He's unable to move at the speeds required in combat so Jyric is his only defense against attacks. The extra arms and legs supported by this armor are Scaedrein by nature and is a product of what is called 'living' armor, the appendages actually grow from the bio-armor after a host is attached to it. The appendages grow to full length in less than three hours but full, fast, and coordinated movements take a little more time. A blend of Kyban and Myie technology Ty'ag is the twisted genius behind this technology.

The captain is a fool blinded by his arrogance. The Myie must die coercing them isn't working, as he suspected, and if the Scaedreins can't get the job done then he will.

Colde's thoughts are of Eve her face burned into his mind as he stares off looking passed the walls and beyond the block he currently occupies, back to when he first persuaded her to help him infiltrate Scaedrei. The first time they kissed and how she initiated it; how she seduced him the first time they made love. When she said "is that his name, this" makes him laugh a bit. The depth in her eyes at that moment swallowed every bit of his cruelty and hatred and in that memory he will live forever. Colde suddenly drops his head and a tear of redemption falls from his eye showing that even in the end someone like Colde is capable of truly loving another.

Eve wiping the tears from her eyes is suddenly feeling very cold and her chest is beginning to hurt. The image of Colde in her mind and the look on his face when she kicked him in the balls makes her laugh a bit, but a flood of other images replaces the laugh with tears. The way he looked at her; the way he touched her; the way he brought out the woman in her and how he raised the peak of her sexual desires, those things she would do with no other man except him. She stands up and begins to pace slowly in the small fifteen-foot cell, only to lie down on the hard bench type seat several seconds later. Eve is suddenly tired and wonders if she'll fall asleep before she dies? In the end, as with Colde, even someone like Eve has the ability to honestly love another.

Kelmu in deep meditation mentally prepares for his death accepting that all things must come to an end, and that their jobs as defenders of morality and life are ending and another has taken its place. The kinetic web of creation works in mysterious ways when viewed through eyes of the flesh, but even those things too small to see and too random to fully understand have significance and purpose. Kelmu begins to feel a buzzing and the metal floor now feels like a cushion of air beneath him, opening his eyes he looks down realizing he is four-feet off the floor. The shock of levitation breaks his concentration and he drops to the floor, immediately jumping up afterward positively perplexed.

Minutes later he realizes six Scaedreins occupy the main station for the d-block but another has just entered, his presence gives off a strange frequency. The guards have an intense hatred of this bizarre presence, it's definitely Ty'agnoome. Kelmu can feel him getting closer as the traitor moves down the corridor toward the cell he occupies; the intent of Ty'agnoome's thoughts as strong as his presence. Kelmu has an idea of why the deceitful delegate has come to see him, and it isn't about cooperating with the Scaedreins or even joining the Khaedrin Nul. Kelmu can't help but feel something drastic is about to happen, and it may not be all that bad.

The heavy gray door slides open Ty'ag stands in the corridor looking in and down at Kelmu, whose now standing up.

"The look suits you traitor," Kelmu looking into the eyes of Ty'ag.

"This look will keep me alive much longer than you."

"Step into this cell and let's test your theory," Kelmu stepping toward the collaborator.

"I don't have time to kill you right now but you can be sure I've all ready tried, you should thank the bug heads for stopping me."

Ty'ag is purposely holding something back, but in essence the former western delegate is screaming at the top of his lungs "let's get out of here and kill each other later."

"Do you have nothing to say?" Ty'ag egging-on the suggestion because his pride won't let him say it.

Kelmu remaining quiet he's a million-miles away in a haze of smoky-gray standing before a massive circle of Myie wearing hooded robes, suddenly in the middle they stare at him; messages of old ricocheting thwatts but not just words or thoughts but of methods *patterns of infinite possibilities* all showing different outcomes where each hooded figure stands. Kelmu looking around the circle from within can still see what he knows to be Myie as these images play like a movie behind and above these older than ancient ancestors, he can see no faces only darkness where a face should be.

Ty'ag pushes Kelmu to get some kind of reaction because he's just standing there staring at nothing.

"What are you doing?" Ty'ag baffled at this odd behavior is too pre-occupied to realize what he's witnessing.

The circle of these mysterious ancestors, a link to a forgotten past, are moving closer as one lowers the hood of the robe revealing his mothers face.

"Kelmu," a familiar voice from behind turns him around before he can even say anything to his mother.

"Billy," how does Kelmu know this person and where did he meet him? Whoever it is the feeling of long and numerous friendships causes his body to warm up and something unlocks within the fibers of his being, something as old and ancient as his friendship with Billy.

"Remember this?" Billy tossing a gleaming metal tube like object high up in the air and though Kelmu can't see it he does know where it's going and what it is.

Kelmu reaches upward as if calling the object to him, landing perfectly in his hand he smiles and without a thought ignites the object. A metal to metal sound is heard before a focused laser beam rises out of the hilt, luminous in the smoky-gray stopping at a point about three-feet from the base of a twelve-inch hilt; the high out-put energy weapon creates a buzzing effect that momentarily vibrates the hilt, and makes him feel very powerful. The humming, its distinct sound, as he slices through the air with the energy blade, brings back a slew of genetic memory that is supposedly dead, junk DNA no longer active.

Ty'ag will be ignored no longer pulling his side arm shooting at Kelmu's feet.

Kelmu yanked back into reality is extremely upset only experiencing a portion of the visions summit, its massive peaks of spiritual knowledge only known by his celestial mind, but it's enough for him to go on.

"Just say what you have to say and go," Kelmu sitting down on the hard bench.

Ty'agnoome looking down the corridor toward the main station and then back in the cell at Kelmu, "I think it would be wise if we set our differences aside for now and deal with our common threat."

"Shame on you for stabbing me in the back but shame on me for letting you do it again."

"I speak of departure and re-location."

"I'm well aware of what you have in mind but there's one problem you seem to have forgotten-the swarm," Kelmu's sarcasm as obvious as his statement.

"Just help me get off this ship and I'll get us passed the clutter of ships in all three systems," Ty'ag speaking very low.

Kelmu not believing Ty'ag capable of such a feat quickly denies the request, "I will die rather than side with you."

"So be it," Ty'ag closes the door with a push of a button leaving Kelmu in the cell.

Kelmu stands up and begins to slowly walk around thinking about the images and emotions from his vision of his mother and these archaic ancestors and this focused beam weapon, once thought of and used but not like his prophetic like episode described. Really the weapon is inferior even in the hand of a master in sword techniques because blaster bolts are long range and these weapons aren't but someone like him could be as deadly with this electrically generated sword, if not more, than a blaster or even an MPFS. He can't help but feel amazed and in awe still wired from the supercharged burst of knowledge the ancient memories emerging as he continues to dissect this revelation to find the words within the fabric of these recollections.

Kelmu walking in a circle around the cell-block he comes to an abrupt halt. A sudden realization has him pounding on the door and yelling, "I remember the Nul," over and over again.

Ty'ag still standing in the main station waiting to leave but his escorts won't quit yammering with the other six guards. Idle time on his hands has him looking at a near-by monitor that shows Kelmu jumping about and yelling but the sound is muted, walking up to the console he turns on the sound hearing the last three words. Remember the Nul? The sound is echoing off the walls and the first word is hard to catch because the reverb is drowning it out; what's Kelmu saying?

"Guard," Ty'ag interrupting the bug heads conversation, "take me back to the prisoners cell."

The two escorts glowering at the fickle human annoyed with his requests, motionless they suggest he go alone this time and that he can open the door on his own.

Ty'ag listens for another second trying to distinguish the missing word before going back to the cell.

Kelmu yelling and jumping wondering if anyone is even watching the monitor, until the opening door stops him, it's about time his throat was getting sore. Ty'ag standing in the corridor on the other side of the door he's looking at the turn-coat, once again.

"You're still here?" Kelmu standing in front of the bench about four-feet from the door advances a couple feet upon his inquiry.

"Tell me what you were saying," Ty'ag pulling his weapon, which the Scaedreins don't know about.

"What are you talking about I wasn't saying anything" Kelmu clamming up.

"You will tell me now or I will blow your legs and arms off and let you live out the rest of your useless life having to rely on everyone but yourself."

"Well since you put it that way I wasn't saying a thing," Kelmu maintaining his silence firmly standing before Ty'ag.

Ty'ag tightened his trigger finger the blaster bolt speeding by a spinning Kelmu who dodges the bolt then a second bolt without even looking at Ty'ag, much less the pulling of the trigger.

"I don't know how you did that and I'm sure you won't tell me," Ty'ag pulling the trigger again, watches Kelmu dodge the third bolt.

"That's impossible," outraged he tightens his trigger finger for a fourth shot.

Kelmu shuffling toward the defector in about half a blink disarming Ty'ag throwing a palm strike right on the lower chin pushing the traitor down to the floor of the corridor in the process, the fourth bolt never making it out the barrel.

Kelmu standing above with blaster trained on Ty'ag, "your failure in grasping the impossible roots from your feeble mindedness you small insignificant piece of Scaedrein dung," Kelmu kicking the former western delegate while he's down.

The Scaedreins in the main station are just now catching on to what's going on quickly running up the steps toward Kelmu, who is now standing in the corridor.

Kelmu throwing up his hands the blaster resting between the waist of his pants and the center of his back, "don't shoot," he calls out trying to lure the Scaedreins closer by acting defenseless.

"Where is the weapon, human?" The Scaedrein on point aiming his MPFS at the prisoner standing outside the cell-block.

Kelmu realizes that's as close as the bug heads are going to get and that he'll have to work with what has been presented to him.

"Relax its right here," Kelmu kneeling down beside the unconscious Ty'ag quickly draws the small blaster and fires at the closest one.

A direct hit to one of the back legs clips it off and the Scaedrein falls back and to the side screeching in pain, blood pouring heavily on to the deck of the detention cell corridor.

Kelmu firing wildly down the corridor fanning the blaster bolts before shooting the outside lock to the cell door, and diving into the room for cover.

"Stop firing," Ty'ag yelling out before pulling himself off the floor hiding his bulky mass behind a protrusion in the wall, looking into the cell and then down the corridor.

"Kelmu you will never get out like this" Ty'ag whispering into the cell, "work with me so we can all get out of here," Ty'ag almost sounding sympathetic and willing to compromise.

Kelmu looking into Ty'agnoome's pleading eyes, "you do this for yourself and not for the lives of the others," Kelmu pointing the small blaster at Ty'ag.

"And is that not my right and privilege?" Ty'ag holding up his hand stopping the advancing Scaedreins while looking at Kelmu.

"I did not want to tell you this now but the Neo-drein have a genetic defect that has accelerated in their DNA and they're dying, the same thing will happen to the others when they have reached the evolutionary rung above the Neo's."

Kelmu not believing a word only laughs at the collaborator, that's a mouthful.

"With your skills in the micro-biology field we can come up with a cure and end this peacefully," Ty'agnoome's tone sounding stressed; but is it for real?

Kelmu laughing over the statement until he senses there is some truth behind what Ty'ag is saying.

"What do you mean?" Kelmu keeping the blaster on Ty'ag, "tell the Scaedreins outside to cease," Kelmu feeling the tension in the air knowing the guards are trying to be sneaky.

Ty'ag raising his hand stopping the guards for real this time glad he was able to calm down the riled Miscreant.

"I am very close to a cure but there are some things that need fine tuning and I need your skills."

"Why didn't you tell me this earlier all this could have been avoided," Kelmu giving in a little too easily.

"Because as I suspected you won't side with me, which leaves one major dilemma if both sides survive, who gets Mieveodrin?"

"I can see your problem with the rightful owners around you can't take it."

"Am I not Myie?" Ty'ag sitting up but not standing, having difficulty moving his newly acquired mass, the stress marks in his tone revealing the physical weakness inflicting Ty'ag looking a way no Myie would want to look.

"You are Nul too me now, a mere presence, your great and divine way is not of hope and prosperity but of death and debauchery." Ty'ag trying to cut off Kelmu but it doesn't work. "And furthermore if you ever call yourself Myie in my presence again it'll be your last words," Kelmu getting riled up tightening his grip around the trigger.

Ty'ag can see that Kelmu is on the verge of committing murder the eyes glazed over and hollow, numb without emotion. "Let me take you to the medical wing and show you what I'm dealing with," Ty'ag trying desperately to reason with the now homicidal Kelmu.

"So you can take advantage of the Myie by using the suffering of others to hide your intentions?" Kelmu stepping closer to the door, "get against the back-wall," Kelmu motioning with the barrel of the blaster.

"Kelmu," Ty'agnoome's tone very different is calming the homicidal urges in Kelmu, "it only affects their young. Now an adult Scaedrein is one thing but these neo-drein children are very different and are just as innocent as Myie children and don't deserve to suffer in such a manner. If we can save the children the Neo's will let us go and ensure our survival for future generations when they take the lead directors chair using the mess we created to dis-credit the current leaders."

"Give me a break you self-righteous, conniving, and vindictive traitor." Kelmu not giving in one bit keeps the weapon trained on Ty'ag.

"Don't you want things the way they used to be before the mass extinction, the Myie flourishing?"

"With Scaedreins around no human is safe because they hate our kind."

"The Neo-dreins are willing to change things and though they do hate all humans if we cure this genetic affliction in their young that opinion could change."

Kelmu sensing a bit of truth in the statement is finally persuaded to at least look at the infected baby Neo-drein's, "if this is a trap you're dying with me."

"If it's a trap I didn't have anything to do with it," Ty'ag standing up as Kelmu steps into the corridor.

The Scaedrein guards clinching up a bit are once again halted by the wave of Ty'agnoome's hand.

"Take us to the medical wing," Ty'ag speaking to the escorts motioning to the only door of this detention block.

"This prisoner will be denied access," the escort pointing out the next obvious obstacle.

"I will worry about that," Ty'ag replying with a suggestive tone looking directly into the eyes of both escorts.

A slight hesitation is followed by the two escorts leading Kelmu and Ty'ag down the corridor leaving the detention-block.

The Scaedrein captain *Straeik* all ready knows Ty'agnoome is heading for the medical wing and is on his way to meet the impetuous human face-to-face.

The door to the medical wing slides open revealing an overcrowded ward filled with Neo-drein children connected to life support within small sealed bubbles, the genetic disease attacks the immune system before it begins to break down the still developing Neo-drein physiology. The first cocooning stage would kill the disease if the young could live that long, at the moment the disease kills in about six to twelve days a few weeks short of the first growth cycle.

"I didn't want to believe you," Kelmu looking around the ward at the human and Scaedrein scientist working together to achieve one goal.

"These Neo-dreins I've learned are quite different from the less-evolved Scaedreins."

"I see no difference between the two," Kelmu looking at one of the dying children underneath the sealed bubble.

"Oh there are slight differences in reasoning capabilities and a few small physical changes almost unseen even by other Scaedreins."

The reasoning part obvious by the looks of the ship, it has steps not ramps and chairs as well.

"Why have you defiled your appearance?"

"This is just a step in my evolution, in time I will no longer need the bio-suit and the longevity of my life will go beyond that of normal humans."

"Your vain attempts will fail because after this you won't be living much longer."

"My work is right here," Ty'ag changing the subject pointing to a console near a half-circle indention by a larger quarantine room with several more support bubbles filled with new born Neo-dreins.

The two are now standing around the console across from one another, Kelmu waiting for Ty'ag to show this work of his.

The Scaedrein captain *Straeik* observing the two from a monitor in a smaller room beside sick-bay. Straeik not pleased with the human Ty'agnoome for allowing the military leader of the Myie into this sensitive area. The two humans saying something about injecting nano-probes that will rebuild the Neo's genetic structure, but the only problem is they can do nothing for who is currently infected with this deteriorating genetic disease. The two are beginning to argue again.

"I need more time than what you're offering," Kelmu looking at the analysis of the simulated effects of these nano-probes on the infant Neo-drein, whose genetic make-up is similar but different in one major way. A dormant gene that may cause accelerated mutation in some of the new born whose bearers have been injected with these probes.

"I don't know if I can give you the time you need, these Neo-drein are even more stubborn than Scaedreins." The door to sick-bay sliding open turns the attention of Ty'ag; it's Straeik.

"If you help you won't die," the Captain raising his smaller weapon pointing it at Kelmu.

"You should know by now that threatening us doesn't work," Kelmu stepping closer to the captain not worried about the weapon pointing at him.

The captain ready to pull the trigger at the audacity of this human is interrupted by Ty'ag stepping between them, "let's not do this let's work this out and end the feuding of differences."

The two looking at Ty'ag like he lost his mind, yet, they calm down.

Ty'agnoome not giving in to the condescending mannerisms splayed all over both faces, "Straeik you gave me your word that proves your willingness to cooperate. Become respected members of the galaxy opposed of the one's most likely to be destroyed when the super powers grow wary of your presence," Ty'ag speaking very quickly so he would not be interrupted.

"I didn't agree to this," Straeik pointing at Kelmu.

"He is here to help," Ty'ag sounding out of character.

"I'm still here you don't have to refer to me in the third person," Kelmu speaking out annoyed and aggravated. "I will do this but you must free all my people and make sure they're safe before I start doing anything," Kelmu implying the demands are not negotiable.

"*Lo' me' ky' nie* Myie," Straeik holstering his weapon then points at Kelmu before leaving the medical lab.

"He's given you the time you requested and your people will be set free," Ty'ag translating for Kelmu.

"I know what he said," Kelmu doesn't believe the bug heads or Ty'ag and if worse comes to worse Kelmu will make sure those two die; even if they're the only two who die.

"I will have one of the humanoid doctors show you around," Ty'ag says turning on the com-system to call one of the doctors in the med-lab.

"He will be here shortly but now I must go," Ty'ag using leisure tones disguising the back hand sending Kelmu's unconscious body across the floor.

"That'll keep you out of trouble until the doctor gets here," Ty'ag leaving the medical lab locking the door from the outside.

Now he must tell the other Myie, despised that he had to change his plans, but survival is a stronger instinct and allows for other options to be conceived or allows time for a circumstantial avenue to open up. A Circumstantial Avenue would be him forcing to reveal to Kelmu information that was supposed to be released later, but Kelmu's break out of the cell block created that circumstantial avenue.

Ty'ag steps out the lift and enters the level where the Myie field units are being held. He enters the control room, which is the first door to the right just passed the lift. He enters the control room and activates the main switch that transmits to every room on that level.

"Your leader has negotiated for your release; I ask you one more time will you side with the Khaedrin Nul?" An onslaught of disapproval pours from the receiving speaker within the control room, the combined noise causing a little feed back before the filters kicked on and silenced the voices coming from the speaker. Ty'ag standing up disappointed to say the least but he expected as much.

Boot throwing his boot at the speaker does not believe they will be released it's just a trap to lure them into a false sense of security so the bug heads can trample on the hope every Myie is clinging to; that's not going to happen.

Colde hearing the news has an unsettling feeling as well, Kelmu wouldn't have negotiated unless he knew for certain his people would be free and out of harms way. Have the Scaedreins agreed to something, not likely, is Kelmu biding time brewing something in that analytical head of his; probably. Colde standing up to move his legs pacing in the small d-block cell; what does Kelmu have in mind?

The NCP's and NCO's are being corralled toward the nearest hanger placed in a ship with no weapons but with reinforced and synchronized energy/particle shields with a 2.3 DDS (Dynamic Drive system) giving it exceptional speed in normal space and as a bonus a DTR (Dynamic Temporal Re-sequencer) with one use before the system fouls out for good.

DTR technology the gold mine that re-fortified multi-planetary business for all business owners is much better than the old method of light travel. The old method of light travel far more risky because it relied on engines producing speeds that fast now the idea is to speed up everything around the ship like ridding within the currents of convergent-space as it's being formed, except the lane doesn't stay open and it closes as the ship travels through it. It sounds risky and it hasn't been around as long as Fractal Magnetic Incursion (FMI,), or Dynamic

Molecular Sequencer but is near perfect with the exception that it's built by imperfect beings.

FMI makes it possible to place an F.M.I. designed magnet in the middle of a pile of steel and attract only one piece and repel the others, as long as the one piece is lined with receiving fibers imbedded in the surface of the metal.

F.M.I. technology was started when large multi-atmospheric mechanized bots ruled the battle field they were called Cyber-frames and this technology was started by the Myie before they were forced to live in space and way before they called themselves Myie, looking for the home they would later name Mieveodrin.

The Myie have an idea of where they came from but for some reason the name of this planet and system has remained elusive and if anyone knows they aren't telling, they sure weren't this Khaedrin Nul Ty'ag is talking about.

Dielan anxiously pacing the floor of his room when the door suddenly opens revealing three Scaedrein guards, "*Deelou yeemu* Myie," the lead Scaedrein's scratchy yet relatively clear tone rolling with more of a rhythm but just a hair different, almost unnoticeable. Dielan taking a good look at these three guards begins to notice a few physical inconsistencies, again, virtually undetectable by the untrained eye.

The guards don't look pleased about the news of their sworn enemy's release. Dielan stepping out the cell and into the corridor eyeing the three ugly insects, these three aren't guards. Hell the bigger one's Nythillic spear is broke at the tip, and those things are supposed to be as hard and flexible as the metal produced by *Zyltherium ore.*

A very old and pure ore that is 300, 000 times the value of diamond and to invest in any efforts involved in this ore is well worth the risk. The D'neirie technique used in refining and smelting this ore into metal is far better than most of the known galaxy.

Dielan walking in front of the three guards can't help but wonder what Kelmu has agreed to concerning the negotiations, and more importantly what is the Colonel planning to do? Dielan knows Kelmu and can see that he's up to something; the question is will it work? He glances back at the guards who tell him eyes forward or they shoot to kill.

"Can I speak with your captain before our departure from this ship?" Dielan addressing the guards using sincere tones with no spiteful intent but he can feel the hatred flowing from the guards.

No answer from the guards, as suspected, he stops at the lift and waits for the three guards to open the door.

The door slides open revealing a lone Jyric standing in the center of the lift. "I'll take it from here," raising his arm pointing a small box at the Miscreant Major.

The guards seem to have no problem with it glad they no longer have too look at the ugly human without being able to kill it.

Dielan steps into the air lift turns and faces the guards.

"Oh, and by the way." Jyric holding the door with his hand preventing it from closing lightly tosses the small metal box at one of the guards, who catches it, "thank you." The door closes before the Scaedreins realize what the metal box is.

The biggest catches it and attempts to throw it but the explosion rips the three bugs apart blackening the walls and floor in a small area of the corridor, sending pieces of bug fifteen-feet away from the impact point.

A large explosion coming from something disguised as a 'shock box' a device that works similar to a tazer, except you can increase the voltage enough to kill someone if necessary, Kyban technology at work again.

"What are you doing?" Dielan absolutely puzzled at the actions of young Jyric.

"Getting us out of here," Jyric quickly replies.

"I will not adhere to your Nul policies," Dielan grabbing Jyric by the throat and slamming him against the wall of the lift.

The traitor unable to breath is trying to say something. "What is that I can't hear you," Dielan tightening his grip watching the lad's eyes bug out, before he releases his hold on Jyric's neck.

"This isn't about the Nul," Jyric coughing from lack of oxygen as the air lift stops.

The door opens to a hanger that seems to be void of any Scaedrein, only the NCP's and NCO's occupy this room.

"What is going on here?" Dielan stepping off the lift yanking Jyric along with him.

"I suggest you let him go," Ty'agnoome's voice is followed by him stepping from behind the only ship in the hanger, about thirty paces from Dielan.

"The Scaedreins are letting you go but Kelmu will have to stay longer he has other pressing matters to attend to," Ty'ag stepping up to Dielan motions Jyric to step away from the angered Miscreant.

"Yeah but your boy there just blew up three of'em."

"I know I ordered him to," Ty'ag with a devious grin.

"Well he should be lucky because I was going to kill him after the lift door closed but the bomb distracted me." Dielan lunging forward is stopped by Ty'ag stepping into the path of the miscreant's aggressive action.

"If you don't decease your hostility I will be forced to tell the Scaedreins you caused the death of those three guards."

"You use the art of deception well." Dielan adhering to the threats, for now, doing what ever it takes to make sure he's around long enough to kill both the traitors.

"You will assist Kelmu in the lab and you will both be each others insurance plan if one is caught trying to escape or tamper with lab results the other will pay the price as well. I am doing everything I can to ensure our survival if we get out of this I hope we can see passed our differences."

"Say what you will but it doesn't change that you're a traitor and have become a mortal enemy of the Myie, and all I'm going to say is, watch your back."

Ty'ag not taking the threats seriously raises his weapon pointing it at Dielan, "You're needed in the lab."

"What of the others?" Dielan showing that he can't be threatened by brute force.

"They'll be in less danger than you; get going," Ty'ag motioning with his weapon.

Straeik just now catching wind of the explosion but not the killing of three neo-dreins is now moving through the ship in an effort to find Ty'ag or Jyric. The human technicians are usually more adept and productive. Are the humans conspiring together, hoping to escape when the other Myie are released? Stinking humans, the time will come when the Scaedrein race will no longer need the assistance of human slaves or any slave the key to success is being self-reliant but at the same time knowing when outside help is needed, but not all the time.

These ideals are considered non-conservative or radical to the Scaedreins and only a ruling class of Neo's can fully usher in this new era of prosperity and a self-sufficient stable economy. This branch of Scaedrein genetics is definitely one in a zillion, and even some Neo's don't fully understand their potential but they can't ignore what they feel and how they were made to feel around the Scaedreins. Ty'ag and Jyric do have something in common with these Neo's both have abandoned their own cultures in hopes to build a new and better way of life. This one common goal will keep an alliance between the Nul the Neo-drein and later all Scaedreins for years to come.

The Myie NCO's and NCP's were released the following day with the exception of Dielan, Kelmu, and Exle. The soldiers now led by Boot released as well, along with Colde and Eve, are reunited with the NCO's and NCP's and transported to a planet where they can be easily reached and watched closely to ensure there are no attempts to conspire against the Scaedreins.

Ty'ag and Jyric's escape plan thwarted by Straeik are forced to stay behind and ensure the progress of the three Myie working on a cure for the Neo's genetic dilemma and although this book ends with a lot of uncertainty there is one thing you can be sure of, this is the beginning of over twenty-five hundred years of history. The only thing left to say now is the Myie, Nul, and Scaedrein races will continue to flourish and that a greater understanding between the three cultures will be realized and a hospitable medium will be achieved until the expense of agenda or convenience runs dry.

The Beginning…

New Beginnings

The re-taking or even maintaining the galaxies current status was not the issue of this piece to the puzzle but the status of those who will one day change the 'order' of things, but these heroes aren't born yet. The next installment will be longer and have more to do with the known galaxies major dilemma, large bugs with gigantic egos controlling a majority of the known galaxy. The other galactic super powers have and will remain silent for the time being but something may indicate their lack of help is but a cover to hide what the known systems have been doing since the Scaedrein's took over, and that is secretly build an army on the planets of these super powers that have "officially" closed their borders to every one. It's obvious these galactic powers would build their armies up what's not so obvious is every known system has sent people over the years through these closed borders to train and become part of the largest army every built through multi-cooperative efforts. All for one common goal to defrock the Scaedreins not necessarily annihilate, unless there is no other choice, but taking that type of control from ego maniacs usually means confrontation results in death or prison. But I've said this once and I'll say it again, Scaedrein Infiltration kept a veil of mystery over my eyes the whole time I wrote it this means the next one should be as equally intriguing if not more because it will cover the galactic picture and not just the races of beings involved. The next story in this history should take place about twenty-seven years after Scaedrein Infiltration.

Scaedrein Infiltration ends with a realization, an understanding, that even the worst enemies can find common ground and work together. "If not for the children then for who?"

About the Author

Born in Lansing, Michigan a military brat who moved from state to state until we came to a halt on the coast of North Carolina. At eighteen I started the process of teaching myself the art of writing with no help from books or even a lot of reading. Eighteen years later and I haven't put the pen down. I have attended no classes for writing or even seminars, I've never left the states, but every night I write I see things that go beyond the galaxy and beyond this flesh that binds us to this world. I don't force creativity it's something that comes to me naturally, I pick up the pen or start typing and it pours out of me like lake's emptying into oceans of creativity. Writing has reinforced my belief that we are more than we appear to be. I am single with no kids and have worked in food service for twenty-years. What I've wrote over these last eighteen years has lifted my spirits and enlightened me in many ways. I sing songs from the books I write and it opens more and more doors into vast regions riding in a boat like roller coaster not created entirely by the imagination; more like looking for the next channel taking a ride conducted by currents from stories long ago, told and forgotten drifting amongst wake of these kinetic oceans of creation.